Ash Slivers

The Land of the O-O

Facts, figures, fables, and fancies

Ash Slivers

The Land of the O-O
Facts, figures, fables, and fancies

ISBN/EAN: 9783744792813

Printed in Europe, USA, Canada, Australia, Japan

Cover: Foto ©Andreas Hilbeck / pixelio.de

More available books at **www.hansebooks.com**

THE
LAND OF THE O-O.

FACTS, FIGURES, FABLES,

AND

FANCIES.

By ASH SLIVERS, Sr.,
LUMBERMAN.

CLEVELAND, OHIO:
THE CLEVELAND PRINTING AND PUBLISHING CO.
1892.

I DEDICATE THIS BOOK TO MY LITTLE DAUGHTER

"Freda,"

WHOM BEING TOO YOUNG TO HELP HERSELF, I FEEL A

PERFECT RIGHT TO DO WITH AS I CHOOSE. I TRUST

THE "SOCIETY FOR THE PREVENTION OF

CRUELTY TO CHILDREN" WILL

TAKE NO HEED OF THE

MATTER.

CONTENTS.

6 *Contents.*

ILLUSTRATIONS.

PREFACE.

I submit this book to the public, not as a literary product of excellence, but purely and solely as the simple story of a wandering lumberman in quest of sights.

"How then," it may be asked, "did you happen to write it?"

I reply briefly, as a soporific.

Let me explain. During the earlier periods of my trip, I conceived the idea of issuing, in a condensed form, an outlined skeleton of my journeyings, both as a trifling souvenir of my travels, and in order, also, to give to my associates at home an opportunity to share in those things I was then enjoying. Acting on this impulse, I proceeded at once to prepare the aforesaid skeleton, and in due time presented it to my family, —six of them—with the fond hope that if it there met with encouraging response, I could thenceforth safely trust it to the kindly criticisms of my friends.

The result, however, was an altogether unexpected denouement; for in varying periods, ranging between four and nine minutes from the time the first leaves of the manuscript were opened, every single one of them fell sound asleep. To fitly describe my feelings of chagrin over this despoiling testimonial to the merits of my endeavor, would be a vain undertaking; hence I forbear. But as the pond-lily often springs from the black and noxious under-soil of the marsh, and the most fragrant blossoms from the mire, so it was with my dejections, for from their dismal depths sentiments arose sweetly perfumed with sympathy for all mankind. And these were the thoughts born of that doleful condition: " The world is full of suffering human beings crazed with insomnia. Here is a panacea for their afflictions, here a blessed relief from their wretched distresses. I will stuff that skeleton, and the world shall have it." The result of that determination stands crystalized in this book.

And now, I beseech you, patient reader, do not condemn too severely, this my maiden effort, or the rough and raw material of which it is composed.

True, there is no halo around it, nor either its workmanship; but still there are many parts which I very well know could never endure such a test. I have renovated what I have put into it to the best of my power, under the circumstances, and will guarantee that there is no deadly infection about it. But the work has not been scientifically done, nor even as well as I have faith to believe it might have been under more favorable conditions; and for that reason I solicit the generous indulgence of those who may come in contact with it.

A. S., Sr.

"The Thistles,"
        (Near Guernsey,)
            Harrison Co., Ohio.

I.

CHAPTER I.

THE REASON WHY.

FOR seven years I had been planning a trip; not to
Europe, for, since boyhood, I had heard so much of the
niches and corners of that country, its old castles, its exhausted dynasties, its marvelous treasures of art and history,
that, to me, it seemed, I was more than replete with every
knowledge of it. The text-books, too, of my youthful school-
days, their later more enlarged editions, and finally, the
copiously illustrated works of travel intended for the library
and the library table, all had made me eminently familiar
with those lands, and I felt little desire to explore them personally. But if, after all these things, any lingering wish had
still remained, the quenchless flow of narrative and description, by those friends who had been over, and around, and
through Europe, would have been amply sufficient to dissi-
pate it, and, as proved to be the case anyhow, would have
inclined me in other directions.

Not an extensive traveler ever, never having been out of
my own country, except across the border to Canada, I had
yet seen considerable of the United States, north and south,
and, being an American of old-time revolutionary stock, had
a pardonable American pride in its progress and glory. I
was always, besides, an enthusiastic lover of the new world.
From Cape Horn in the south to the illimitable in the north,
and from ocean to ocean, America, to me, was God's own
special domain here on earth, and before all other lands I
most desired to see its boundless wonders.

Seven years ago, the pot of travel began to bubble in my bosom, faintly, at first, it is true, but quite enough to induce me to begin looking seriously over the field. A year later, I found myself deeply engrossed reading Lieut. Page's thrilling report to our government, of his explorations up the La Plata river of South America. Following this came Darwin's journeyings around the world, fifty years or more ago, in his account of which he gave much attention to our western hemisphere, especially Argentina, that most thriving of all the young Republics of the Spanish constellation south of the equator. Then came Professor Orton's account of his explorations across Ecuador, and down the Amazon, with everything else I could find in book-store or library bearing on the subject, until, finally, I came to be known as " The great South American enthusiast who travels wholly in imagination; " a cabinet photograph of myself, thus inscribed, having been placed in a sightly spot on the parlor mantel, where it persistently stared down at me in shame-faced mockery, as if to prod and incite me.

At my place of business, also, this oft-repeated promise of " a trip," which at first appeared to be really genuine, afterwards came to be looked upon as a huge joke, and ultimately almost as a mild form of lunacy, liable to evoke manifestations of concern and sympathy whenever referred to ; while on one occasion, during mention of the subject at home, I now distinctly remember a groan of pain that came from a remote corner of the room, with a smothered explosion of " rats ! " from one of the younger off-shoots of the family. None of these things, however, for a single moment deterred me, so immovable was my resolve to take " that trip."

Moreover, I had my plan of campaign all laid out, and this was my itinerary : First, I was to proceed from New York to Para, at the mouth of the Amazon river, and thence, following the channel of that mighty stream up toward its

DREAMS, NEVER REALIZED.

sources, stay my steps only when the snow-clad heights of the Peruvian Andes should check their further progress with the command : " Thus far shalt thou go, but no farther ! "

Then I was to retrace my course; down through impenetrable shadows of verdant umbrage, of tree and vine, that hold forever in twilight darkness the choicest riches of Nature, though all that surrounds them dazzles with tropical brightness.

I would study, also, the aborigines of that land; those descendents of the Incas who once in the flight of time, ere the introduction of eastern civilization had been known among them, brought more nearly to perfection than any other race in ancient American history, the completeness of human government; now living worse than beasts of the field in those deserted places.

I would see those things that Humboldt saw and that Darwin revelled in. I would try to unravel the secret that brought Wallace there, and that for seven long years of uninterrupted study and research kept Bates away from friends and England ; things which, to me, had ever been full of alluring and mysterious enchantment.

In that rich paradise of the naturalist, I should see millions of gaily plumaged birds, and ten millions of insects more gorgeously arrayed than " Solomon in all his glory." I should listen to the whiskered monkey howling in his own fastnesses. I should hear the crocodile bellow, the turtle blow, the anaconda splash. All these were things before me, in my mind's eye, when I took " that trip."

Then I would travel on to Rio Janeiro and its far-famed harbor, its magnificent scenery. And to Montevideo; where I should view gardens and flowers of unexcelled perfection, beautiful signoras and signoritas, walled habitations of the dead, and glorious sea-views. Then, to Buenos Ayres, the New York of South America ; rich, pushing, progressive.

Then up and down the La Plata and Parana ; among islands where grow, wild, the choicest fruits—oranges, pomegranates and figs—to Paraguay ; that fairest land under the sun, now almost depopulated by the misrule of a tyrant during the last half-century. Paraguay ! where patriot women, for the sake of home and country, took up arms, like men, and fought in the ranks to drive back the invaders.

Those places I had planned to visit. And then to cross the continent to Chili ; to scale the summit of the ragged Andes ; to sweep along the watery base of those great Cordilleras of the south ; and then, by a series of flights through Central America and Mexico, after a six months' tour, return to the place of my beginning and my lumber piles, gratified and satisfied. All this I expected when I took "that trip."

Finally, after seven years of waiting—like the young man spoken of in the Bible, waiting for his sweetheart—the auspicious hour arrived. But alas for my idols! They were shattered. All South America had suddenly burst into an eruption. Revolution was rampant in Brazil. Likewise in Paraguay. The Argentine Republic showed very little better, and Chili all at once became so horribly formal in her respect for the United States as to render the prospects of travel there decidedly frigid.

What then was to be done ? For seven years I had waited. The cabinet on the mantel still stared down at me in mute, uncomplaining silence. It seemed to me, I could actually discern tears in its eyes. The sound of "rats!" too, echoed in my ears. What was I to do?

"Go!" said everybody ; "go, by all means! Don't let anything on earth deter you! Take 'that trip'!" So I succumbed, but nevertheless, not without changing, largely, my plans.

Though I had studied the Spanish language for years, I now laid it all aside ; and abandoning every fair vision, dis-

encumbering myself of every fond enchantment, I threw
overboard the whole South American scheme of promise and
bought a ticket for San Francisco, undetermined from there
whither I would go, but bound to take " that trip."

The flight across the continent, though a story oft told, to
me was a pilgrimage filled with intense interest and the
utmost pleasure. I left Chicago on the Santa Fe, night train,
November 12th. The Pullman in which I had secured accommodations was filled with travelers, my nearest neighbors being an elderly gentleman and his daughter, anxiously hasten-
ing to the suffering bedside of a wife and mother at Pasadena.
In the section next to them, was a young bride returning
to her idol in California; and accompanying her, her sister,
an enthusiastic, bubbling, wholesome young girl of sixteen,
fairly running over with the exhilarating excitements of a first
journey from home, who, from one end of the trip to the
other, was a beam of fragrant sunshine illuminating every
heart in the car.

There were people from the east in our car, others from
the far west, and foreigners; but we all soon became
acquainted, and then the time flew fast, the little coterie thus
formed providing genial and harmonious pastime, which
added greatly to the comfort and enjoyment of the whole
journey.

We arrived in Kansas City the following morning after our
departure from Chicago, and then away to the west flew our
insensate train, like some hurrying thing of life; through
the immense prairie farms of Kansas; through Topeka and
Trinidad; and over the vast ranges of unoccupied lands
which intervened, until at length we rested on the highest
point of the continental divide, in full view of the white-
capped summits of the Spanish Peaks, ready to take our
final plunge downward to the flowery gardens of the Pacific;
the land of palm trees and of sweet valleys; of the orange,

the blossom, and the vine; where the breath that fans the pilgrim-traveler is always the breath of gentle deliciousness and repose—peerless California.

Mountains were passed and alkali plains; scattered huts and "dago" villages. Mighty canyons yawned beneath us as we leaped across their frightful abysses; and herds of cattle, and half-tamed horses, and flocks of sheep, skurried away to right and left, as the whistle of our engine reverberated among the hills or was lost in the far, flat distance of the pampas.

At length Los Angeles was reached, busy, bustling Los Angeles; city of the bright sun; lying hid among fruitful verdure half way between the mountains and the sea. And then we hastened northward to San Francisco, five hundred miles further on.

Here I spent three weeks, radiating daily to different points of the compass into the surrounding country; drinking in its delicious atmosphere; luxuriating in its sweet-tempered, rural delights. Here, too, I visited those places for which San Francisco is so widely known: Chinatown, that celestial ulcer of a beautiful city, buried, like a consuming canker, in its heart, feeding on its vitals; Sutro's gardens; the Cliff House; the Alms House; the House of Correction; the City Prison; and finally, the Morgue; where, in one month, sixty-five dead bodies, many of them suicides, with pale and unknown faces, lay on the dripping marble of that homeless place, the victims of a desperate last resort, of want and crime, in this modern Sodom and Gomorrah, this wickedest city of America.

And then I prepared to embark for the Sandwich Islands, more modernly known as the Hawaiian kingdom, for a sea voyage.

CHAPTER II.

THE distance from San Francisco to Honolulu, Hawaiian
Islands, is twenty one hundred miles. The fare, for
first class cabin passage, is seventy-five dollars. The time
required for the passage is seven days; two days, at least,
too much, and ought to be shortened. There is no competi-
tion, however, so it is not likely to be done.

The Oceanic Steamship Line is composed of four very
comfortable boats, though not by any means such as are
found on the Atlantic. They are of about 3000 tons burthen
each, and have, uniformly, very musical names; the Ala-
meda, the Monawoi, the Mariposa, and the Australia. All,
except the last, ply between San Francisco and Sidney,
Australia, touching at Honolulu, Samoa, and Auckland; and
are so regulated, that one or the other leaves each end of the
route every four weeks. The Australia is confined between
San Francisco and Honolulu, and departs from each place,
on an average, about once a month. This arrangement affords communication with Hawaii fortnightly.

I left San Francisco on the Steamer "Mariposa," Friday,
December 11, 1891, at 3 P. M. The day was an exceptionally
fine one, the sky beautiful. Nature, in all her moods,
seemed to smile with warmth as we rocked idly at the ship's
dock.

As the afternoon hour of our departure approached, the
crowds on the wharf perceptibly increased; greater hurry

and bustle prevailed, both on board and ashore. Passengers were arriving, friends going; there was rush here and there among the boat's crew; and these commotions, mingled with the shouts of hackmen and the rumble of trucks and conveyances over the hollow, wooden floor of the ware-house, created a din and excitement that were intense.

As all things that have an existence must somewhere have had a beginning, so had this trip of the Mariposa; and finally, the signal came for the boat to start. Hasty caresses quickly followed; hand shakes; words of precious endearment and tears; and then the gang-plank was dropped from the side of the vessel, the slackened lines were cast off, and we began slowly drifting, out into the bay of San Francisco.

A solid phalanx of out-turned faces along the wharf followed us, and multitudes of fluttering tokens, waved as white messengers of love and parting by those we were leaving behind, were answered from our boat as long as they could be distinguished; even after, many a kiss burdened with sighs of emotion was dispatched to the shore, although those for whom they were intended could no longer be identified in the distance.

Once fairly out on the bay, our steamer headed to the south, and then, like a coroneted duchess withdrawing from the presence of her sovereign, swept gracefully round to the left in a broad semi-circle, followed by her sparkling train in the water, as if to make a parting salute to the mountains, which lay to the east, gray and majestic, before starting on her long and perilous voyage.

Hundreds of sea-gulls surrounded us, as we picked our way out through the shipping that dotted the harbor along our course. Some of them were gray in color, others black and white, but not a note did any of them utter; scarcely perceptible was the flapping of their wings, as they floated through the air, over and about us, like couriers deputized to see us safely out over the bars of the harbor and bid us " God-speed " on our journey. These beautiful, harmless creatures are wisely protected by law; and yet it seems indeed surprising that any law for their preservation should be necessary; for who could wish to wantonly injure or destroy them? They constitute one of the principal attractions of the bay of San Francisco.

Numbers of pelicans were also observed, as we steamed along, poised on unsteady wings over the water, or dropping into it like meteors with loud splashes, or in the act of rising to their former aerial heights, to again scan the depths below for the prey they were eagerly hunting.

Porpoises, too, gamboled in our wake, as we passed noiselessly by Alcatraz and under the threatening guns of the Presideo, and long before night all traces of the land we had left were lost to sight.

We struck rough weather at the very portals of the Golden Gate, and for four days, nine out of ten of all the passengers aboard were sea-sick. Happily, and unexpectedly as well, I chanced to be one of the fortunate few who escaped, and was thus able to enjoy what to the greater majority was the inexpressible dread and horror of their voyage, the raging sea.

Never shall I forget the multitude of misconceived notions that everywhere greeted me during my trip of two months to Hawaii, but none of them exceeded those of the Pacific Ocean, sweet-tempered, graciously-disposed, placid,—as it had been told to me it existed—and that boiling, seething, mighty cauldron of rolling water which we actually encountered. Never shall I cease to remember its yawning, cavernous gulfs, nor their frightful, storm-whipped, angered and slippery sides, down which we plunged as if to sure destruction. Nor the ride back again; up, up, up from those threatening valleys of death, until, hanging to the guard-ropes of wire, it seemed to me I could almost scan the whole watery universe, so high was our altitude above the wild flood that surrounded us.

For four days our staunch boat was shaken, hammered, battered, beaten, rolled, pummelled and drenched; lashed by the hissing winds, stung and bitten by the pitiless rain; and then old Neptune relaxed his fury and the storm abated.

During the period of its greatest commotion, a young boy from Buffalo, seventeen years of age, died. He was the son of a former Associate Justice of Hawaii, who had died several years before, and whose remains were interred on the Islands. The boy was wofully out of health, and his mother was bringing him back to the scenes of his early boyhood hoping he might be benefited. But the strain of the rough voyage was too great for him, and he succumbed in mid-ocean. Everything that could be, was done for the broken-hearted, widowed and childless mother, both by the officers of the boat and by sympathetic passengers, but her grief was beyond the reach of words or pity. The body, contrary to the usual custom requiring burial at sea, was subsequently encased in ice and carried through to Honolulu, and the funeral, two days later, was attended by several of the passengers of the Mariposa, who thus manifested their sympathy.

> Ay, many flowering islands lie
> In the waters of wide agony."

After the sea had quieted, the passengers began coming out on deck, and during the few succeeding days, before our arrival in Honolulu, many pleasant acquaintances were formed.

There is nothing quite so conducive to smiles and good-fellowship on ship-board, as recuperation from the throes and agonies of an extended grapple with sea-sickness; for, however disgruntled or miserable the victim may be at such times, he is nevertheless certain to cover up his feelings and try to be gracious and civil. And, oh! what a deliciousness there is in rest, on such occasions; after those terrible periods of spasm and upheaval, when one feels that his poor, abused gizzard has been turned inside out and completely despoiled of its sweet-breads. One wants nothing else on earth then, but to lie perfectly quiet, and look at things and loll.

We who had escaped the dread malady, being duly grateful for our good fortune, were disposed to do whatever lay in our power to entertain the others; and feeling as did the old lady in the legend, that we could offer our services " with perfect impurity," we made free to do so.

There were quite a number of prominent people on board, among them the Hon. C. R. Bishop, banker and capitalist, of Honolulu. Mr. Bishop is most conspicuously known in the world, as has been many a noted man before him, by reason of being the husband of his wife. Many years ago, he wandered out to the Sandwich Islands from New York state. He was a penniless lad then, but he had plenty of courage and the spirit of adventure boiled and sizzled in his blood. For a while he was a clerk in one of the early established mercantile houses of Hawaii, and it was probably during this time that he got in his fine work with the Chiefess Bernice Pauahia, a young and fascinating female member of the royal family, whose ancestor, Kamehameha I, was the fighting founder of the present dynasty, and married her.

Kamehameha was a great warrior, and likewise a sagacious ruler, and everything relating to the history of the Hawaiian Islands, at the present time, runs back to him, and then, like grandfather's clock, stops short. There is nothing on earth, prior to his reign, that interests the average Kanaka an iota.

Before his time, there were numberless rulers scattered

over the Islands; petty chiefs, who governed the natives in squads, and who were forever at war with one another.

Kamehameha took it into his head that the supreme sovereignty of the entire group wasn't any too great nor too good a thing for him to handle, and he accordingly went for the other fellows like a turkey gobbler after grasshoppers.

For many years, the struggle of contending factions kept all of the islands in a state of perpetual strife; but finally, about the close of the last century, the last remaining cohorts of the enemy, bunched in opposition on the island of Oahu, were run over the cliffs at the Pali; and then, tradition says, Kamehameha, wiping his barbed war-spear on the fern-clad hills of the Nuuanu valley, bounded to the top of Tantalus and crowed over all creation. A fine, bronze statue of him, which from its proud demeanor would seem intended for that very moment, stands by the gates of the Government, building in Honolulu.

Kamehameha continued to rule for thirty-seven years, and died in 1819, in the eighty-second year of his age. After him came five succeeding rulers of the royal family which he had established, each a little more feeble than his predecessor, in prowess and governing ability, until, finally, the stock got to be as thin-spun as a Honolulu strawberry short-cake, the only remaining legitimate heir being Mrs. Bishop.

Her taste for kingdoms evidently had not been properly cultivated, for when the crown was offered to her she declined it with thanks. Thereupon an election was held and a new branch of royalty was created; and thus it came about that the present reigning sovereign possesses the throne.

I was told by several persons who knew Mrs. Bishop personally well during her lifetime, that she embodied in an eminent degree the richest qualities of pure and noble womanhood, and was in every respect a most accomplished and beautiful character. At her death, which occurred some

STATUE OF KAMEHAMEHA I.

years since, she bequeathed all of her large estate to the cause of education of Hawaiian youth, and the fruits of her noble benefaction are already apparent. Several of the buildings of the school established from her legacy have been erected, others are in process of construction, and the entire institution is in a flourishing, hopeful condition.

Mr. Bishop has supplemented his wife's magnificent gift, by generous donations, to the same school, from his own individual purse, and it was my good fortune to be present when a large preparatory building, built and presented by him, was turned over to the trustees. It is of gray lava-stone, quarried near by, neatly ornamented, and is admirably fitted throughout for the purpose intended. The school is established on the theory of manual training.

On the occasion referred to, I heard the boys sing, and also listened to a number of addresses delivered by eminent persons of Honolulu. Among them was one from an American resident of prominence. His remarks very properly urged upon the boys the vital importance of labor as an instrument of success in the world. He also dwelt with much fervor on the virtues of life, bearing down specially strong on the evils of intemperance.

Figuratively speaking, he rounded up the rum traffic after the most approved western forms. Mounting the fiery steed of his hot, impetuous eloquence, lariat in hand, he commenced circling at full swing round and around his scattered herd of arguments, until he had the individual members well clustered together and corralled; then he lassoed a few and hung on to them determinedly till the boys could come up and look them over; after which he gave them a little fatherly advice.

His voice was a trifle husky, and while speaking he kept a glass of water by his side, with which from time to time he moistened his blazing lips.

"Now, my dear boys," said he, still dwelling on the question of temperance, "let me urge upon you, never, under any circumstances, to enter a saloon; do not even go near one of those horrible, soul-destroying dens of infamy and destruction. But if by any chance you should ever be compelled to do so, under stress of circumstances such as are liable to occur, even to the most virtuous and temperate, take my advice and do this"—— and the speaker very deliberately raised the goblet to his lips and took a long draught of its contents. Then he proceeded with his suggestion, which it is needless to say was not fashioned after the object lesson he had so funnily and unwittingly exhibited to his audience.

While there, I was offered the opportunity and gladly availed myself of it, to examine the work of the boys, both in wood and iron, executed in the shops of the school. It was exceptionally well done, and displayed evidences of mechanical aptitude quite remarkable. Taking into account their antecedents, it was really quite surprising. They were, besides, duly appreciative of their skill and very proud of it, and crowded thickly about me as long as I remained, exhibiting their specimens of handiwork.

Mr. Bishop has also contributed a museum building to the school, and a large and choice collection of Hawaiian and other curios, the possessions of himself and wife, gathered during the many years of their lives together; but it is not yet in place in the building, nor catalogued.

The institution is known as the "Kamehameha School," and its site is one of the most commanding and delightful anywhere about Honolulu, embracing, as it does, extended views of sea, and mountain, and plain. Mr. Bishop is a courtly, polished gentleman, and in his conversation, is free from all ostentation and very friendly. He stands high in the community in every relation.

CHAPTER III.

ANOTHER passenger on the Mariposa was an ex-governor of the state of Vermont, going out to Samoa as United States Commissioner, with England and Germany, in the settlement of land titles. I found him an extremely genial and companionable man, and being, like myself, proof against the ravages of sea-sickness, we spent many pleasant hours together.

He had in his possession a recently published book, written by an ex-British Consul to Samoa, giving his experiences in that country during his term of office. Among other descriptions of native customs which the book contained, was that of making "ava," the national beverage. The liquor is manufactured from the root of a certain herb which grows plenteously on those islands, and which having first been chewed to a pulpy mass in sufficient quantities by young women, is mixed with water and then left to stand until ready for use. After the decoction has passed through the requisite stages of preparation, it assumes a greenish, unwholesome color, and if one is a "tenderfoot," the thought of drinking it is worse than the small-pox, with sea sickness and the Salvation Army included in the dicker.

The natives, however, regard it with such zealous consideration, that to refuse it, particularly when tendered as an offering of hospitality, which in the highest degree it is presumed to symbolize, is next door to a serious affront. One must either drink the stuff or run the risk of their disfavor.

We chaffed the governor a good deal, over the perplexing problem how to avoid the drink and still retain the esteem of the people, and considerable rambling fun was evolved from the situation.

The subject was again revived a day or two before our arrival in Honolulu, one of the passengers in the smoking room volunteering the opinion that limburger and onions, properly administered in sufficient doses, would act as an antidote, and recommending the governor to try it. Another thought laughing-gas just the thing; but the favorite remedy, and the only one that seemed to strike the new commissioner as at all suitable, was "to die first."

I ascertained afterwards, that this drink is not confined to Samoa alone, but is used quite considerably in the Hawaiian Islands as well, especially among the older natives, and during my visit I met a number of tourists and others who had seen it manufactured and drunk by the people. It, however, is not popular among the later generation.

Still another passenger of the Mariposa was a Mr. S——, formerly an active business man of Detroit, Michigan. He was quite out of health, and one's first impressions on being introduced to him were, "hands off 'till invited!" How often even the best judges of human nature go awry in their opinions of men, he who travels most best can understand. A more agreeable, chatty, or better informed, companionable man, it would be difficult to find. Rich in the diversified experiences of years, scientific in his tastes and cultured, he was able to bring into conversation subjects of interest which were always entertaining, and which rendered him a universal favorite in whatever circle he moved. Besides, he had traveled much over the world; yet not as most men travel, with no other purpose in view but to wear away time amid strange scenes and incidents; for, as an idle tourist, life to him would have been unendurable.

To illustrate: A few years since he spent some months in Japan; and while there, busied himself and gratified his aesthetic love of the beautiful, by getting together the largest collection of Japanese curios and other products of that country subject to art decoration now in America,—sixteen thousand specimens. It may be seen in the art museum of Detroit, the gift of its generous donor to his native city.

While in Hawaii, he was giving expression to his love of the natural, in the pursuit of marine shells, of which he had already gathered fifteen thousand specimens.

He retired from active business a number of years ago; but he could not be idle. The occupation of a collector in the realms of art and nature furnishes him with congenial employment, keeps alive and bright his keen, nervous temperament, and preserves him against that oxidizing process known as "rusting out;" a disease exclusively confined to wealthy men and tramps, who, laying aside the cares and burdens that afflict them, sit down indolently to rest till the heat of their life-day is over.

From San Francisco to Honolulu, seven days and seven nights, twenty-one hundred miles, not a sail of any kind was sighted. The ocean was a perfect blank. This was largely due to the fact, that the ocean steamers plying between those points do not follow the same course of travel as do the sailing vessels; and furthermore, to the limited number of all kinds of sea crafts, wherever radiating, that run out of San Francisco, compared with the great breadth of water they must necessarily compass. Even the steamers of the Oceanic line rarely sight each other, and the management, it is said, makes no effort to have them do so. The traveling public, it would seem, ought justly to be conceded greater consideration in this regard; for no watery waste on the footstool is more inhospitable, and certainly every means possible should be provided for interchange of reports between ships of the same line, that go out upon its bosom freighted with human lives.

The people of the Hawaiian kingdom are anxious that their islands should be known and visited; but they can depend upon it, that until the disadvantages and perils of travel in their direction are reduced to correspond with others, it will be up-hill work to induce tourists that way to any great extent.

They have, indeed, magnificent attractions to offer, of climate, and scenery, and marvellous natural wonders, and open-handed, generous hospitality. But there is a land to the east, full of alluring enticements, where the distance is no greater and the perils of reaching it much less; and there are, besides, the Bermudas, and Cuba, and Jamaica, and Mexico. If the modern tourist-for-pleasure is to be lured to Hawaii, the best of everything is the sweet, tempting bait that will accomplish it, and nothing less will.

On the sea the nights were glorious; the moon at its full. While the storm lasted, masses of beetling clouds begrimed the sky, but during fair weather, Luna rode sublimely through the heavens, illuminating with her gentle effulgence the great body of water over which we were voyaging, as if it were day.

Her grandeur thus was a new revelation to me. Strange it was that the moon and the heavens should so have impressed me. Certainly there was nothing new about the moon. I had known her always, but it had always been on the land. There, her face had been familiar to me in all weathers, and seasons, and in many places; in storm, and in the quiet of the night when " the stars sang together."

I had seen her, I thought, everywhere; where mountains were, and meadows, and vernal, green pastures, and fertile plains; and, years ago, among the southern woodlands, where the mocking-bird warbles in the night, enticed to rapturous song by her radiant graces. In all of those places had I seen her, but never before, face to face with the mighty ocean; never before, crowned, garlanded, and ablaze with the glory of the firmament, had I seen her come down from her lofty place and station and kiss the wrinkled sea.

As I stood on the deck of the Mariposa, and gazed at the magnificent spectacle above, and beneath, and all about me, I could not avoid feeling deeply impressed with the grandeur, the solemnity, and the order of the universe, as I never had felt it before. There was a newness, a novelty of experience about it, that drove the sensation down deep into my heart, there seeming to release the spirit of a new consciousness and send it with a thrill of exultation, like a winged messenger, caroling to the skies. It was a song that electrified, a picture that inspired me, drawing me up closer than ever before, to that Deep Mystery, by whose mighty hand all things are fashioned, governed and controlled. Thus powerfully are we sometimes influenced by the wonders and mysticisms of creation.

On the morning of December 18th, I was up early and out on deck, for we were expecting land; but until seven o'clock, it was nowhere discernible. In order to see the sun rise and to get the full freshness of the morning, I went out on the prow of the boat, forward, and for some time stood there alone, in the presence of the great silence all about me. There was a soft mist on the sea, a thin, dewy fog, calm and passive only, disturbed by those deep, smothered breathings below, which forever deny either rest or repose to the ocean. Not a particle of air was stirring.

The atmosphere was as gentle as June, and the laughing whispers of the water, as it crept in flaky undulations along the sides of the ship, were the only sounds to be heard. Occasionally, flying-fish darted here and there over the dark, smooth surface of the deep, glistening like tiny, silvered spectres in the hazy morning sun ; but aside from them no other signs of life did it offer.

Presently, across the port side of the boat, away in the distance, a black cloud seemed to rise up out of the sea and overcast the heavens faintly ; but as we proceeded, it grew more distinct, and finally assumed the form of an elevated body of land outlined against the horizon. This was Molokai; and we were nearly opposite that portion of it devoted to the leper settlement, about five miles distant to the south. A little further on, as we progressed, the island of Oahu loomed up to our right ; and very soon after, " Koko-Head," a fierce, barren promontory, the remains of an extinct volcano, pushed its brazen face boldly out into the channel before us.

For awhile, the whole shore of Oahu assumed a rugged, brown aspect, affording, through the field-glasses, fine opportunities for observation of its rocky formations. Then, " Diamond-Head," the point whence all true Hawaiians take their bearings to the uttermost parts of the earth, came into sight, dark, threadbare, corrugated, and shortly after, our course bent round its southwestern boundary and we were ushered into the waters of Honolulu harbor.

The entire landscape, before rounding Diamond-Head, had been brown, broken and forbidding, with scarcely a vestige of verdure about it ; now, all, like an act of Aladdin, was suddenly changed to magnificent green. I was afterwards frequently reminded of these striking contrasts, by the peculiarity of garb of the state prisoners, daily seen parading to and from their work through the streets of Honolulu, one side of their suits being plain brown, the other, a solid, dark blue ; and I wondered if it was another illustration of the tendency of man to copy unconsciously the object lessons and examples of nature, so manifest in many ways the world over.

FIRST VIEW OF OAHU.

The son of a prominent attorney of Honolulu, a bright, gentlemanly young boy, stood by my side as we entered the roadstead, and entertained me, pointing out places of interest: Kaala, the highest point of the island, away to the west, his sleepy crown hidden in banks of floating cumuli; Manoa, the rainbow valley; Mt. Tantalus, his spiral roadway bent, like a creeping python, in and out among the green foliage, from base to summit; Waikiki, the Long Branch of Hawaii, cocoanut-fringed by the sea; and Punchbowl, as prominent in the eyes of Honolulu as is the volcano of Kilauea in those of Hawaii.

Besides these, the spires and lofty places of many of the prominent buildings could be seen, shining white in the sun above the thick mass of greenery where the city lay, an inviting picture of quiet peace and comfort, resting against the slumbering foot-hills, between the mountains and the sea.

But who can describe the mountains themselves; those ancient battlements of fierce, gigantic forces that lie stretched along the shore? To me, there was nothing more fascinating than the study of them. In some places they were grandly ribbed, like columns fashioned to uphold the sky, now fallen prostrate. In others, they were furrowed with deep fissures, until the two effects, combined, might be compared to the fluted robe of some Titanic empress, which, at the waist, seemed to dissolve and vanish amid the shadows of their pinnacled peaks. Add to these, the light green of the kukui trees patched on the darker shades of the other dense foliage, which like a soft carpet lay over the mountains, and the scene, all in all, was simply enchanting.

We arrived in the inner harbor about ten o'clock. The sun was well up towards the zenith and had scattered the mists completely. All overhead was now a melting azure-blue. The waters about us were blue; and these, with the rich emerald-hue of the shore, and the flecks of white buildings peeping out from the tree tops, made a combination of color and design charming beyond description.

As we approached the wharf, a native pilot came out and boarded our vessel, and as we rode up to the dock, myriads of canoes, out-rigged in native fashion, were seen going in and out to the fishing fields on the reefs. A number of foreign vessels were lying at the various docks, loading and unloading, and a short distance out in the harbor, riding at anchor, was the United States war-ship Pensacola, painted black as the distresses that her duty engenders, but bearing at her mast-head that flag of all flags to thrill the patriotic American heart in foreign lands, the glorious Star-Spangled Banner.

It was indeed a lovely panorama ; and yet as I stood on the deck of the Mariposa and looked out over it, a sense of lonesomeness somehow crept across my heart ; for I was doomed to remain there a month, and it appeared to me a very few days would exhaust all of its resources. How happily I was disappointed the sequel of my story must show. Seven weeks did I spend there, seven weeks of delicious satisfaction ; and leaving, I carried away memories that can never be effaced while I live ; so sweet and delightful were my pleasures, so many the benefits I derived in the recuperation and rest of my stay.

CHAPTER IV.

AS soon as our boat touched the shore, we were inter-
viewed by a custom-house officer of the kingdom, to
whom we were invited to surrender up the keys of our
trunks and valises, and the numbers of our checks. I re-
luctantly did as requested, and on arrival of my baggage at
the hotel, was, much to my surprise, thoroughly convinced
that it had not been either opened or tampered with. The
fastenings were exactly as I had left them, and as a further
evidence, indisputable, and which could not possibly be
gainsaid, a small flask that lay exposed in my trunk, with a
slight quantity of Bourbon prescription still remaining in it,
had not been sampled or even touched. Who, after a test
such as that, could for a moment doubt the absolute ineffi-
ciency of the Hawaiian officials to protect the revenues of
their country ?

Babel was waiting for us when we went ashore, and such
a chattering as went up from the multitude of hackmen on
the street could only equalled by the thoroughbreds of San
Francisco. A big, off-hand, open-hearted fellow from California who was going through to Sidney, started to walk with
a crowd of us up the street to the hotel. The loud voice
and boisterous manner of one of the drivers attracted him,
and in his overflow of good spirits and humor, he stopped
and spoke to him.

"Do you charge anything to ride up town?" he asked.

"O, yes sah; yes sah; twenty-five cents, sah; get right in, sah!" quickly answered the versatile driver, preparing for his customer to embark.

"What, only two bits?" replied the traveler in a somewhat surprised manner; "tell me, now, Kanaka, one thing, and I'll ride up with you. How in the world does it come, that you can afford to waste so much good, merchantable, high-proof wind, and everlastingly dislocate your suspender buttons, bawling here as you are on the street, all for the paltry, miserable little sum of only two bits?"

"Excuse me for living, boss, but it's jes this way," promptly responded the quick-witted driver, taking off his hat and bowing very low; "you see it's fer charity, jes charity, sah, that we does it;" and his mouth broadened with a grin that was contagious. "If we doesn't do something to induce you Yankees to ride, when you comes out here among us, every blessed one of you will chase yourselves sick in de sun, and we'll have you all in de Queen's hosspistol; see? charity, boss, jes charity."

The interlocutor made no further attempt at argument, but followed by a volley of laughter from the balance of us, got into the carriage and was whirled away, while we who preferred to walk, even at the risk of getting sick at some body else's expense, started afoot for the "Royal Hawaiian Hotel."

As a rule, everybody of any standing in Honolulu rides, the degradation of walking being confined solely to those too poor to muster twenty-five cents, and to animals; and the consequent contempt with which we were surveyed by the hackmen was correspondingly pitiful.

As we advanced back from the dock into the business portion of the city, the shadows of drooping foliage of a variety of kinds, and a brisk, stirring breeze down through the gorges of the valleys, cooled our paths refreshingly; and dense shrubs, vines and flowers spread their beauty and their fragrance about us.   Having never before been among such scenes of luxuriant vegetation, I could only hold my breath in mute wonder, stare at what was before me, and wait what was coming, every fibre alive with delighted emotion.   It seemed like a vision of fairy-land.

Finally, we arrived at the hotel.   It is a solid building of

ROYAL HAWAIIAN HOTEL.

pleasing exterior, two stories high, built of concrete and wood, large, airy and commodious, and has broad piazzas numerously provided on all the floors. The establishment is located on a square of land of about four acres, in the very heart of the city, close to the royal palace, and is covered with tropical and semi-tropical trees, palms, algerobas, and others. A variety of shrubbery also adorns the grounds, and vines, some of which clamber to the tops of the tallest trees, thickly embowering their branches in festoons of flowers. Attached to the hotel are several tasty frame cottages, one of which was assigned to me during my temporary stay in Honolulu.

The Hawaiian kingdom is a constitutional monarchy, the present sovereign being Queen Liliuokalani. She came to the throne in January, 1891, next in line of title to King Kalakaua, of whom the most charitable thing that can be said is, he is dead.

Liliuokalani is a large, coarse-appearing, copper-colored woman, not at all such a person as one would naturally idealize in a queen; yet she bears herself gracefully in public, and in her official relations deports herself with becoming dignity. Seen on the streets in the States she would attract no particular attention, except it might be from some thrifty housewife in search of a good, strong kitchen domestic, or a fairy for that realm of home industry where soiled linen chiefly predominates; but for either of those places she would be considered a howling success. She is said to be, however, like all of her race, a woman of warm sympathies and generous impulses; but whether merited or not, it is a deplorable fact, that her private character is unblushingly bandied about, in a shameful manner, by the people of her own dominions who talk; and general sentiment seems to consider the castigation deserved. She is about fifty years of age, and a widow; her husband, a white man, having died less than a year since.

At the death of the present queen, Her Royal Highness, Princess, Victoria-Kawekiu-Kaiulani-Lunalilo-Kalaninuia-hilapalapa, will succeed to the throne; unless in the meantime she dies, or a political thunderbolt pulverizes the kingdom, which from present appearances is not wholly improbable. She is sixteen years of age, and at present is residing in Europe, where she is being doctored for her name and educated.

There are eight members of the royal family, or "Court," besides which the Queen has a cabinet of four ministers,

THE PRINCESS AND THE QUEEN.

and a " Privy Council " embracing a number of her most influential subjects. Other officers of the government, executive and judiciary, are plentiful, and the diplomatic and consular representatives of Hawaii abroad, numerous. There are about eighteen hundred salaried employees on the pay-roll of the kingdom.

The United States has an Envoy Extraordinary and Minister Plenipotentiary accredited to the country, at a salary of $7,500 per year; Mr. Stevens, of Maine, a fellow townsman of James G. Blaine. He is quite an agreeable gentleman, and has an enviable reputation for being ever zealous in any appropriate service he can render to his countrymen.

There is also a "Consul General," with a salary of $4,000, and several others occupying minor places. Nearly, if not all of the great European nations likewise have representatives; also China and Japan.

The salaries paid to the officers of the little kingdom, especially if one takes into account the number of its people, appear to be large. The last census of 1890 states the population to be 89,990. Appropriations for expenses, covering bi-annual periods, are made by the legislature, which consists of two branches, patterned after the British Parliament, and designated as Nobles and Representatives.

From "An act making appropriations for the two years ending March 31st, 1890," I copy a few of the more prominent items, viz.:

His Majesty's Private Purse.	$40,000 00
His Majesty's Household Expense	16,000 00
His Majesty's Chamberlain	6,000 00
Salary of Cabinet Officers, (each)	10,000 00
Salary of Envoy to Washington	12,000 00
Band, Flags and Salutes.	37,000 00
Salary of Chief Justice	12,000 00
Salary of four Associate Justices, (each)	10,000 00
Salary of four Circuit Justices, (each)	3,000 00
Salary of Police Justice, (Honolulu).	6,000 00
Salary of twenty-two District Judges, (each) 800 to	2,400 00

The total budget amounted to nearly three and a half million dollars.

The Queen's residence, known as "Iolani Palace," is situated on King street, in the central part of the city, in the middle of a square of land containing about ten acres. It was formerly enclosed by a high concrete wall, but in 1889, or thereabouts, an attempted revolution of the natives, under a man by the name of Wilcox, demonstrated its availability as a rampart of military defense for the enemy; hence, it was soon after shorn down, and now stands only about three feet high, a simple line around the royal prem-

IOLANI PALACE.

ises. The grounds are abundantly shaded, and ornamented with trees and shrubbery.

In one corner of the palace grounds, is "The Bungalow," a low, latticed building, reminding one of the architecture of India as seen in books. It is occupied as the private apartments of the sovereign.

The palace building itself is a plain, substantial structure of concrete, 100 x 140 feet, with a tower 84 feet high in the center, and contains forty rooms. It is stated to have cost half a million dollars; but if that be true, there must have been a luscious fat-fry in the contract for somebody, a thing more than likely anyhow, if reports are to be relied on, as jobbery is said to have been conspicuously active in Hawaii, wherever public improvements have distributed the people's money, for many years past.

King Kalakaua himself wasn't above petty peculations, and during his reign, acquired quite a reputation for always having a finger in the poi whenever Public Plunder held the calibash; a liberal supply of pelf, it is alleged, invariably sticking to his fingers when the day of division came round among the ringsters.

In 1887, public corruption became so rank that an uprising and overthrow of the government was seriously threatened, and had not the king, at the time, put himself into the attitude of acquiescence he did, under the reform constitution framed and forced upon him by the better element of the people, his reign would have been of short duration.

The following extracts from a series of resolutions adopted at a mass meeting in Honolulu, June 30th, 1887, which were presented to him, and which he had the wisdom to answer on short notice and defer to, will show the temper of his subjects during that period and, in part, what they complained of:

Resolved, That the administration of the Hawaiian Government has ceased, through corruption and incompetence, to perform the functions and afford the protection to personal and property rights for which all government exists.

In order so far as possible to remove the stain now resting on the throne, we request of the king that he shall cause immediate restitution to be made of seventy-one thousand dollars recently obtained by him in violation of law, and of his oath of office, under promise that the persons from whom the same was obtained should receive the license to sell opium, as provided by statute of the year 1886.

In addition to this pointed " request," his subjects further demanded from him a specific pledge that he would not thereafter interfere with elections; that he would not attempt to unduly influence legislation ; that he would not interfere with the constitutional administration of his cabinet ; and that he would not use his official position and patronage for private ends. And as a final wind-up, they demonstrated to him " the divine right of kings," after the American fashion, as follows :

" And said committee is hereby instructed to request of the king that a personal answer be returned *within twenty-four hours*, and to further inform the king that his neglect to answer within said time will be construed as a refusal of the said request."

The principal promulgators, organizers, and executive forces of this revolution, which proved to be a bloodless one only because the king conceded to their every demand within the time granted him, were prominent white citizens of the kingdom and determined men; and the moderation displayed by them, when they had the reins of government substantially in their own hands, showed conclusively their law-abiding purposes and disposition. Their forbearance was certainly commendable in the highest degree ; for Kalakaua had so demeaned himself, and had so shamefully disgraced his reign, that he could have found no just cause of complaint had they even gone so far as unceremoniously to kick him off the throne and run him out of the country. It was a lesson in home rule and royal discipline demanded by special exigencies, and the men engaged in the castigation were courageous enough to administer what the king deserved without fear or favor, and they did it promptly.

Being in themselves essentially radical, revolutionary measures, when successful, are always liable to breed reforms of individual selfishness and bear fruits of injustice. It was so in this instance. The constitution forced upon Kalakaua and the country demanded stringent educational and property qualifications in electors, and its practical workings have been to disfranchise many of the native sons of the soil.

This occasioned great dissatisfaction, and provoked much ill-feeling against the white foreigners of the kingdom, and looking at the matter through the eyes of one who favors the utmost protection of the rights of universal suffrage, the indignation seems to have been amply warranted; for so long as life and liberty continue to be valued as of more worth than wealth, so long will disfranchisement, for such reasons, be considered a wrong and an injustice. Besides, it was little less than an outrage to take from those people the precious right of self-government on their own soil and give it to foreigners, and if they have a drop of common manhood in their veins they will never amiably submit to it.

I was in Honolulu during much of the time that the campaign of 1892 was being fought for representatives in the legislature. Three parties were in the field; the " Reform " or " Missionary " party and the " Liberals " being the two extremes relative to repealing the educational and property qualification clauses in the constitution of 1887, which was the main issue, and the " National Reform " party, that claimed to be conservative. A good deal of prejudice was engendered, and a foment of bad temper aroused between whites and natives much to be deplored.

Political meetings were held almost nightly, where addresses were made. The absurdity of some of them was amusing. I copy a few, taken from the *Daily Pacific Advertiser*, made by natives, candidates for office.

J. W. Bipikane said : " I am an ignorant man ; yes, too ignorant to take bribes. Former legislators have sold their brains for money. I solemnly swear before the goddess Pele and the Shark-god that I will not receive bribes. Some one has asked me how we are going to obtain the new constitution. If we cannot get the Queen to sign our constitution, let the forty thousand Hawaiians send a petition to France, and other powers, asking them to aid us to get a new constitution. If elected, it is your duty to watch me. If I take bribes, do not hesitate to shoot me."

C. B. Maile said: "I am not a fluent speaker. My only platform to show you is equality. I don't know anything about law. You can find me every day at the fish market."

C. H. Cummings said: "My grandfather was a chief, and he owned an ahupuaa at Makawao. The missionaries induced my grandfather to sell his estate for twenty-five cents an acre. My grandfather became a drunkard, and vicious, and was ruined. I think he is now in hell. A national bank will remove our present monetary crisis. England, Russia, France and Italy are flooded with bank-notes."

Hon. L. W. P. Kanealii said: "The constitution was really republican because there were two sovereigns, the queen and the cabinet."

The credulity of the Hawaiian natives is phenomenal, and is only equalled by their simplicity and ignorance. Hence, intriguing men readily find in them pliable instruments for their knavish schemes and designs, and of late years have manufactured much mischief among them. To an unbiased outsider, it seems scarcely possible that a kingdom so inefficiently governed and puerile as this can long exist, or retain its autonomy, especially amid such contending forces as here prevail. It can offer no assurances of stability or protection to any one, but like a frail nest on a frail bough, is itself forever beaten and lashed by every fickle wind, and is liable at any moment to fall and be dashed to pieces. Capital fears, and no one has any confidence in it.

CHAPTER V.

A FEW STATISTICS AND THINGS—RECIPROCITY—THE SUGAR
INDUSTRY—JAPANESE AND CHINESE
CUSTOMS—ETC.

THE territory over which her majesty, Liliuokalani,
reigns, is composed of eight islands, lying midway in
the Pacific Ocean, just over the border line of the tropics.
Geographically, they may be found between the 19th and
23rd parallels of north latitude, and from longitude 155 to
161 west.

Five only of the islands are important: Hawaii, Maui,
Oahu, Kauai and Molokai; three are indifferent, and devoted principally to sheep grazing, viz.: Lanai, Niihau and
Kahoolawe. The aggregate acreage of all of them is about
4,000,000, of which Hawaii embraces five-eighths and Oahu
less than one-eighth. In point of population, however, Oahu
ranks first, containing more than a third of all the inhabitants of the kingdom; Hawaii, in this respect, ranks second.

The climate is simply perfection. A summary of observations taken by Professor Lyons of Oahu college, Honolulu, for the year, from July, 1890, to June, 1891, shows an
average temperature of 75.05; the highest average of any
month being 77.55, the lowest 68.92. The rain-fall on the
east or windward side of the islands is plentiful and in some
sections excessive; but on the leeward side it is ordinarily
very dry, and for purposes of agriculture, artesian wells or
irrigation from the mountains must be resorted to.

The total valuation of the real and personal property of

the kingdom, for taxation, is in round numbers about $35,000,000; and from this about $500,000 is collected annually; equivalent to about six dollars per capita. High authority estimates the government cost of collecting this amount to be more than eleven and one-half per cent. of the whole sum collected. This in itself is a heavy burden on the wheels of Hawaiian progress, and, if continued, must sooner or later wear out the grease of its axles and make the old cart squeak.

The load, too, it is said, rests very unevenly on the people; the poor, as usual, doing most of the paying, while the rich possess pretty nearly everything in sight. The great sugar interests, it is claimed, hold fully two-thirds of all the property values of the kingdom, and yet they pay only about one-fifth of the taxes.

The principal revenues of the government, however, are not derived from internal taxation, but from customs duties, which bring to the coffers of the kingdom, directly and indirectly, about $700,000 per annum. Under a treaty with our government, which has been for many years in force, nearly $4,000,000 worth of goods are annually imported from the United States free of duty; while of all that are brought in from all sources, seventy-five per cent. comes from the the United States and sixteen per cent. from Great Britain.

The aggregate amount of exports from the kingdom for the year 1890 was about $13,000,000; of which more than $12,000,000 was in sugar, one hundred and thirty thousand tons; and more than $500,000 in rice. All of the exports of the country went to the United States, except five tons of sugar and one hundred pounds of coffee. This illustrates in a striking manner how closely their business and industrial interests are allied to us.

And here is a lesson for agriculturalists in behalf of Yankee protection.

Prior to the year 1876, the Hawaiian kingdom was in a state of woeful depression; every industry was clogged and at a standstill; and her exports, as given by one of the best-informed business men of the islands in a recent speech, amounted only to about a million dollars per annum.

Labor was in no demand and the people were poor. Many embarked in the sugar business; the soil was excellent, the climate unsurpassed; but failure almost invariably followed such investments, often bankruptcy. The country and the people were poverty-stricken.

By a happy stroke of good fortune, at that particular time, a treaty was effected with the United States, under which our government acquired for a term of years, certain rights in the Hawaiian Islands which we alone were to enjoy and which were not to be granted to any other nation.

In consideration of these important concessions in our favor by Hawaii, our government took that little nation under her protecting wing, and gave to her substantially every privilege and right of free commercial intercourse that exists between the different States of the American Union. Her products were to come into the United States free of duty, and our goods were to be admitted into her ports in the same untrammeled manner. Not absolutely all articles were so admitted, but the treaty covered so nearly all that those not included have since cut very little figure.

Hawaii, thus, to all intents and purposes, became a protected colony of the United States; a sort of step-sister, so to speak, in the proud young family of the American Republic. She took the same attitude in her trade relations with us, as if she had been really annexed; her sugar planters especially (and sugar is the only industry worth speaking of on the Islands) were on an exact footing with ours of Mississippi and Louisiana. See the result!

Immediately every industry began to thrive, and money by the millions commenced flowing to Hawaii for investment. Enormous plantations were established, involving in some cases stupendous sums; sugar-mills sprang into being; steamboat lines radiated among the islands; and vessels owned by Hawaiian subjects soon spread their white sails all along her shores. In a few years wealth and luxury prevailed where before had been poverty and distress; everybody was happy; and from a single million of dollars exports, the amount ran rapidly up, until, as before stated, it exceeds thirteen millions.

The Sandwich Islands now blossomed as odorously as do the wild roses that bloom on Hawaii. Labor at once became scarce; consequently, when the toiler worked he got well paid for his services. The rich went to Europe, and either there or in America educated their children. The poor rode in carriages. Comfortable homes came to be the patrimony of all; many had luxurious ones.

In 1890—unfortunately for Hawaii—the McKinley bill passed the United States Congress, and its practical effects were to place that little protege of fifteen years' careful nursing, now fully developed into a vigorous, buxom maid, back into the cold, cold world, to scrub for herself, and take her chances along with the rest of her foreign sisters, in their chase after doubtful prosperity. For under the provisions of the McKinley bill, the sugar interests of Hawaii came to be no longer protected; the similar product of every other nation being, by that enactment, thereafter admitted equally as free, as had been hers exclusively for so many years past.

Now see another transformation! The Hawaiian Islands in financial distress; business stagnant; planters despondent of the future; embarrassment staring them in the face; and labor, already cut fifteen to twenty-five per cent., threatened with more; or worse still, the importation of coolies. Where could be found a better object-lesson than this for our farmers?

The liquor traffic of Hawaii has rough roads over which to travel, and yet enormous quantities of the stuff are consumed. The imports of 1890 were valued at about $320,000, the tariff bringing to the treasury about $340,000. It will thus be seen that the duty exceeded, by quite a tolerable sum, the original invoice cost of the goods. A license of one thousand dollars per annum is also exacted for the privilege to sell.

There are probably, all told, not a dozen saloons in the kingdom; but what there are, notwithstanding the high price of their tarantula juices, seem wonderfully to thrive. Everything goes at twenty-five cents a drink; cock-tails, gin, lemonade or beer. McKinley is not the only enemy that the islands have got, nor leprosy their only disease. " Give the devil his due."

Like everything else in Hawaii, the cost of living has been and still continues to be very expensive; but the present, general depression will undoubtedly modify that, after a time, to correspond with other conditions, for the luxuries and extravagancies of the past are unquestionably on the eve of a decided change all along the line. The hotels in particular give emphatic expression to the scarcity of the food supply of the islands and the consequent high value at which it is held, and the least said about them, therefore, the better. If, however, I were going to offer advice to a friend, who chanced to be contemplating a trip to Hawaii, I should say: Take everything with you which you generally carry when traveling in America or Europe, except your appetite; leave that at home or in San Francisco. For unless you can feast and grow fat on views, curry and rice, with an occasional noon sandwich of climate and cold mutton thrown in, you will very likely waste avoirdupois during your visit.

The principal industry of the islands, as before stated, is sugar. The largest plantation is at Sprecklesville, on the island of Maui, the Hawaiian Commercial Company, otherwise Claus Spreckles, proprietor.

To describe this plantation and its mills would take up many pages of space; hence I will summarize. It is located on an arable plain at the foot of the mountain slopes, close to the sea, and was formerly an arid waste; but by the outlay of enormous sums of money in irrigation, and of energy and labor, it has been brought into great prolificness. The capital stock of the company is $10,000,000.

In bringing the water from the mountains for distribution over the twelve thousand acres of land constantly under cultivation, thirty gulches are crossed, some of them more than two thousand feet wide and four hundred feet deep, and twenty-one thousand feet of 42-inch pipe is required to span those places alone.

The water is conducted to the plantation through flumes and ditches, of which, in all, there are sixty-one miles, capable of delivering eight million cubic feet per day. There are also five reservoirs located at different points on the premises, convenient for storage, the largest having a capacity of forty million cubic feet.

The company owns forty thousand acres of land in this one tract. Twenty-five thousand acres of it is suitable for cane, not, however, all under cultivation. The balance is only good for grazing. One can travel for fifteen miles in a given direction, through its growing mazes, purple-crowned, sweet and delectable, and yet not exceed the limits of the plantation.

The mill on the premises is capable of producing one hundred tons of sugar per day; just think of it! 200,000 pounds! How is that for a honeymoon? And yet, while this is the largest plantation in the kingdom, it is not, by any means, the only one.

There are thirty-eight incorporated companies engaged in sugar production in the Hawaiian Isles, whose aggregate capital stock exceeds twenty-six millions of dollars; more than twenty-two millions of this is American. There are, besides, about thirty companies that are not incorporated, whose estimated value is six millions of dollars; half of it American.

The labor of the plantations is Chinese, Japanese, and Portuguese; the latter commands the best wages. The Kanakas, although more in point of numbers than all of the others, combined, do not figure conspicuously in any of the details of sugar production; they are so outrageously shiftless and lazy. And this reminds me of a conversation I once had in Honolulu with a very shrewd, eccentric, old Spaniard, who used occasionally to bring figs to my cottage. He was a chattering old expert of life-long failures, but withal, a man of considerable experience and observation in the world, and above all things else, was particularly fond of ventilating his own opinions. The mother tongue of every nation on earth, he said, was in some manner specially adapted to matters of grave import, and each in some particular respect excelled all others.

The English and Americans, for instance, were bluff and outspoken, always right to the point; their language was that of business, and through it they had conquered the commerce of the world. The French, on the contrary, were suave in conversation, smooth and polite in manners, and possessed of an innate faculty to say and unsay whatever they desired in a single sentence and in the self-same breath. Theirs was the language of diplomacy. The Germans were gruff, stuffy and short-winded; their speech was only fit for horses.

"But," said I, "you have forgotten your own language, my friend; how about the Spaniards?"

"O!" he replied, clasping together his hands and rolling his eyes to heaven, "Spanish is the utterance of love; soft, sweet, gentle as the breezes among these algerobas. Spanish is the discourse of angels; the only articulate sound worthy to be whispered into the ears of women; it is the dialect of music, of poetry, of art and of song."

"Very beautiful!" I replied, laughingly, charmed by his eloquent and patriotic enthusiasm, "but now how about the Kanakas, what is the peculiar fitness of their native tongue?"

"Bah!" he blurted, throwing up his two hands and opening wide his mouth, "Bah! good for nothing, good for nothing but to bellow for gin on the street and bawl in their shanties for poi." And in this he has many to confirm his judgment.

The Portuguese workingmen on the plantations live like civilized people, and have, ordinarily, comfortable homes. Their women, also, sometimes work in the fields with them (for they are an industrious people), and the Japanese women, too, are occasionally seen there; but the Chinese never.

The Japanese people delight in their homes, their simple abodes, rustic in pattern, being invariably toned by the spirit of the Mikado's kingdom. These resemble, in many respects, the ancient grass houses of the Hawaiian natives. But no matter how cheap or insignificant the structure may be, they never fail to incorporate into it that rude, indescribable sentiment of the beautiful which so strongly illustrates the art tendencies of their race. They also have the economics of life thoroughly studied, and their practical application is observable wherever you see the abode of a Jap.

A custom, frequently observed among them, consists in planting running vines, which bear edible fruits, close around the foundations of their little, thatch-roofed cottages. These, when they begin to grow, clamber up the sides and over the tops of the houses in a prolific mass of verdure, cool and delicious, and later on, when they bloom, decorate the entire roofs with the charm of flower and of color. At maturity, what before was esthetic, materializes into food supply, and is utilized for that purpose. Does not this one illustration alone tell much of the story of the world-renowned art-culture and thrift of this wonderful race?

A JAPANESE HOME.

No other eastern civilization has so readily responded to that of Christendom as the Japanese. May not this be due to the common motherhood of Art, around which the sympathetic children of all nations cluster, as do particles of metal round a magnetized center, no matter how widely distributed, or howsoever far they may be set apart by race or condition?

The Chinese, on the contrary, seem to be almost akin to the animals, and like animals they burrow wherever they can find a hole to crawl into or a room to store a bag of rice. Yet, perhaps, there is no other nation on earth whose people are so uniformly industrious. They swarm together like ants, and like them go in and out of their miserable quarters, day by day, bringing back from their expeditions of search whatever of crumbs they can pick up.

They have no sympathy with any other race of people, and desire no affiliation or association with them. Nor have they much of the " milk of human kindness " for each other. Ages of struggle for the bare necessities have crystalized in them the art of simply living; they have reduced to the minimum the cost of maintaining a human life, and they know exactly just how many grains of rice are daily needful for that purpose.

An old physician who for a number of years sailed between San Francisco and Hong Kong, and whose experiences thus brought him into very close association with the Chinese, especially the emigrant portion, told me they were so supremely selfish, and so utterly indifferent to the sufferings of one another, that rather than render the trifling service necessary to feed one of their number, too sick and weak to feed himself, they would stolidly permit him to lie on the deck of the boat, and die before their eyes from neglect. And this, he said, was the rule rather than the exception.

But in case of death, no matter how poor the fellow-passenger might be, if he were only a Chinaman, thirty dollars to embalm the body and carry it back to China, could be raised by subscription among them in less than five minutes. This, however, was not due to humanity, but to religion; for Confucius wrote : " Every Chinese must be buried in his own soil."

The Chinese are forbidden by law to come into Hawaii,

except as laborers under contract, and when they come, —and the Japs, too, for that matter—are obliged to deposit a sufficient sum of money to defray the expense of their return passage home when their term of service has expired. And when that time comes they must go. Neither race is granted citizenship, and viewed in the light of self-preservation, wisely so ; for if the immigration of either were permitted unchecked, they would soon monopolize every branch of industry, and overrun the island like rats.

CHAPTER VI.

NATURAL ATTRACTIONS OF HAWAII AND ITS VEGETATION—
FISH—FRUITS—BIRDS—BUGS—INSECTS
AND REPTILES.

THERE is much that is beautiful in all of the Hawaiian Islands. The sky is forever glorious, both in its magnificent, varying tints of blue, and in the delicate massiveness (if such a paradox is permissible) of floating clouds, which somewhere over the broad vault, or along the mountain tops, or close down to the sea, can at all hours of the day be observed, idly drifting, like the enchanted squadron of some fairy corsair, where the current is calm and where there is neither breeze nor motion.

And, in addition, there are the mountains with their creeping cloud-shadows, which, as one transparent, fleeting shade dissolves into another, divert the imagination to those iridescent stones often displayed by dealers in their mirrored windows, ever changing color as we stand and watch them.

The ocean, too, always grand in its far-reaching amplitude, ever full of life, motion and mystery, now caressing the shore with soft murmurs, and now storming it with furies which are appalling, holds much that absorbs the mind and chains the thought with worlds of endless fancy.

With one who by taste and disposition is fond of the versatilities of nature, the keen relish and delight of such experiences seems never to change or pall, the picture never grows old. What was new yesterday is new to-day, and will be new tomorrow. The glory of it all is boundless; it is not of the earth earthly; even the sky does not hem it in.

The fanciful imagination of man is unconfined either by boundaries or space; but, wandering alone in illimitable fields of beauty, it builds castles of its own out of its own raptures, richer in fabled charms and grandeur than ever the eye of mortal man beheld.

One can scarcely conceive of a country more abounding in natural attractions than are these islands of Hawaii. All of them winningly invite the tourist, but some there are, which, in addition to those inducements common to all, hold others still, specially confined to themselves; like rare souvenirs whose duplicates no one possesses.

Kauai is known as "the garden island," and boasts of Hanalei valley, and its rivers and waterfalls. Here, too, are the "Barking Sands of Mana," which emit a growling sound when one treads over them on the beach. Scientific men say that this phenomenon is due to their peculiar conformation; but the natives shake their heads, and declare that it comes from no such thing, but from the "uhanes," or spirits of their departed ancestors, who take this method to manifest their displeasures at being disturbed.

The Island of Maui contains a rare combination of wonderful opposites; the lovely, picturesque valley of Iao, nestled like a stray bit of Swiss scenery here in the tropics, and the mighty extinct crater of Haleakala, which, like an awful, black hell, lies sunk deep in the crown of the mountain, ten thousand feet above it. Haleakala is by far the largest volcanic crater in the world, seven miles across, twenty miles around it. Within this mammoth basin are fourteen distinct sub-craters, each of which in times past spouted separate columns of fire and smoke high into the air, lending igneous fury to the lurid sky for leagues around. Now they stand cold, moody and silent on its broken floor, two thousand feet down, and though each is five or six hundred feet high, appear to the observer, from his lofty summit, nothing more than trifling, insignificant mounds ; so deep are they buried in the heart of this great upheaval.

Immense gorges, too, are slashed in its wrinkled sides ; precipitous canyons leading down to the sea, along which seething torrents of hissing flame once rushed in frantic fury, and plunged into the deep, in the days of its mighty convulsions.   Now when ocean storms gather, as they frequently

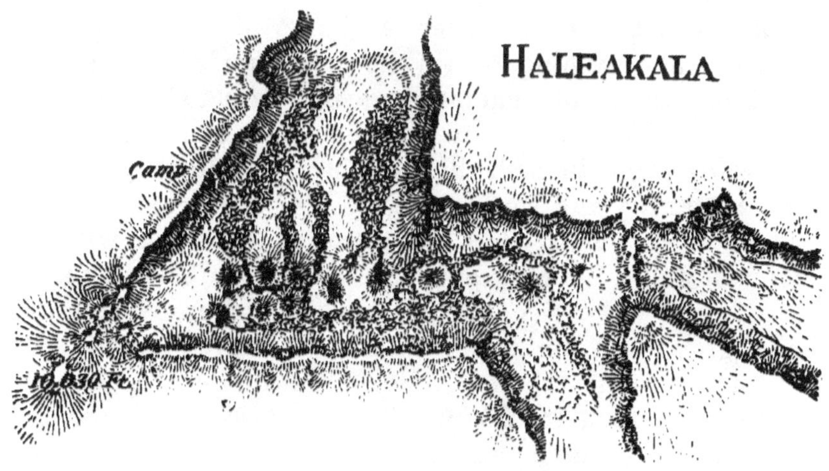

do in this tropical, torrid-swept zone, those hollow places fill with battling clouds, which, marshalled in sweeping columns, roll up their jagged defiles, till the crater of majestic Haleakala is deluged to fullness, and naught can be seen of his giant basin but a sea of white, as if here were gathered the shearings of all the fleecy Cotswolds of the world.

And then up from below come the fierce trade-winds, or konas, rushing, like demons, in pursuit of the clouds that have fled before them, twirling, squeezing and twisting their vaporous volumes into eddies and whirlpools, until crushed and dissolved, they flow back in torrents, down over the old-time channels of fire, to mingle again with the sea.

The island of Hawaii, for its special attraction, has Kilauea, the largest active volcano in the known world, the boiling pit of fire which it contains being nearly a mile in circumference.

Oahu has Honolulu, the Coral City of the Pacific; built on coral, fringed with coral, and with coral colorings, pink and white, forever radiant, like a precious gem dropped from a perfect sky.

Molokai is the sweet sister of charity of the group, ever holding to her weeping bosom the great grief of the nation.

The luxuriance of vegetation everywhere to be observed on all of the islands is a never-ceasing source of pleasure to those who delight in such things; it is so wonderfully profuse both in quantity and variety.

There is the eucalyptus forest-tree of Australia, with its medicinal gums, which grows to a perfection here, equal to that of its own native heaths; and the algeroba, another choice growth, whose delicate, fern-like leaves tremble fitfully in the faintest breeze, among multitudes of pods that furnish alike fuel, refreshing shade, and food for animals. This tree is not indigenous, but on account of its numerous utilities, is believed to be one of the coming sources of wealth of Hawaii.

Along the mountain sides grows the kukui tree, whose nuts are brought into service in many ways by the natives, both as food and for personal adornment; and the koa, from which furniture is made, the grain being exceedingly close and firm, and susceptible also of a very high polish. It would consume altogether too much time and space to enumerate in detail all of the native arboreous growths that are found here, hence I will confine myself to a few of the more prominent ones only.

THE WINE PALM.

The banyan is found in many private enclosures, the largest specimen, probably, on the premises of Mr. Cleghorn near Waikiki. This is fully a hundred and fifty feet in diameter across its branches, which are supported from the ground by several auxiliary trunks. It was interesting to observe how those trunks are formed. Hundreds of slender rootlets are perpetually putting out from the laterals of the tree, and dropping like the suspended threads of insects to the earth. Only a few of them, however, ever reach or fasten there, but occasionally one does, and ultimately becomes a large upright stem. In this manner, the whole space under the branches of a banyan is sometimes thickly occupied with trunks, like a miniature forest.

The hau is a gigantic shrub of rank quality, whose leaf-less arms, like huge serpents, wind writhingly together in an inextricable maze over large spaces of ground, their tops embowered in foliage. It is often trained for arbors in private grounds, producing excellent canopies of protection against the sun. The hau, in reality, is a native species of the hibiscus, and, like all shrubs of that kind, is superb when in bloom.

Then there are the palms, how many varieties, I do not know, but every yard is full of them. There is the "royal palm," erect as a polished column, the upper portion of its trunk bright and shining green, its head crowned with a tuft of waving, fern-like leaves, in my estimation, the king of all tropical trees.

The "wine palm" stands next in beauty, bearing at the base of its clumpy, thick foliage, large, sinuous masses of chain-like fiber-plumes, which hang in loose, unraveled clusters from its trunk, like the curls of a young child's hair. The "screw palm" also figures conspicuously everywhere about Honolulu; and the "date palm," whose species produces the fruit of commerce; and the

" traveler's palm," which bleeds, when tapped, an abundance of water sufficient to satisfy thirst, from which peculiarity it derives its name ; and many others that, to me, an ignorant denizen of the wild-woods of the North, brought confusion of memory, and a general struggle of the mental faculties to bear up decently under the multitude of their names.

Among shrubs there is likewise great variety, first, in my esteem, being the hibiscus. It constitutes many of the dividing lines between residences along the main streets of the fashionable parts of the city, forming a lustrous, green hedge, bespangled with scarlet blossoms, which, at a distance, look like birds of brilliant plumage scattered over it. The "oleander" is another vigorous, out-door plant, bearing its pink flowers high in the air, in great quantities. The " heliotrope," too, grows to a large size, and blossoms odorously.

It would require a botanist to name even a part of the plants one observes while passing along the streets of Honolulu. There was one that particularly attracted me, but the name of which, in spite of repeated inquiries, I could not ascertain. Its beauty was in its leaves ; it had no blossom. It was a flower unto itself, a beautiful, variegated mass of color, pink and white predominating.

Wherever you go, through the principal thoroughfares, immense, crimson leaves peer up at you over the fences, and shrubs of endless hue and fancy glance shyly out from hidden cloisters of rare umbrage, giving, altogether, a resplendency to the lawns that dazzles and bewitches the novice.

Of climbing vines, there were honeysuckles, and nasturtiums, and convolvuli, and, it appeared to me, every other common, clinging plant of flowering sweetness I had ever seen grow in the States, or elsewhere ; and there were besides many others. Some of the varieties, rare to me, ran to the very tops of the trees, great algerobas, or others equally as tall, smothering their branches in purple clusters of bloom, till they resembled huge nosegays of florescent beauty as large as hay-ricks. These were the Bougainviliers.

Another vine which greatly attracted me, bore infinite

MANGOES.

clusters of long, yellow, finger-shaped flowers, which completely covered the roofs of the buildings where it ran (its preferences seeming specially to incline it to such places), thus presenting a spectacle at once peculiarly odd and brilliant. The Mexican creeper, the passion flower, and the jasmine also abounded.

The abundance of all sorts of flowering life of the islands is wonderful; roses, and tuberoses, and moss roses, and climbing roses, and geraniums of immense size, and lilies, and what others I shall not attempt to enumerate. There are said to be eight hundred and forty-four species of blossoming plants in Hawaii, and this number, I think, can be safely relied on, for any attempt at prevarication would certainly have made it an even thousand. The century plant grows wild, and the lantana curses the soil wherever it gets a foothold, with its aggressive spread and growth.

The fruit products embrace nearly every known kind that thrives in the tropical zone, and many of the temperate as well.

Oranges of fine quality grow spontaneously, and there are twenty different varieties of bananas from which to select. Cocoanuts, bread-fruit, custard-apples, dates, figs, lemons, limes, pine-apples, mangoes, pomegranates, melons, and strawberries, all are found; and they are only a part of the number and variety.

The mango is said to possess certain qualities and characteristics purely its own, and which eminently justify the high regard in which it is held by the natives, but as it was not in season during my visit, I was unable to verify the statement personally. I have, however, the testimony of reliable parties bearing on the subject, and will repeat it as it was given to me.

It transmits a flavor to the taste that reminds one strongly of turpentine; in fact, it is said so much to resemble that resinous liquid, that rheumatic individuals, uninitiated into its secrets and mysteries, have, after taking a first bite of the fruit, been known to immediately rub the balance of it over their bodies. History has failed to record the result, but the instinct of the application would seem to bespeak merit; at all events, there is a sum of comfort in the story for those who now dance to the rythm of such music.

Notwithstanding this first repugnance, after awhile you acquire a taste for mangoes, just as you do for poi ; and then you hunger for them, as did the children of Israel for the flesh-pots of Egypt.

When, therefore, thou hast arrived at that blissful state, prepare thyself, O man! for new harmonies, and attune thy crop to the divine afflatus ; for esculent symphonies or rare joy are about to be let loose on thee!

Now order a bath-tub, and then unloosing every fretful garment, command that the fruit be brought. A peck is said to be a very moderate allowance for one sitting, and when you have finished it (if you still continue to exist), you will have inbibed worlds of happiness, and more mango juice than ever you thought it possible a human body could contain. The Kanakas have a tradition that just inside the gates of Paradise is a mango grove, where the faithful obtain their first taste of celestial joys.

Another of the products, found in abundance in Hawaii, is the guava. Hanging unplucked on its native bush, which is quite like that of the lemon, it has much the appearance of that fruit and is every way luscious to the eye. The rind, however, is thick and acrid, but inside is a seedy mass of pink-colored pulp, very grateful to the taste, and from this a delicious jelly is made, equal to apple, or quince, or currant.

The papaya is another oddity of vegetable nature. The tree resembles the palm, or more nearly, perhaps, the cocoanut, and at the top of its tall, slim trunk, which shoots to a considerable height up from the ground, is an umbrella-shaped crown of dark-green leaves. The fruit which it bears is large and smooth, and in color, when ripe, a bright yellow.

To the eye, it very closely resembles our musk-melon, except in the matter of shape ; in that regard it is more like an
apple or plum.   To see great numbers of these clustered
together in masses around the trunk of the tree, high up
under its leaves and branches, is a novel sight, and on one

GUAVAS.

occasion, nearly drove an American granger, who was visiting the islands, to distraction.   He hadn't any use, he said,
for any such heathenish country.

   "Punkins belonged on the ground, and there was suthin'
wrong, sumwhere, when they got to plantin' 'em on the

trees. No wonder they had earthquakes, and leprosy, and McKinley! The hull thing was rotten, and out o' regular, and jest as likely as not to fly to pieces any minnit; and by the nickel-plated dumb-bells of Xanthippe! he was a goin' to git out." And he got.

Birds are not very abundant around Honolulu, except the ubiquitous little English sparrow, which somehow has found his way out there, and the " mynah."

I have always been a very fond admirer of the English sparrow. Wherever I meet him I am sure to be his friend. He is so richly endowed with those independent character- istics which human nature always extols. He attends to his own knitting, fears nobody, loves his family and friends, and gets possession of just as much of this world's good things as he possibly can. Let the growling biped who doesn't like these qualities throw stones at the English sparrow; he can't possibly hurt him; for a man of that type won't have energy enough to throw more than once, and the force of his missile, even should it strike, couldn't do much dam- age to so brave a little Trojan.

The " mynah " is an importation from India, and is very abundant about Honolulu and on the island of Oahu. He is about the size of a small robin, is proud and shy, and his yellow beak, and wattles of the same color behind his eyes, render his appearance very ornamental. The main part of his body is brown, tinged with black, with white markings on the tail and wings. He has a peculiar habit of grating his bill together, that sounds like a man in the agony of fits, and his song is about as musical as a cat-fight. He is a great " scrapper " though, and he and the English sparrow are at it a good deal of the time, nip and tuck; but the sparrow, despite the disparity of their sizes, is said to be too much for him.

The English sky-lark was imported into the country some

years ago, and is doing well and increasing in numbers. It haunts the regions round about Pearl Harbor, where its glorious carols ravish the early-morning dawn with exultant melody.

There is a wild dove, quite common in Oahu, that resembles very much our turtle-dove; its "coo," however, is entirely different, though characteristically plaintive. At higher altitudes of the mountains, other varieties of birds are seen, but they do not take kindly to the lowlands along the sea.

There is a bird called the "O-o," that formerly inhabited the islands in considerable numbers. Its plumage is glossy black, except a few feathers under the tail coverts, and a little tuft on each shoulder; these are golden yellow, and from them, in ancient times, royal robes were made. A garment of that kind is now in possession of the Queen, and one is in the Bishop collection. They are valued at incredible sums, as the species is virtually extinct. If you chance to ask a native anything about birds, he is sure to tell you of the "O-o;" but after that he doesn't know the difference between a bald-headed eagle and a blue-jay.

The O-o (Moho Nobilis) is scientifically classed under the order of "Climbing Birds," and is grouped with the family of "Brush Tongues" (Melaphagidæ), its distinctive branch being the "Honey Eaters." It is closely allied to the family of "Sun Birds," and more remotely to its minute cousin, the "Humming Bird," and nowhere else on earth except on the Sandwich Islands is it known to exist.

By a beautiful contrivance of Nature, the O-o carries, at the tip-end of its tongue, a peculiarly equipped, delicate and sensitive brush, by the aid of which it extracts from the calyx of flowers the honey-pools there to be found; and this constitutes largely its main supply of food. It is not confined, however, to that rich sustenance alone, but combines with it the wild banana of the islands, and other dainty fruit-

age, and besides, on occasion, sometimes mixes with these
a fresh, meaty entree of insects, or a choice salad relish of flies.

The mountain regions of Hawaii are its favorite haunts,
and here, hid among the dense growths of those unfrequented
heights, it breeds and rears its young, unmolested. In the
times when it was much sought for, before the resplendent
cloths of modern Europe and the other fair and fabulous
fabrics of fashionable feminine fancy of the present day were
known to the Hawaiians, it was snared with bird-lime, its
few, long, costal ornaments were plucked from its sides, and
it was then turned loose to continue the production of those
rare golden gems, ten times more precious to the natives
than any other thing of value that the earth contained.

The song of the O-o is said to be low, sweet and melodious,
and to resemble strongly the Baltimore Oriole. Its strains,
however, are short and fitful and are seldom ever heard.

The fish that are found in the sea around Hawaii are
almost innumerable in the number of their species, and the
brilliancy of many of them in color is wonderful. They also
assume a great variety of forms.

I used frequently to visit the fish market in Honolulu, for
the purpose of examining them. After a south wind, or
" kona, " as it is called, they are generally abundant on the
stands. Blue and gold are the prevailing colors, but if there
is a shade in the rain-bow that hasn't its duplicate in some
fish of Hawaii, I am not aware of it.

One which I frequently met, and a favorite always on the
market, was shaped like a striped bass, thin and deep, its
sides gorgeously frescoed, up and down, in a multitude of
hues, principally blue. Its mouth was a curiosity, a regular
beak ; and being hooked at the tip, like a parrot's, was wonderfully similar in appearance to one of those birds.

Insects did not appear to be very abundant, but as I was
there in the winter-time, that to me may account for the ex-

ceeding scarcity. I saw but few butterflies and they were all of one common variety. Ants were abundant, and cockroaches; but where on earth are they not, except it be on some glacier of Alaska, or at the North Pole?

I quite frequently observed bumble-bees feeding with much characteristic buzz and confusion among the efflorescent lawns, and on such occasions, invariably felt a deferential impluse to clutch my hat and shy respectfully round to the other side; so forcibly do the painful remembrances of early days impress themselves on memory. Honey-bees were rarely seen, but they are cultivated, in a small way, and I had an opportunity to test the quality of their sweets, the finest, by all odds, of any I have ever tasted. It is so rich in saccharine matter, however, that it soon candies if left standing in the dish. The name given to it there, "orange-blossom honey," in itself suffices to make the mouth water.

Mosquitoes are thicker, in Honolulu, than the pretty little stars in the milky way. One can hear them by the score, in the dead stillness of the night, serenading, like a band of taro-patch fiddlers, outside his canopy. This device probably works all right to lure the natives, but as I wasn't at all musical in my tastes, it didn't work on me. I simply lay still and smiled, while they fluted.

From a close estimate, however, carefully prepared under a shower-bath, I am morally dead-certain that in spite of all my precautions and watchfulness, they ultimately got the better of me, and by one mean, under-handed device and another, during my stay, finally robbed me of at least three quarts of good, healthy, life-giving extract. But I succeeded in getting away with the other quart and deemed myself lucky.

Much has been said of the deadly scorpion, and the poisonous centipede. Both are found in Hawaii. The latter is a sort of wormy pedestrian, who scratches his way along through the world by means of a number of expanding, wiry legs, set in pairs on the under side of his body, like the underpinning of a fashionable parlor table.

In a quarrel with the centipede, it is always eminently desirable that you keep him as much as possible together; for just so sure as you cut him up into pieces, just so sure you increase the number of your enemy. Each section, then, starts right off on its own account, and the first thing you know you are surrounded. The centipede, though, bless his dear, ornery nature! doesn't go outside of his way to pick a fuss with anybody; but if by chance you should ever happen to want a " scrap" with him, all you have got to do is to send in your card. It won't even be necessary to divide the gate-money.

His only weapons are a pair of formidable jaw-nippers, and these he always carries with him as courageously as ever Kamehamcha carried his war-club. If he ever sets them into you, look out for new sensations; mad-dog bites tinctured with the double extract of chain-lightning, and things of that kind.

The bite of a centipede, however, doesn't kill; and that's where the keen deviltry of its spite comes in. My guide, from the Volcano House down at Hilo, said he had been twice bitten by centipedes. He was a blacksmith and had a blacksmith's ideas of suffering. He compared it to a pair of red-hot, horse-shoer's tongs, securely fastened to the suburbs of the body near the sirloin steak.

The fangs of a centipede can, with care, be extracted, and then he is as harmless as a school-marm in love. A wag dropped one thus denuded of his strength, into the sack-coat pocket of a crack billiard-player, at the Hawaiian Hotel parlors, along with the chalk which the player was using. The next time the victim put his hand into his pocket for chalk, he was highly elated, and in a dickens of a hurry, for he saw a chance to carom and make two; but when he took it out again, the first hurry, to use a vulgar aphorism, wasn't "in it" at all.   He saw a chance then, to make about a dozen, and like a snorting kangaroo stuffed with india-rubber car-springs, he made every one of them, over the billiard table and out of the back door.   When they caught him at Beretania Street, he was divested of all but one garment, and with eyes wildly staring, was tugging at that, like a long-shoreman at a boiled shirt, trying to get it off.   But they finally quieted him.   The popular young man who devised the entertainment came in for his share of the applause, later on, and for some time afterwards rusticated at rural Waikiki, to recover from the shock which struck him twenty minutes or such a matter later.

There are neither snakes, toads nor frogs on any of the Hawaiian Islands.

CHAPTER VII.

OAHU is the third island, in size, of the group; forty-six
miles long, twenty-five broad, and contains about three
hundred and sixty thousand acres of land.

Like all of the others, its climate is superb, never hot and
never cold, the trade-winds of the Pacific, from the north-
east, ever sweeping across its narrow boundaries to modulate
and equalize the temperature.

Like all of the others, also, it has its lofty mountain summits, rugged cliffs, beautiful valleys teeming with picturesque, scenic effects, and its fertile plains.

I have been up and down its delightful places; I have
stood on its over-towering pinnacles, and have drunk in its
breadths, and heights, and depths of glory and of beauty; I
have basked in the spacious shadows of its luxurious re-
treats; I have imbibed its climate, sweet as the breath of a
child asleep on its mother's bosom, soft as its slumbers; I
have bathed in its clear ocean-waters, both at Christmas
time, and on New Year's Day, the temperature of air and sea
so nearly akin, that not even the skimmer of a chill was perceptible, as I passed down from the land into its pellucid
bosom; I have heard the breathing music of its proud palms,
the gentle witchery of its pattering, warm showers at night;
I have looked upon its clustering blossoms of infinite color,
that greet the eye enchantingly wherever one goes, whether

in city or country; I have heard the hospitable voices of its people; and to me, no place of all the Hawaiian group can ever offer the same attractions or allurements as the charming island of Oahu.

At its southernmost part is Honolulu, an opal gem of many colors set in a diadem of jewels; a city of refinement, and

ONE OF THE FINEST.

culture, and beauty, containing twenty thousand souls. Yet, viewed from the standpoint of American cities, Honolulu is a very tame place indeed. It is a city without city attractions; a congregation of rural homes and industry, condensed in a small compass; as if some wizard power had cast a net over the land, and drawing it through the Nuuanu pass, had planted what he thus snared here by the sea.

Honolulu maintains quite a comfortable opera house, capable of seating several hundred people, yet it scarcely has a theatrical performance once in six months. Concerts, too, are rare, and generally the product of home amateur talent. Occasionally, wandering troops, passing through from the states to Australia, or vice-versa, stop off and give a series of entertainments, but this does not often occur; when it does they are usually well patronized.

There are only a few liquor saloons in the city, but what few there are keep industriously at work entertaining the natives; there is not a dance-house or dive in the place.

The social element of the city is almost exclusively white, and mostly American, and one meets many polished, cultured men, and charming, gracious, lovely women, bright and intellectual, if to that charmed circle he fortunately be permitted access.

They have hard, clean streets all over Honolulu, and neither dirt nor garbage is allowed to gather about their premises; those spots which in other cities are set off for the storage of refuse being here studiously reserved for flowers. One can sit on the uncovered ground, either in the front or back yards of their homes, without being besmirched.

I know, too, that they give much concern to their church relations, and are engaged in many works of Christian charity and godliness; for I find recorded in my " Guide," a number of benevolent missions and societies, as well as several other organizations, of kindred character, in connection with the names of many prominent people of the city, of both sexes.

Native Hawaiians are great for holidays; they never allow any to get away if they can possibly help it; and if any outside nationality chances to celebrate any particular day, or occasion, the home population is sure to turn out in force and help them do it.

Christmas is a holiday of course; so is New Year's; and

there are besides eight other holidays. Among them is the
Birthday of the Queen, the Birthday of the Queen of Great
Britain, Hawaiian Independence Day, American 4th of July,
and American Decoration Day; and I was told by a citizen,
that although there are scarcely a dozen Irishmen on the
Islands, St. Patrick's Day comes up smiling every spring, and
McGinty is heard in the land.

Riding is a pastime greatly resorted to by all classes of the
community, especially horse-back riding ; and music and song
enter conspicuously into all the pleasures of the people.
These things, together with their natural love of flowers, and
those other harmonies which nature has so lavishly bestowed
upon them, tend to render them, to all appearances, happy and
contented.

There is a line of street-cars in Honolulu that runs, or
rather crawls, east and west through the city. If one wants
to take a good, long, land-voyage, no better trip than this
could be selected ; you get such an extended tour for such a
little sum of money.

If you should ever decide to take it, follow my advice: go
out to the west end of the line and travel eastward. You
thus get the trade-winds in your face, and are thereby frequently lulled into the sweet illusion that you are moving.
This is a thing which you cannot most always otherwise defi-
nitely tell, unless you take bearings out of the window, or go
to the door bodily.

There is ordinarily a native driver aboard, but if the car
isn't a " bob-tail, " the chances are the conductor will be a
white man, and he is liable to be from any part of the habitable globe.

The passengers who travel back and forth are of all orders,
castes, colors and degrees, and the study of them greatly interests the stranger.

If a native Kanaka comes in, he is almost sure to bow to

you, and greet you with such a genial, good-natured " aloha ! " (my love to you) and smile, that you involuntarily raise your hat to him, out of respect for his sweet-tempered, sunny disposition. The chances are, you will go even further, and answer his salutation with " aloha-nui ! " (my great love to you) hoping thereby to add just a mere mite more to his already redundant supply of rich, wholesome humanity.

After awhile a Chinaman gets aboard. More than likely he will have two huge baskets with him, which he carries suspended at each end of a pole over his shoulders, when he walks or paces. In one of these, possibly, will be some ducks, or maybe a pig, or anything else on earth that a close-fisted barbarian of easy appetite would be likely to put into his stomach; in the other, some soiled clothes, or any of the thousand and one traps a Chinaman is forever gathering. He takes out a nickel and " drops it in the slot, " or into the conductor's hand, with a sigh that ought never to be heard, except over a grave. And then he curls up in one corner, and is as motionless, almost, as the car itself.

Finally, a Jap comes along and gets in. He looks frightened ; all of the Japs do. They have a habit of cutting their hair pampadour, and that adds to the illusion. He begins watching you the minute he takes his seat, and keeps it up till he leaves the car, as if you were a deputy-sheriff or some officer on his trail, and he didn't propose you should catch him napping.

If a white man gets aboard, he does it with about as much self-respect as a peddler would manifest reading door signs in San Francisco : " No Peddlers Wanted. Scat ! " but after he is seated, he is as proud as the usher of a two-bit theater. He looks at you then as if he owned you, takes a chew of tobacco, crosses his legs, and spits on the floor.

When you get down into the business part of the town— mind, *when* you do—the car stops and the driver lights his pipe. Then others get aboard, maybe a batch of hula girls going out to Kapiolani Park, or to the beach for a plunge in the surf, and you spin along at the rate of a mile every once in a while.

If it isn't asking too much of the imagination, finally you arrive at the end of the road, four or five miles down along the borders of the harbor, close under the lowering shadows of Diamond Head. I will not weary you to return; imagine yourself walking; it will rest you.

There is another line that runs out Fort street, and ends somewhere under the trees, up the Nuuanu valley, towards the Pali. The road is owned by English capitalists, who paid for it about four times its cost, and who discovered, too late, that they were in the toils of jobbery. This is the kind of a street-railroad system which renders profitable a hundred or two licensed hacks, drawn by one horse, at twenty-five cents a trip around the corner, or a dollar and a half an hour.

Most of the residences of Honolulu are low, frame structures, of cottage style, with broad, roomy verandas in front. Some are two stories high, with "lanais" above; a lanai, in such cases, being simply the second-story porch of the building, either enclosed with movable glass, or latticed, or open, as best suits varying fancies. A profusion of vines and blossoms invariably adorns the lower porches.

There is a " Free Library and Reading Room " of eight thousand volumes occupying a neat building on Hotel street, which is very creditable to a city of this size; and the Y. M. C. A. building, directly opposite, two stories high, of brick, is one of the best in the place.

Of eleemosynary and benevolent institutions, there are quite a number, one of them, "Lunalilo Home, " being devoted exclusively to the care of aged, infirm, and dependent Hawaiians. The building, a beautiful structure, is located in the picturesque valley at the foot of Punchbowl, from the road

A COTTAGE HOME.

to which many delightful views may be obtained of its quiet seclusion and restfulness.

Another, the " Queen's Hospital, " is situated in the central part of the city, and is surrounded by a magnificent wealth of arboreal growth, equal to any portion of Honolulu. Here every comfort is provided for the sick, and while foreign-

ENTRANCE TO THE QUEEN'S HOSPITAL.

ers are admitted to its privileges, they are, contrary to the rule as applied to the natives, charged fixed rates for service and attendance.

About a mile from the center of the city, on Nuuanu Avenue, is the Royal Mausoleum, built in the form of a cross, in the midst of beautiful, park-like grounds. It is a plain, unpretentious structure, and is conspicuous neither for size nor elaboration. Many of the dead monarchs of the nation rest here, among them Kalakaua.

In company with several others, I took occasion, during my stay in Honolulu, to visit the Oahu prison. It occupies a slightly-elevated plat of ground, on what is known as " The Reef, " near the water's edge, in the west part of the city, and to all of us appeared to be extremely insecure against involuntary detention. We were informed, however, that escapes are exceptionally rare. The surrounding walls are of the customary concrete and about ten feet high, the tops being thickly imbedded with broken glass to keep the fiery Kanakas from climbing over. The place was scrupuously clean, and we were accorded most courteous attention by those in charge. The prisoners are industriously worked on the public highways and other improvements, and many of the most attractive features of the kingdom are due to their hands.

There are a number of schools and colleges in and about the city, and matters of education are given liberal encouragement. The natives are zealous to learn, and proficient in study, and while they are said to have a special aptitude for oratory, when started, they are like Tennyson's brook ; they " go on forever. "

Churches of several denominations are scattered over Honolulu and through the rural districts, ample, presumably, for the ordinary moral demands of the people. Some of the church building are fine structures. The Congregationalists had one under process of erection while I was there, to cost, when complete, more than a hundred thousand dollars.

Some of the church organizations are devoted in their memberships exclusively to the Hawaiian natives, the services being conducted wholly in that tongue ; but reliable authorities insist, that Christian faith, as the average Kanaka sees it, is a remarkably volatile substance, and one that bears exceedingly light on them between Sundays. As a makeshift and pastime it answers well enough, and they enjoy it ; but after the singing is over, they have little further use for it, and if any happens to stick to them, they easily brush it off on the church steps, when the services of the day are concluded.

Honolulu is lighted by electricity, supplied by the government from water-power derived from the mountains through Nuuanu valley, the principal street-crossings being illuminated by arc lights. There is, besides, a private company, that supplies incandescent light to some of the principal buildings. Water also is furnished by the government.

CHAPTER VIII.

CHARACTERISTICS OF THE NATIVE HAWAIIANS—THE HULA
—HULA-KUI—AND HULA-HULA—WITH A FEW COM-
MENTS ON POI.

THE population of Hawaii is cosmopolitan; the natives, in round numbers 35,000, predominating. After them come the Chinese, 15,000; the Japanese, 12,000; Portuguese, 8,000; Half-castes, 6,000; and Americans 2,000. Besides these, there are about 7,000 "Hawaiian-born-of-foreign-parentage," largely Americans, and a mixed population of several other nationalities.

To the tourist and stranger, the native population presents an untiring picture of never-flagging interest. When Captain Cook discovered the Sandwich Islands in 1778, he estimated the population at 400,000, and while that number was probably over-drawn, the evidences remaining of a once large number of inhabitants, at a period not far remote, is conclusive.

Taro-patches and fish ponds by the hundreds, that are now abandoned and over-grown with wild-wood vegetation, tell in unmistakable language of the enormous food supply they formerly provided; and the story of modern statistics clearly affirms and verifies the rapid decline of the race in recent years.

A thoroughbred Hawaiian is of a dark, copper-colored complexion, and ordinarily of fine physical development. His hair is jet black, thick and straight, and his eyes are dark. The men are usually rather good looking, but the women, as a rule, are coarse, slip-shod, and lacking in personal charms. Some of the half, and quarter castes, and later dilutions, however, are beautiful.

The race is of a happy-go-lucky disposition, passionately

AMALGAMATED GEMS.

fond of everything that affords amusement, and enthusiastically averse to any kind of toil ; and this characteristic of their natures seems to have been honestly acquired. As they were formerly situated, before the invasion of the whites, in a magnificent climate where neither dwellings nor raiment were demanded to protect them against the elements of nature, and where food grew spontaneously on almost every limb, and in the sea, it is not to be wondered at, that they lapsed into a condition of sloth and idleness, or that the habit, ultimately, through generations of time, came to be an inheritance of the blood.

Even civilization itself, with all its developments of our race, has never yet been quite able to eradicate from the noble Caucasian a longing desire for rest ; and it is true of us all, as Garfield once said of himself, that every blessed one of us is just as deliciously lazy as he possibly dare be. And if this be true of us, with all of our boasted spirit, and peerless ambition, spurred on, in addition, by the mercilesss stings of greed and necessity, how much more should it be true of those poor, ignorant, wayward children of the sun, scarcely yet emerged from the swaddling cloths of barbarism.

The love of music is one of the strongest proclivities of the Hawaiian race, so mirth-loving and gentle are they in their natures ; and scarcely a man or woman of native blood can be found, who is not proficient with some kind of a musical instrument. It may be the accordion, or it may be the taro-patch fiddle, a diminutive guitar of four strings, or it may be the violin ; but nine times out of ten it will be the guitar. Music to them is more than church, or Bible, or creed ; and however much of poverty may exist there, one or the other of those instruments will be found in almost every home, even in their grass houses ; and wherever the occupants travel the music goes with them. I have seen men and women, unwashed and disheveled, sitting together on their cottage verandas, as early as 7 o'clock in the morning, before breakfast, playing on the guitar and singing as if not a care in the world troubled or annoyed them ; and I presume it did not.

They grow to be quite expert musicians, as one naturally

THE KING'S DANCERS.

would suppose from their inborn tastes and talents, but it is said to be difficult to confine them to notes, preferring, as they do, to wander after their own harmonies. Hence they organize themselves into clubs and bands, and sing and play together after their own fashions.

To the novice, their music is delightful; it is so low, dreamy and gentle; reminding one continually of the voices of birds. There is a sameness, though, about it, that might, after awhile, become monotonous and tiresome, like the equally uncivilized chickety-chickety-chickety-chatter of an imbecile mandolin. They take, very fondly, to the light airs of the variety stage, and ballads familiar to American ears are quite common among them, " Annie Rooney, " " Sweet Violets," and other choice effusions of their kith and kin.

A number of years ago, a German musician by the name of Berger wandered out to Hawaii from California. He was a natural leader in music, and the result of his visit was the "Royal Brass Band," an organization composed wholly of native talent, which is supported at the expense of the government for the entertainment of royalty and the people. It plays in one or the other of the parks of Honolulu (of which there are several scattered about over the city) a number of times every week, and generally at the wharf when steamers leave for San Francisco. At a contest of brass bands in San Francisco, a few years since, it carried off first honors; an ample testimonial of its merits. Each concert concludes with " Hawaii Ponoi, " (Hawaii forever) the national air. It was composed by Berger, but is so interjected with snatches from our own grand master-piece of patriotic melody, " America, " that it has been fitly dubbed " America played backwards. "

The natives are extremely fond of dancing, but like all people of recent barbaric origin, prefer to exercise the pastime free from set figures or forms. Their dance is known as the "hula, " and, as in the Italian tarantella, and the Mexican fandango, it is every fellow for himself and the devil take the hindmost. It however admits of a number of variations.

The style formerly danced before the king, was often seen in public, during the time of Kalakaua, on the grounds in front of the royal palace ; and nothing afforded the old sinner greater amusement than this pastime. The garb worn, on such occasions, by the female terpsichoreans composing his majesty's retinue of trained dancers, consisted of a narrow band of cloth about the loins, from which depended a short, fussy skirt of thick fringe, made from a flexible grass of the islands, the whole dyed in various brilliant hues.

Anklets were also worn, and ornaments about the arms and wrists ; the legs and upper portion of the body being mostly bare. Wreaths of flowers adorned the head, and leis and garlands were festooned about the shoulders and around the neck, making, when the outfit was complete, an exceedingly striking combination of pleasing color.

The dance consisted of a confusion of short steps, postures and motions, many of them disgustingly suggestive, accompanied by the beating of large, dry, hollow gourds containing rattles, and other tom-toms, and instrumental and vocal music.

The old king used frequently to give these dances at his seaside home at Waikiki, for the entertainment, largely, of his American friends. On such occasions, potations of gin were freely distributed to the dancers, and what was commenced in moderation, almost invariably ran into a wild orgie before it was through ; those of the invited guests who had any longings whatever for ultimate salvation, generally going home before the thing was half over.

There is an aggravated form of the hula, which is secretly resorted to by the vile in Honolulu, but it is strenuously hunted down by the authorities, and for that reason does not often show its head. It is the same old devil's quickstep as

THE HULA.

the French can-can, only more obscene, and is set to a different scale and key to fit Hawaiian methods and demands.

From what I was able to glean, during my experiences in Hawaii, I have figured out a theory relative to this people, which runs back even to the beginning, and which, it may be, is entitled to be classed with the speculations of Darwin and Huxley, and of other great philosophers, bearing on the subject of the origin of man. I give it as I have formulated it, for the benefit of sages and theologians the world over.

After this universe was framed, and all of the nations composing it had been distributed to the different quarters of the globe, where, according to the judgment of supreme intelligence, each was best fitted to belong, Shem here, Ham there, and the other brother over yonder, then, and not until then, the " hookupus, " or gifts of Christian virtue were given out ; love, faith, tenderness, charity, benevolence, modesty and morality ; together with all of those numberless others, which adorn the world, and which render it a place endurable to live in for a series of consecutive years.

I also imagine that when that distribution was made, somehow, or in some manner, purposely or otherwise, the Sandwich Islands were left out to the last ; and then, all of those gifts which had accumulated, were, either in a hurry to get through or for some other reason, jumbled together and dumped helter-skelter on to them.

There was probably a surplus of some things, such for instance as human generosity, and faith-in-man ; and too little, undoubtedly, of others, like common intelligence, and love-for-work ; but, like the prince in the Mascot, " it was just their luck, and they got it, " and have ever since had to make the best they could out of the situation.

One article, I am sure, must have run completely out before their turn came ; or at all events, so nearly out, that it has failed to cut much of a figure in the history of the race from that time down to the present. I should say that the whole tribe of Hawaii didn't get more than an ounce or two at the utmost. The article to which I refer is what is usually known under the style and title of " common morality. "

They have, it is true, been picking up driblets of this priceless commodity, here and there, since, and have of late been giving unusual attention to the encouragement of its production ; but from present appearances, it will be many centuries yet, before they will have acquired much of a stock on hand ; it certainly will, if they have to depend on the average white tourists who nowadays go among them, for an increased supply.

Among themselves, the natives dance the hula without any sense of impropriety or shame ; brothers and sisters, fathers and mothers, wives and husbands and friends, dance it together ; but whenever a haole (white man) appears on the scene, modesty presumes to enter and forbids the revel.

Gin, however, the devil's nickname, overcomes all scruples in the Sandwich Islands as elsewhere ; and wherever its destroying fever creeps in, all restraining virtues are disposed to fly. As the natives acquired squalor and disease through the advent of the whites, likewise acquired they the love of the white man's strong drink ; and now, struggling in its toils, whenever any saving influence of good comes to their rescue, to snatch from wreck and ruin their fast decaying race, even though it be only so fragile a god-send as acquired modesty, all that is necessary, on the part of those who seek their destruction, is to touch the gin bottle ; the devil does the rest.

There is a chaste form of the hula, called by the natives, " hula-kui, " which embodies all of the graces of the hula, without its vulgarities. I saw it danced, on one occasion, by a half-caste young lady, a teacher in one of the government schools, after an evening luau.

She was attired in a plain, white, loose-flowing " holaku, "

HULA-HULA, I. E., THE TOURIST'S DELIGHT.

which, by the way, is simply an ordinary Mother-Hubbard
gown, and the prevailing costume of most of the native wom-
en of Hawaii, and of many others there besides. The dress
was composed of some light, fragile stuff, and was worn with
a train, and the graces of the dancer's supple body exceeded
anything of the kind I had ever seen. The music was supplied by a string band of six pieces, violins, guitars and taro-

HULA-KUI.

patches, the players, natives, and the air that peculiar, repe-
titive melody which once heard is never quite forgotten, and
which is the invariable accompaniment of the hula wherever
it is seen.

The space occupied by the dancer did not exceed eight feet
square, but that eight feet was all occupied, every inch of it,
and in a manner so bewitchingly graceful and modest, that

had it been the presentation of an American stage the audience would have been driven wild with enthusiasm.

The homes of the natives, as a rule, are plain, some of them, indeed, comfortless, large numbers of people often herding together in spaces wholly inadequate for so many. But

TARO.

as this has ever been a custom of the race, and as they live out more than in-doors, close quarters and impure air have probably become second nature to them, and are no longer hurtful. Their houses, ordinarily, are whitewashed outside, and present a tidy exterior. Some few, in the rural districts, still live in grass houses, but that class of structures is rapidly going out of date, and not being renewed.

For food, " poi " has been the staple so far back, " that the memory of man runneth not to the contrary ; " and it still holds its supremacy over all other edibles.

It is the product of a species of the calladium lily, called on the islands " taro, " and is grown like rice, in the mud. When mature, the root gets to be enormously large, like a potato of abnormal size, or an immense rutabaga, and when broken apart, in its raw state, presents a mottled appearance, purple and white, that renders it very toothsome as an article to be eaten. The leaf, too, is utilized along with the tuber, and makes excellent greens for the table.

The first process of preparation for food is by cooking, which often is done in the ground ; the skin then slips off, after which the inner portion is broken into fragments and is known to local commerce [as " pai-ai. " The process of reducing pai-ai to poi is simple. The former is placed on a broad, smooth surface, usually a plank or stone slightly hollowed, and then with a stone mallet, which the operator manipulates sitting cross-legged on the ground before his work, the mass is beaten into a thick paste. Another reduction, by the application of water, brings it to a dough-like consistency that resembles gray mush ; and this is poi.

When ready for the table, it is served in calabashes, and is eaten with the plain, unvarnished fingers. On many home tables—which by the way are often not tables at all, but simply the bare, uncovered ground—only one calabash is provided, and out of this all of the family eat in common.

Some like their poi thick, so that a sufficient mouthful can be gathered up on one finger; others prefer it thin. It goes, therefore, by the name of one finger, two finger, or three finger poi, according to its consistency. The man who in one or the other of these three ways, is incapable of gathering up enough to fill his mouth, is given a trough in the back yard and an extra litter of straw.

The adhesive quality of poi is remarkable. It makes an excellent paste for putting on wall-paper, and is warranted to stick to the appetite, like bad luck to an indolent man. It is not, however, generally relished by foreigners, on first acquaintance, it is so cold and unsocial; but one quickly

MAKING POI.

acquires a taste for it, and if he can only avoid going where it is manufactured by the Chinese, will soon learn to enjoy it.

There is, perhaps, no vegetable more nutritious than poi, and none that has greater sustaining qualities. On my trip to the volcano, I was much entertained watching the boatmen of the Inter-Island Line of steamers eating it; great, strapping, muscular models they were of perfect physical development and strength. It was served in wooden butter-tubs and pails, and was carried forward by them into the bow of the boat, where it was eaten. They were tidy fellows, those Kanaka sailors, and would not for the world commence a meal until, according to the ancient customs of good Hawaiian society, they had first laved and purified their fingers for that osculatory process. This they accomplished, in a novel way, by dropping overboard one of the ship's lines into the sea. When it came up dripping, they caught the fleeting fluid that adhered to it, and ere it could again escape into the great deep, bathed themselves luxuriously in its spongy current.

It was astonishing to see what an amount of poi could be elevated on two fingers by one of those burly deck-hands, and deposited, without waste, inside the capacious limits of his open "waha;" yet that feeling of surprise nowhere compared with the interest aroused on seeing him eat it; or on hearing the long-drawn-out, sweetly smothering sighs that lingered at the door, when the digits again appeared after carrying in the last truck-load. I really do not know to what harmony I should compare it, except it be the final, trembling refrains of an exhausted bath-tub, gasping for breath through its last few pints of water.

The Kanakas are natural sailors, and in the days when the Sandwich Islands were noted as fitting-out stations for the North Pacific whalers, were greatly in demand for that service. It is about the only line of work they will cheerfully follow, and they will not follow that steadily.

CHAPTER IX.

CAPTURE OF A DEVIL-FISH—HABITS, CUSTOMS AND SUPER-
STITIONS OF THE PEOPLE.

ALL native Hawaiians are fond of the water; they learn
the art of swimming in baby-hood, and both sexes are
equally proficient in it. One of their favorite amusements,
years ago, was surf-riding. This they practiced among the
breakers, standing up on single pieces of plank, as the waves
dashed in over the reefs. This amusement, however, is of
late years rarely resorted to.

In former days they wore little or no clothing, after the
habit of tropical savages, and were consequently always ready
for the water; besides, their food being largely the product
of the sea, they were of necessity much of the time in that
element, almost as much as on land. They still retain their
old-time tastes in those directions, and many of them therefore are fishermen. They also eat pretty nearly everything
found in salt-water, and they are not very particular, either,
whether it is cooked or not.

Fish are eaten raw, and are so preferred by many at the
present day, although they are also served cooked. They
have a process of preparing them, by boiling in " ti " leaves,
a plant very common on the islands. This plant, besides its
utility in that way, is used as a substitute for paper, in wrap-
ping up various articles, particularly fish on the market. Its
fibre is strong and very flexible, and the leaves, in boiling,
impart a flavor to the fish that is fragrant and palatable.

There is also a manner of serving raw fish by lomi-lomi-ing, or kneading into a mixed morsel with tomatoes and onions, which makes a preparation greatly relished, even by many of the whites.

Snails, crabs, shrimps, mussels and small fish are not infrequently eaten alive. I saw a little girl catch a fish from among the rocks on the island of Hawaii, and devour it then and there, all except the head, in a jiffy; and I was told by a gentleman who came down with me on the steamer Kinau, from Hilo, that he had seen a native sailor, one of the crew of that boat, do the self-same thing only a short time before. He was at work unloading, and while so engaged, caught the fish, quite a large one, out of the water. Biting off its head, he took the balance of the body in his mouth as a smoker would a cigar, and holding it there between his teeth, consumed it, little by little, paying no heed whatever to its antics, (for it kept up a continual flapping round his jaws) until every particle of it had passed in and been swallowed up.

I saw a young native boy, seventeen or eighteen years of age, catch a cuttle-fish, or "squid" as it is called by the natives, on the reefs at Waikiki. Why such a horrible creature should be called a fish is a wonder to me, for it is more like a hideous reptile, an eight-pronged, hydra-headed snake, hateful, repugnant and devilish in every aspect and form. The ocean about Hawaii contains great numbers of them, but they are principally found among the reefs near the shore. They are fished for by the native fishermen, and are sold on the market, both fresh and dry, where they can always be seen.

They are specially alert and active in the water, darting from place to place with wondrous agility; and in addition to this method of avoiding harm, carry with them a sack of inky-black fluid, which, on occasion, they have power to eject, thus, in case of danger, beclouding the water against their enemy. The force of this ejection also acts to propel them away from their peril.

The squid is a veritable devil-fish, bristling with suckers along its entire tentacles from body to tip; and its eye is as vicious and malignant as that of a shark. The one I saw caught measured about three feet from out to out of its extended arms, and a more detestable, ugly looking object was never dragged out of the sea.

Did you ever read Victor Hugo's account of the devil-fish, in his novel, " Toilers of the Sea?" If not, I advise you to do so, and you will get a faithful, graphic picture, by a master hand, of this most foul and horrible creature which I wish to describe.

In the story referred to, one of the characters is drawn down into the water, by one of these monsters, and destroyed. Another, the hero of the tale, is likewise assailed; the octopus has seized him with its far-reaching, slimy, powerful hooks; their suckers have begun to fasten on his flesh; he feels them creeping along his body like ribbons of fire, biting, gnawing, devouring, and holding him fast in a grip of steel, while the wicked eyes of the reptile glare savagely before him, as though they belonged to some pitiless demon of hell.

Fortunately for the victim, he happens to know the one, only assailable point of his foe, the one weak spot where it can be attacked and conquered; and unsheathing his knife, he plunges it with the quick, fierce thrust of desperation, into its head, slashing out both its eyes and killing it.

The head of the devil-fish, about the eyes, is indeed its weak point, and when the boy at Waikiki captured the one there, he grabbed it quickly as it lay resting in shallow water on the bottom, and dragging it hastily out, dispatched it. But in doing so he did not use a knife; instead, he used only his teeth; and these he fastened, like a fierce dog, into the head and eyes of the reptile, biting and shaking it to death.

THE DEVIL-FISH.

Immediately after, he brought it where a number of us, ladies and gentlemen, were standing on the shore. It was not yet dead, but for some time continued to move its tentacles in and out, in a writhing, tortuous manner, until finally it expired.

Anxious as I was to test its powers of grappling, and its capacity to adhere, I could not, for quite a while, bring myself to take hold of the body; it was so vile, and clammy, and the twisting movements of its gaping tentacles, which it kept turning inside out like the fingers of a kid glove, were so foul and disgusting. Finally, however, I was tempted to do so. Even then, dying as it was, with life almost extinct, it grabbed and clung to my hand so tenaciously that considerable effort was required to release myself from it. It was like a double row of leeches plastered to the flesh.

While we were yet examining it, a native fisherman came where we were standing, and at my request, took it from the hands of the boy, in order to uncover and exhibit to us its feeders.

The muscular strength of the creature, even in its then exhausted condition, was something truly surprising. It required all of the power that the man possessed—and he was a strong, vigorous fellow—to disclose to us the thick, gristly mouth underneath, densely studded with stiff, tooth-like projections, pointing inward, which formed in part its frightful equipment of destruction.

Desiring to show us still more, David continued to tear away at the body with his hands, but finding them insufficient to overcome the resistance of the tissue, he had recourse to his teeth, with which he gouged and bit into the thick, cartilaginous coat, till he burst through into the black, filthy contents of the stomach, emptying them out through his mouth upon the ground.

The ladies screamed and ran away, and even we who were

blessed with stronger stomachs, found it difficult to retain
the poi of our last meal; but David simply laughed at our
consternation, and wandering down to the water, rinsed out
his mouth, as a great Newfoundland dog might have done
after dealing with some disreputable subject; after which he
went on his way rejoicing.

If the native Hawaiians, however, in some respects border
nearly upon the animal, in others, they are shining examples
of virtue, which many civilized people of sonorous preten-
tions might, with profit, copy after.

They are honest. One can leave his valuables freely exposed in their midst, and fear no danger from their pilfer-
ings. This was so notable, that it was a frequent subject of
comment among tourists and strangers, and I often heard
white residents of the islands bear testimony to the same
high order of integrity among them.

They are also a very tender-hearted, kind and credulous
people. The sufferings of the unfortunate find warm sympathy in their bosoms; they will not desert a friend; and
they trust implicitly the word and advice of whoever has
their confidence.

They are generous. There is perhaps no trait of their
character more prominent than this; they will never turn
away the needy unaided, if they themselves possess the
means of relieving him, and they will share the last crust
with a friend.

The white man, who carries on his breast the cross of
Christ, and who talks so glibly of the sweet, universal brotherhood of the race, that should bring together all men of all
qualities and colors under the one glorious banner of a common humanity, and who holds himself proudly pre-eminent
as belonging to a civilization far in advance of all others,
needs but to survey his own heart and conscience honestly,
in comparison with some of the noble traits of this people,

to hang his face with shame in the presence of their superior virtues. Yet we are Christians, they barbarians.

The aboriginal race of Hawaii is doomed to extinction; and, at the present rate of decline, will soon be numbered among those tribes whom the white man and the doctrine of "the survival of the fittest," which his religion, according to his own construction, warrants and defends, have exterminated.

Taking into account the population, this decline is rapid. For twenty-five years last past it has averaged nearly a thousand souls per year. The half-castes, and quarter-castes, and eighth-castes, and the further amalgamations, however, are multiplying, and on them Hawaii must hereafter rely for the glory of her native sons.

The Kanaka tongue sounds, separately, each letter of the Hawaiian alphabet, and to the ears of a new-comer, has a very odd expression, like a confused jargon of windy gutterals, minus sense and rhythm. But, after awhile, one gets used to it, as he does to everything else with which he is obliged constantly to associate, and then it goes with the rest on the islands, embracing nearly every nationality of the globe.

The letters of their primitive alphabet, as the language was formerly spoken in its old, original purity, were few; only thirteen I was told. Their words, too, were quite limited in number. At the present, however, they are more profuse. Still to interpret from English into their more voluminous, modern vernacular requires a good deal of linguistic circumlocution, and to express the same thought, time, almost double, is necessary, although, as a rule, their speech is much more rapid.

It is amusing to watch the practices of a Hawaiian mixed political meeting. The three leading nationalities of the islands are generally represented in force, English-speaking,

Hawaiian, and Portuguese. Very few of either understanding any but their own tongue. Two interpreters are therefore imperative.

If an English speaker occupies the rostrum first, it is his privilege to mix the forensic dough, into whatever condition of fitness he desires, and hurl it, in short sentences, at the audience. Then the Hawaiian interpreter gathers up the fragments and works them over for the benefit of the natives; and when he has finished, his Portuguese successor gets what is left, and, third-hand, distributes it to his people.

This arrangement is subject to various combinations, readily discernible, and dependent largely on who first has the floor. Whoever that may be always has an advantage under the system. This, in the first place, is explained by the fact that two-thirds of the audience is totally ignorant of what the speaker is talking about, and he therefore gets the first whack at their ignorance. And then, again, there is a long breathing spell between weighty effusions, while the interpreters are working them over, and this affords him an opportunity to rub down his thoughts and blanket them, ready for the next dash.

Like all people, civilized and uncivilized, enlightened and savage, the Hawaiians are superstitious.

There is a certain, small, red fish in the Pacific, which they believe comes to their shores in countless shoals of millions, whenever a great personage of the realm is about to die, and at no other time.

The ancient priests, or "kahunas," of Hawaii, were medicine men as well as priests, ministering alike both to body and soul, and for this reason obtained great influence over the people. There are still a few of them on the islands, who practice among the older inhabitants. It was formerly thought, and is still so believed by many, according to the testimony of physicians and others who are intimate with

PRAYING HIM TO DEATH (BARBARIC).

the facts, that these kahunas possessed supernatural powers, and were able to pray to death those whom they sought to destroy.

It is not infrequently the case, even at the present day, that natives, taken suddenly ill, imagine themselves under the potent influence of some unknown kahuna, and so believing, and considering resistance of no avail, give up and die.

This varies somewhat, in practice, from the modern faith-cure method, of praying back into health those who are sick and dying, the cart being a trifle before the horse; but that makes little difference after all; what now appears most to be lacking, in both cases, is reliable, trusty evidence of some kind, that the horse is in fact a real, genuine, living thing of vitality, and not a refuse dummy of riff-raff sweepings and straw.

In former times the king was a very sacred personage. If a poor, unfortunate devil of a subject chanced by accident to pass between him and the sun, and his shadow fell on royalty, immediately he was liable to be slain.

There used also to be a "sacred cuspidor" in the kingly outfit, devoted exclusively to the use of his majesty, and a "high and mighty chamberlain," whose duty it was to carry the precious article around and hold it firm and steady, at a convenient distance, whenever the royal mouth puckered to explode. Then, in the dead hours of the night, this mighty official of the sacred cuspidor, would steal forth into the great stillness, and in some secluded glade, or out on the boundless main, would empty its garnered wealth, free from the ken of all observing men. This profound secrecy was demanded, in order to protect his majesty against the kahunas; for it was believed, that if they should ever discover the contents of the sacred cuspidor, they would thereafter be able to pray him to death, the same as other mortals.

In 1881 there was a great lava-flow from the side of Mauna-Loa which threatened to destroy Hilo. Prayers to the "Goddess Pele" proved of no avail; the molten mass of liquid fire continued steadily down the side of the mountain, towards the little city, carrying destruction in its path wherever it traveled.

Princess Keelikolani of the royal family was informed, and being an enormously large personage, weighing some three or four hundred pounds, it is presumed she felt proportionately the distresses of the people. At all events, she hastily got together some white pigs, and hens, and one or two other rare and costly offerings, and lit out for Hilo.

Immediately on arriving at what appeared to be the doomed city, she repaired at once to the scene of desolation, and there offered up her treasures in appeasement of the angry goddess, by casting them alive into the boiling flow. Two days after this circumstance, the flow absolutely ceased, and Hilo was saved. Who for a moment can doubt that this salvation was wholly due to the offerings of Princess Keelikolani?

Madame Pele, the "goddess of fire," is supposed to have her home in the burning volcano of Kilauea, and when I was there, an old, native woman, ostensibly visiting a friend, was frequently observed, her face turned to the burning lake, making signs of supplication and beseechment from the front porch of the hotel. Such pilgrimages are frequent from different parts of the kingdom, pigs, chickens and other gifts being brought, which, with prayers and petitions, are thrown into the fiery pit, to propitiate the goddess.

There is a point on the shores of Hawaii, which is exhibited to strangers as the place of former sacrifice to the "Shark-God." Here, at periodic times, certain of the natives voluntarily immolated themselves, by diving from a rampart of the rocks into the sea. The old shark-god, it is

PRAYING THEM BACK (MODERN).

said, soon got on to these regular barbecues, and was always
on hand to receive his guests as soon as they struck his dominions.

There are in Honaunau the remains of an old "City of
Refuge." Tradition speaks of it as a place where criminals,
and others who were pursued, found safe shelter and protection from the spirit of Keawe, the deity of the place, until
they were either dismissed by the kahunas or attached themselves to their service.

The walls of the enclosure were twelve feet high and fifteen feet thick, which would seem to give warrant to the be-
lief that Keawe relied not a little on good strong lava-stone,
well laid up, for the protection, until his return, of any
refugees who might arrive in his absence. Certain it was
that the kahunas were always present to wait on the gate.

CHAPTER X.

A RIDE TO PUNCHBOWL.—PEARL-HARBOR—FISH-PONDS—
BANANA-PLANTATIONS—TANTALUS, AND RAINBOWS.

AFTER I had been in Honolulu a few days, and had
visited its chief streets, and such of its delightful attractions as a cursory view along its main thoroughfares afforded, I one morning took an early horseback ride to the top of Punchbowl. This is the crater of an extinct mud-volcano, about five hundred feet high, against whose base, and between it and the harbor, the most beautiful residence portion of the city lies.

The horse that I rode was a young, mahogany-bay gelding known as "Commodore," from one of the livery stables of the city. And here I may remark that in no other place I have ever visited, have I found, uniformly, a finer class of showy, stylish horses, in public conveyances and in the livery stables, than in Honolulu.

Commodore was as clean of blemish and as symmetrically formed as a Kentucky racer, his limbs all bone and muscle, and he was overflowing with good spirits and style. His face was a picture; broad between the eyes, which were large, wide-awake and lustrous, and tapered beautifully to the muzzle, where the nostrils, thin as a thoroughbred filly's, expanded nervously with pride and excitement.

His ears told the story of his breeding and quality, pointing continuously forward in that eager, spirited way always so much admired in a horse, and which is never found in any but an intelligent one; and he was kind as a dog and as easy as a rocker.

My gallop, for a mile or such a matter, lay along Beretania street, and then I wheeled to the left, where, after passing Lunalilo Home, the ascent of the hill began.

The length of the road, from the base of Punchbowl, is something over three miles, winding deviously back and forth in ascending terraces to the top. Much skill has been displayed in its construction, and as one ascends, a succession of striking panoramas, varying in character, are constantly presented to the eye. In one direction may be seen the mountains, drifted into enormous windrows, up and down and along their sides, by the eternal wear of ages, and forever clothed in changing shadows of perpetual green; in another, the view is down to the lowlands and the city, and over the frilled waters of the harbor to the boundless sea.

Never again do I expect to feel just the same wild thrill of Arabic delight, which I did on that beautiful morning, as filled with the exhilaration and beauty of my surroundings, I cantered to and fro along the mountain side, through flowering fields of lantana, clusters of green cacti, and native verdure, every turn lifting me higher and higher, till I finally arrived at the summit. There, one takes a whirl round the edge of a smooth, circular parapet, overlooking a great stretch of land and water, and the trip up is finished. There is still a somewhat higher elevation, to which one may ascend on horseback, where a large, chiseled, gray-lava stone has for some purpose been planted in the ground; and after a few moments consumed in surveying the scene from the lower altitude, I proceeded up there, where alighting, I permitted Commodore to graze, and absorbed with rapture the magnificence that was spread out before me.

Most conspicuous of the features there presented was Diamond Head, a recumbent sphinx, bronzed, fierce and sullen, its face projecting far out across the water to the south. Over its back and shoulders glowed the morning sun, torrid with ardor, while the ocean, sedately solemn, lay like a silver desert all around.

To the west, the water shone blue and calm in the distance; but closer to the shore, over the reefs, it was emerald green. Still closer, cocoanut trees and a white fringe like a broad band of filmy lace, told to the view where the waters kissed the land, and between them and the place where I stood, gleaming fish-ponds, shimmering like up-turned mirrors in the light of the sun, and taro-patches, and banana plantations, were set thickly over the landscape, giving life and beauty to the scene. Following along the cultivated levels by the water, still farther west, Pearl-Harbor was seen, and back of it, the far-off, distant hills topped by Kaala, the highest point of elevation on Oahu, robed in a haze of Indian-summer blue.

Back of me stood the mountains, outlined against a sky so perfectly that I dare not attempt to describe them; an azure canopy, unflecked by a single cloud, through which the glories of the translucent heavens, like an unseen mist, seemed softly dropping to the radiant earth.

As I turned again and looked to the south, a broad spectacle was presented; the crescent harbor, floating vessels, and clear to the horizon's edge, the quiet calm of the sea; at my feet, Honolulu. Down over the city, the scene was one of supreme, picturesque simplicity, like some village reproduction of rural "Old England," such, perchance, as that of which Goldsmith sang ere it had been deserted; the distant hum that came up from the dotted, white places below, among the thick green, denoting the abodes of the cottagers. Doves, in circling troops, swarmed in the air, and church spires, and other lofty tops of prominent buildings, glimmered in the sun through the deep foliage.

I sat in the voiceless silence of the high place I was occupying, and vainly endeavored to catch some note, that should

A VIEW FROM PUNCHBOWL.

tell me there was a modern, populous, little city at my feet, humming with industry, alive with the enthusiasm, the loves, and the passions of men ; but aside from the monotones of low melody which occasionally rose, and the wild screams of the mynah birds as they darted along the hillsides, none came up to me.

Thus I remained until noon, riveted amid scenes of beauty,

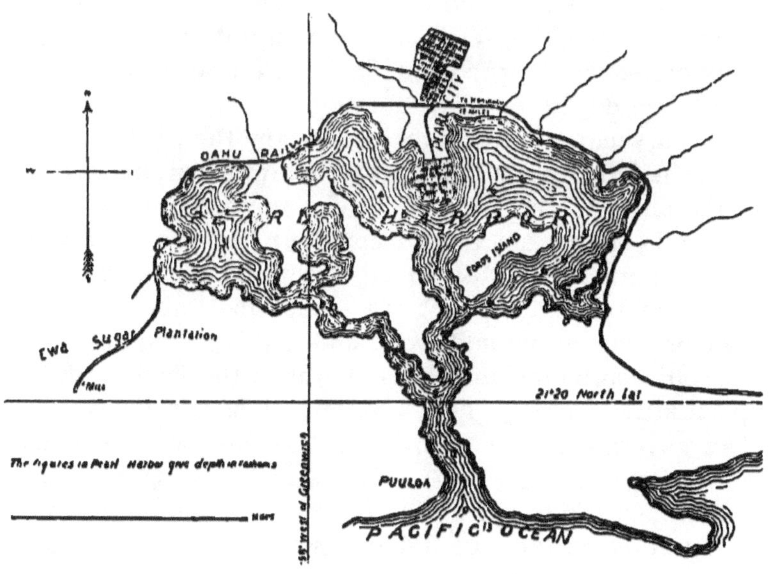

PEARL HARBOR.

and absorbed in reflections over the lavish profusion with which Nature bestows, gratuitously, her charms ; then, remounting Commodore, I wended my way back by another route, on the opposite side of the hill, to the city.

A few days after my visit to Punchbowl, I went with a couple of gentlemen to Ewa, to visit the sugar plantation and mills at that place. Our trip was over the only railroad of Oahu, twelve miles long, and the nucleus of what is promised to be a line that shall ultimately encircle the island.

Part of our way skirted the borders of Pearl-Harbor, that little inland bay which at the present time is the subject of so much confusion in the minds of all Hawaiians, and which some of them consider absolutely essential to the peace, progress, and perpetuity of the American Republic. It embraces a few hundred acres of land, has shallow water over the reefs covering its entrance, and might, with a sufficient outlay of money, be made to float quite a respectable navy.

The United States, for a number of years, has been anxious to secure it as a naval station, and the wisdom of such a desire is fully warranted by the future maritime hopes of the nation; for the time is surely approaching, when the white sails of the American Republic will more thickly stud the high seas than those of any other people on the globe. It is therefore prudent that we should look ahead, and betimes provide accommodations and coaling stations for our vessels of commerce and ships of war in the Pacific; for the opportunities for such places are few, even at the best.

Our government has appreciated all this, and has endeavored to demonstrate to the Hawaiians, by special favors shown them during the last fifteen years, amounting to nearly a hundred million of dollars, which side of their bread was buttered and who buttered it.

But they were wilfully obtuse, and until the McKinley bill showed it to them, obstinately refused to see. Now, however, every man woman and child on the island can discern their mistake as clearly as though a pair of nautical glasses were strapped to their eyesight.

It is the old school-book story over again: "if you won't come down out of the apple-tree through moral suasion, we will try what virtue there is in stones." The stones have been flying pretty lively during the last year, and have raised many a welt on Hawaii; and it looks now as though they had about concluded it would be just as well to come down. They begin to see their past folly; and while, like the boy, who, contrary to fatherly advice, continued to play with the heels of a fractious colt and was kicked into smithereens, they may never again be as beautiful as they once were, they are likely hereafter to have a mighty sight more sense.

There is a little railroad station on Pearl-Harbor, but the name of the town and the railroad station were about the only things we saw there worth mentioning.

The town-lot schemes of the real-estate hustlers of Honolulu take on peculiar fancies. The government, too, has recently been trying its hand in the same direction; laying out town lots from base to summit of Tantalus, 2,013 feet high, part of them above the clouds. They are nicely surveyed and staked off, and as goat pastures will undoubtedly be greatly sought after in the near future. There are too many other beautiful spots for building purposes, more accessible to Honolulu, for those to come very soon into demand as the habitations of men.

Along the road to Ewa are many rice-fields, taro-patches and fish-ponds, mostly the possessions of the Chinese, whom we saw plowing in the mud with their single, black, hornless oxen, preparing the ground for rice. We also saw them thrashing out the seed, in the good old antediluvian fashion spoken of in the Bible, with trampling herds of horses; also, winnowing it in the air. After the last process, the grain is known as "paddy," and has then to be milled and cleaned, when it is ready for human digestion. It constitutes the chief article of food for the labor of the plantations.

The fish-ponds are enclosures, either of stone or earth, along the borders of the harbor, through which flood-gates admit a circulating flow of fresh water to and from the sea;

and in them, millions of fish, mostly "ama-ama" or mullet, a species resembling our chub, are cultivated for market.

The taro-patches and rice fields are composed of small squares of land, fenced with low retaining-walls, generally of earth, a foot or two above their levels. After the crop is set, they are flooded with water from the mountains, and so kept until it matures.

Along the marshy places close to the sea, where formerly naught but rank bulrushes grew, the Chinese, of late years, have trenched out the earth and thrown it up into rectangular beds above the water; and on these they cultivate all manner of garden vegetables. Besides, some of the finest banana-plantations about Honolulu are here established. In the water, between the beds, gold-fish are raised in countless numbers, and to see them gleaming in the bright sunlight, flitting hither and thither like flames of fire, is indeed a beautiful sight. Where the edges of the banana-beds touch the water, taro is planted; and thus every foot of the soil is to some advantage utilized.

The banana plant bears but one bunch of fruit and then must be cut down, the leaves and stalk being left on the ground to fertilize it. A new stalk immediately shoots out from the root, and in the course of six months, another bunch is ready for the market; there being thus two crops annually. All of the bananas of the island that are exported go to San Francisco, bringing from twenty-five to fifty cents per bunch on the docks in Honolulu. Nothing in all the category of tropical fruitage can be more beautiful to the sight than a well kept plantation of growing bananas; their great, ragged leaves, waving in the air, have such a thrifty look of refreshing, indolent plenty.

We spent most of our visit to Ewa in the new sugar mill that had just been erected there. It was planned on the modern system of extraction by diffusion, which is giving quite a percentage more of saccharine matter from the cane than under the old roller method.

The stalks are first chopped fine by machinery and then go to the diffusion vats. The extracted juice is afterwards treated, by a succession of processes, until the sweet, watery solution, which is first sought to be obtained, ends in a heap of yellow, brown sugar on the floor of the mill, where it is shoveled into sacks ready for market; 259,000,000 pounds were exported to the United States in 1890; and yet that is only about four pounds for each man woman and child of the country; hardly enough to sweeten the old maids of Lynn. Heavy, powerful rollers squeeze out whatever of moisture remains in the cane-rubbish after it leaves the diffusion vats, and the dry, fibrous portion then goes as " trash " to the furnaces for fuel.

Accompanied by a friend from Los Angeles, I went on Christmas-day to Waikiki, and together we took a plunge in the Pacific. It was the first time that either of us had ever experienced an open air bath in any body of water in midwinter, and in order that there might be no mistake about it, we went down again on New-year's-day and repeated the dose. The water, on both occasions, was as mild as an August river, and one might, without discomfort or chill, have remained in it all day long. It was simply the perfection of salt-sea bathing.

On December 27th, twelve saddled horses, in military array, were drawn up before the Royal Hawaiian Hotel, and eight ladies and four gentlemen stood on the broad verandas, ready for a jaunt to the top of Mt. Tantalus.

Not a single horse of the whole dozen wore a side-saddle; and that for the very sufficient reason, that in Hawaii ladies and gentlemen alike all ride astride. The custom, at first, is rather apt to shock the stranger unpleasantly, but he soon gets accustomed to it, and then it no longer electrifies the senses.

The better class of native women robe themselves specially for horseback riding, in costumes exclusively designed for
this exercise, called " puas."   A pua is a divided skirt, generally of some cheap, tawdry material of brilliant color, and
hangs gracefully over the limbs, in becoming folds, almost to

LOS ANGELES.

the ground.   To see a number of ladies, so arrayed, riding
through the streets, reminds one instinctively of the Grand-
Entree at the beginning of a circus, and the inclination immediately follows to prick up the ears and listen for the
brass band.

None of the ladies to Tantalus wore puas, but they nevertheless all rode astride. To obviate, however, the disadvantages of their usual skirts, they folded them in a satisfactory fashion—which modesty very chillingly forbade me to explore—between them and their saddles; and thus we went dashing through the streets, and around the base of Punchbowl, like a chase of English huntsmen with the game in sight.

The road up was a sightly one, offering, as we progressed, many rare vistas and delightful views; but the day proved to be rainy, and on that account we did not continue our trip to the summit. As it was, we all got drenched through and through, two or three times over. There is, however, a peculiar sponginess to the atmosphere of Oahu, which causes it to absorb moisture, when the rain abates, about as rapidly as it emits it during a storm; and as the wind was stiff, only a brief period was required, after each shower, until we were sufficiently dry for the next course. We nevertheless tired of these repeated alternations, sooner than did the weather, and as the latter persistently hung on, we finally gave up the tussle and returned home.

It often happens in Honolulu, that the sun will shine brilliantly through quite a heavy rain-shower; and, often again, while it is pouring hard in one spot, scarcely a drop will fall in another not half a mile distant.

These mixed combinations of sun and shower naturally result in rainbows, and somewhere in the valleys, or along their borders, the most magnificent displays are almost of daily occurrence. Oftentimes the entire gorges between the summits of the hills will be so suffused with the rich outburst of brilliant shade and color as to be wholly incomparable.

We saw dozens of rainbows on our ride to Tantalus, just such enormous, sweeping, perfect specimens, I have no doubt, as was the one cast across the heavens in the days after the deluge, when Noah, forewarned that the end of his voyage had come, felt perfectly safe in letting out the ducks and goslings.

Of all the rainbows I had ever seen, these excelled in every particular. All others had been anchored far away in the sky, dropping to the horizon only in the far distance; but these came familiarly right up to our feet, and gave to our riding-boots a new and radiant polish. Some of them appeared to be perfect circles.

How often, by some commonplace circumstance in the after-years of life, do we find the winsome traditions of childhood ruthlessly shattered and dispelled. One of the most lingering of all the household fairy legends of those happy days, with me, was the oft-repeated tale that at the end of every rainbow lay a bag of gold; and with many a journey backward, in memory, as I rode along, I thought of that romantic fable. Yet right here, now, close to my hand, was the resplendent substance of one, that like an arch of many-colored jewels spanned the sky; one end resting on the steaming hill-side, plump up against my path, the other across the valley.

Still there was no gold there; nothing but blossoms of lantana, and wild flowers, and green grass, and a world of magnificent, auroral flame beyond the power of brush to picture or of pen to describe. And then the thought came: " perhaps those treasures that I thus was promised were not to be of gold, or silver, or of any other precious metal ; but instead, I was to be given the wealth and riches of the rainbow itself; " for true it is that sometimes, even in this narrow age of hungry avarice and greed, the charms of Nature far exceed those of Mammon in the hearts of men.

CHAPTER XI.

NEW-YEAR'S-DAY, in Hawaii, is a general holiday much exceeding Christmas.   It is more like the 4th of July than any other day in the States, the rattle of crackers and display of fireworks creating a similar confusion over the city.

On New-year's-eve, serenading parties patrol the streets, visiting friends with song and merriment, and hilarity everywhere prevails.   During the night I was there, I counted from the front porch of my cottage where I was sitting, six different bands, in as many different parts of the city, sprinkling their melodies of string and song till the air was fairly suffused.   The Royal Band was also out among the more prominent people.   It was a season of feasting, singing, dancing and gin.

On New-year's-morning, Los Angeles and myself went down to Waikiki.   The road was lined with natives, all on pleasure bent.   "Aloha" was on all their lips.   One, from their actions, would naturally have inferred that not a single blessed Kanaka of the whole lot was worth less than a cool hundred thousand dollars; so easily are they rendered happy, and so happy are they when they are happy.

Every fellow appeared to have a girl, every girl a leis, and every leis, somehow, before night, seemed to find its way to the hat-band or neck of the gay Lothario, to help complete the circuit of their perfect bliss.

Luaus were spread in many of the native homes, where, through the day and night, feasting and revelry prevailed; and into one of them Los Angeles and myself, by a little adroit practice, managed to get our first peep.

It was at a rustic, half-civilized hovel near the villa of Waikiki, alongside of which a rough temporary lanai, or pavilion of palm and cocoa-nut branches had been erected for additional room.

We arrived shortly after noon, and when we drove up to the door, any fears we had formerly harbored that possibly we might be considered intruders, speedily vanished into the hearty good-will of our reception.

The first table had already been served, and the guests having feasted, had retired to the adjoining building, where music and dancing now prevailed. Before proceeding there ourselves, we decided to pay our respects to the second table. For fear of losing prestige in the eyes of my reader, I desire, to say that the first table of a native luau signifies nothing; the scriptural injunction, "the first shall be last and the last first," fits the case more nearly to the point; for while the day lasts, to "eat, drink and be merry" is the rule, and night brings no change in the programme.

The banquet was quickly re-arranged, and on invitation, we took our seats on the ground beside it, our feet doubled up Turk-fashion beneath us. The table consisted of rough boards resting on "horses" of wood about a foot from the floor, and was covered with a thin spread of clean, fresh fern-leaves, which answered admirably the purposes of a table-cloth; and on this the different articles of food were spread in abundance.

The first course served to us was a calabash of poi, rattling good poi it was, too; and then came raw fish, and roast pig, fresh from the ground-oven in which it had been cooked, sweet and delectable, and half a dozen other dishes, besides, that I knew nothing about, but all clean and palatable. Not wishing to be considered "tenderfeet," we partook of everything freely and in native fashion, eating poi, pig, and all, with our fingers, as if to the "manner born."

In some portions of the Islands, particularly on Hawaii, young puppies are roasted and eaten the same as pig, and are considered great gastronomic delicacies; there is no question about this or concealment of it. They go by the name of "poi-dogs," for the reason that they are fattened exclusively on poi for this purpose. Besides, it is very difficult to tell one from the other, when they lie steaming in the pan; or even by taste.

While we were eating, I looked over at Los Angeles. He was reaching across the board, right and left indiscriminately, and was playing general havoc, with everything he could get his hands on, particularly with the roast pig, and it seemed to me, if he kept on, there wouldn't be a smell of that article left for the next table, to say nothing of the remaining day's feast. So drawing his attention with a low whistle, I riveted my hands tightly together over my stomach, and whispered in a subdued tone of voice, " poi-dog."

Those two, brief, suggestive little words answered every desired purpose with a vim, and Los Angeles' appetite fled as precipitately as though he had actually seen the dried-up, fuzzy spiketail of a genuine poi-dog sticking up out of the platter. His meal was done. But there was pop in bottles, and California wine in a demijohn, and with these we washed down our suspicions "with fear and trembling" and kept mum.

We remained for an hour afterwards, smoking the pipe of peace with our hosts, and watching the hula which was being danced; but we shortly noticed that our presence acted as a restraint to the full enjoyment of the festivities by the others, so we retired.

A few days subsequent to this event, we found ourselves the honored recipients of invitations to a similar entertainment; this time in Honolulu. It was to be quite a fashionable affair, and we looked forward to it with much expectation of pleasure.

The young lady at whose home it was given was a half-caste, and her family was one highly regarded in the city. She had been one of our party to Tantalus, and this luau, in part, was the outgrowth of that occasion, in order that my friend and myself might have an opportunity to see correctly the customs of the better class of the native people.

There was a large number of invited guests present, some of them from prominent Hawaiian families of high official distinction, and a string band of six pieces, placed in the upper lanai, received us on our arrival with strains of instrumental music, occasionally interspersed with choice vocal selections.

We were first shown to a room assigned to the gentlemen, and after laying aside our hats and re-adjusting our toilets, were then escorted to the parlor, where we were presented to such of the ladies and other guests as we had not previously met.

After all had arrived, the gentlemen were invited to a side part of the lanai, where each was presented with a choice leis of roses and flowers, delicately interwoven with sprigs of fern, the hostess herself placing them about the necks of her guests, where she dexterously fastened them, by lacing the ends together; then we again returned to the parlor. A short period of conversation followed, after which, provision having been made for the proper escort of each lady, the line of march was taken up, in couples, to the dining hall, a detached building on the first floor separate from the main house.

The table, in the customary manner, was laid close to the

floor, and at a given signal, each took his place beside it. It cramped some of us, who were not accustomed to sitting on the ground at our meals, to remain long in this position; but we arranged our legs as comfortably as we could, under us, or under the table, occasionally propping ourselves back on our two hands, and in these ways found helpful and refreshing relief from our difficulties, that carried us through to the end, free from undue criticism or disgrace. The service was spread with white linen and napkins, very tastefully, and at each place was a calabash of poi.

Then there was the inevitable roast pig, without which a luau would be no luau at all; and there was chicken, roasted, like the pig, in the ground; and ama-ama, cooked in ti leaves; and salmon; and crab; and devil-fish, very palatable devil-fish, too, the way it was served; and sea-moss as a relish; and raw-taro-and-cocoa-nut pudding; and starch-and-cocoa-nut pudding; and kukui-nut jam; and oranges; and bananas; and pop; and ginger ale, in bottles, laid at each place; and last but not least, as will be shown hereafter, live shrimps in goblets, with sea-moss to keep them wide-awake and cranky.

These, in part, were the dishes from which we were expected to help ourselves in the native fashion; there being neither knife, nor fork, nor plate, nor spoon, on the table. Poi was lifted from the calabashes on the fingers, and was thus carried to the mouth; devil-fish ditto. Roast pig, and chicken, and jam, and raw fish, were likewise picked up in alternate tid-bits, between the fingers and thumb, and so took their places in the long procession of epicurean delights that led on to satiety.

I enjoyed everything. It was all clean, and it really tasted good, and I went through it, course after course, in royal form. In fact, when I had finished, it appeared to me I had done full justice to every single dish set before me, and had

acquitted myself with such credit, that no one who had observed me could for a moment insinuate I was other than
a thoroughbred.   I felt completely satisfied with myself, and
with my record as a luauist.

I had eaten pig and poi, and poi and pig, and poi and
devil-fish; what more could be asked?   Was not this sufficient to elevate any man above the groveling plane of a low-
bred tenderfoot?   Most certainly it was! and with a grim
sense of satisfaction, I leaned back on my two hands, and
with just the slightest little tinge of a shudder running up
and down my spine, recurred to the things that were then
inside me.   But I had them down, and I was on top; that
constituted the main strength of my position; for with that
advantage, there wasn't the remotest doubt, in my own
mind, that I could remain there through thick and thin.

While I was thus cogitating, my thoughts for a brief
moment drawn away from consideration of things that were
going on around me, I chanced abstractedly to cast my eyes
down along the line of the table.

Shark-Gods of Kamehamcha! what was that I saw them
passing?   Could it be that goblet of live shrimps?   Immediately I bolted upright, pricked up my ears like a scared
coyote at the first alarm of danger, and began watching the
proceedings with the intentness of despair.

I hadn't long to wait, however, for sure as fate, it was the
shrimps, and right gayly they were coming down the line,
each guest, as he passed the goblet to his neighbor, merrily taking out one or two from the moss, and after snipping off their
heads with his teeth, shoving them down to kingdom come
along with the roast pig and poi that had preceded them.

For the first time since I sat down to the repast I began
to tremble; in fact, I am free to confess, I never before in all
of my life was so disgustingly frightened; but what to do I
hadn't the faintest conception.

By this time the goblet had arrived and been handed to me; and as I held it up to the light, and looked through at the miserable, crawling, tail-snapping vermin within, I wondered how it was possible that such a smile as I then tried to put on should fail to smash the glass to flinders, or crinkle up the whole sickening mess it contained, like a peacock-feather struck by lightning.

After awhile, however, I gathered pluck to look over the company. Everybody was eyeing me; some tittering, and some holding their breaths expectantly to see what I was going to do about it; while Los Angeles, the unmannerly sneak, was hanging to his short ribs as if he had heart trouble, and laughing and roaring like an Irish member of Congress.

That irritated me worse than anything else that had thus far occurred; but I hadn't much time for reflection. One of two things I had got to do, that was certain; either refuse the dose absolutely, and show myself a contemptible tender-foot, or take it like a native and prove myself a thoroughbred.

I began to reflect. If live shrimps were the custom of the country, why shouldn't live shrimps go, the same as devil-fish, or poi-dog? Why should I kick against them more than against raw fish?

My mind was made up; and without further ado I reached down into the glass and took out the homeliest, meanest-looking bug in the gang. Raising it gayly between my thumb and forefinger, "aloha!" I shouted; and then, shutting both my eyes, I sent it flying somewhere, I know not where. All knowledge I have of that part of the |proceedings was a subsequent titillation in my throat, and a coughing spell that succeeded it, lasting some seconds, which nearly strangled me.

Everybody screamed when they saw the act; "bravo!" "bravo!" "well done!" "good boy!" and immediately I became the lion of the occasion. But I deserved it, every bit of it; befuddled, driveling idiot that I was, to make such an ass of myself.

Los Angeles insisted that the shrimp he took was as big as a mullet, and that it crawled right out on the edge of the glass, and at the word of command, jumped for him, like a Kanaka boy diving for nickels, lighting first on his diaphragm, and from there dropping "kerflummmux" to the bottom without touching a tooth. And I believe every word that he said; for how it could have been otherwise, with that mouth of his stretched to the proportions it was, is beyond the comprehension of man.

A few days after the luau, Los Angeles took his departure for home, on the Australia. I was very sorry to lose him and his genial, sunny companionship; but "'twas ever thus." In travel, there is a continual making and breaking of friends, which is apt to keep one who is "going it alone" in an ample supply of the blues.

There is a most delightful custom in Hawaii regarding the departure of friends. It is an ancient heritage of the aborigines, but to the credit of their successors, be it said, has been so studiously cultivated and preserved since their advent, as to have become a fixed habit among them too. It consists in the decoration with flowers of those who are going away.

On regular days, when the steamers of the Oceanic Line are about to clear, especially those for San Francisco, (although the custom is not confined to those boats alone) bouquets, in profusion, are brought to the dock by friends, and wreaths, and garlands of sweet-scented "maile," and flowers of every color woven into leis, and these are placed lovingly about the necks and persons of those who are about to depart; the gentle offerings of a gentle people to the universal goddess of human love and affection.

Sometimes so abundant are these floral gifts, that ladies

are obliged to sit down under the load thus heaped upon them, utterly unable to carry the weight; resembling, on such occasions, great, weeping bunches of animate blossom

THE LUAU.

in mournful repose. Often, too, the whole land side of the steamer puts on the airs of a moving conservatory, as if it, likewise, had caught the infection, and was conscious of it.

The band is also on hand, and plays; one of the last of its selections invariably being "Auld Lang Syne," "shall auld acquaintance be forgot;" and hundreds of people gather till the boat starts. It is difficult to understand how touchingly music, flowers, tears, kisses and embraces can appeal to the heart of the wayfarer, in the midst of merry surroundings in a strange land, unless one himself has witnessed such a scene as this. Los Angeles came in for a liberal share of decoration, and for a multitude of regrets, as the Australia drifted back into the harbor and we lost sight of him in the distance.

Whenever a steamer goes out, numbers of boys may be seen swimming in the water, waiting for nickels and dimes to be thrown to them by the passengers. They seem never to tire of the exercise, and it is a rare thing that they ever miss any piece of coin cast to them, if within a reasonable distance.

Honolulu appears to have more domestic fowls to the square acre than any other place on the habitable globe; ducks particularly. The Chinese especially delight in ducks, and you can see waddling droves of them wherever there is a stray bit of water. Chickens are said not to thrive, but if you could be transported there in a night, and waken amid the clatter of their voices in the morning, you would, I am sure, form a very different opinion. So furious are their crowings and cachinations, that in the States, if the same practice prevailed, some one would be found on short notice ready to put a stop to it by ordinance, as they do steam whistles.

To me, it was a titillation of my rural tastes, that was truly quite wholesome and refreshing.

Right over the fence, back of my cottage, in another yard, roosted a proud, young chanticleer with his family; and, at the first glimmer of day, every morning, he would fairly crow himself hoarse, trying to keep pace with the balance, whose clarion notes could be heard all over the city. Sometimes he would rouse in the night and crow, to avoid, I presume, being behind time with his fellows.

A rooster always reminds me strongly of certain sorts of men. He goes about quietly enough while on the ground, and attends strictly to his own business, making no noise; but the minute he takes a notion to fly, and can reach the top rail of some tall fence or other, he makes such an awful fuss and confusion over it as to attract the attention of the whole hennery. And that isn't all.

When he was on the ground, the farmer's family didn't notice him much, except, perhaps, to figure a little on him for some future dinner; but when he begins to flap his wings from a high elevation, and crow, he appears, in their eyes, to be little less than a great, grand, radiant peacock, and they throw up their hands, and declare him the finest bird they ever saw in all of their lives, and insist that he shall be spared, even if every other chicken in the yard has to be slaughtered.

For myself, I could never see much difference in a rooster, whether on the ground or on the fence.

CHAPTER XII.

A HORSE-BACK RIDE AROUND OAHU — THE PALI — DE-
SERTED VILLAGES — AA FIELDS — SEPULCHRES —
JUMPING-FISH AND LOMI-LOMI.

BY pre-arrangement, a friend called for me one morning, for a horse-back ride of twenty five miles over the island of Oahu. Commodore had been secured, and before the sun was far risen, we were speeding away in high spirits, out through the flush of the early day, along the charming valley of Nuuanu.

The ride to "The Pali" was glorious; leading up, as it did, between the lifting hills, clothed in wavy vestments of eternal green, among the homes of the cottagers, to the summit height, 1,207 feet above the level of the sea.

Taro-patches, running streams of pure water, and high elevations of land on either hand, were the chief auxiliaries of a morning magnificent in every attraction of sunlight, and bracing atmosphere, and clear delightful sky; but they were not the only ones; for the way was bordered with flowers, and the deserted places with lantana blossoms, yellow and purple intermixed, as thickly as are sometimes the fields of New England, when clad in their autumn robes of white-capped buckwheat-bloom.

After a ride of six miles, during which my attention was frequently called to the decaying remains of former Hawaiian industries—which by the way have been entailed, and are still doing a large percentage of the decaying—notably the ancient sluice-ways, through which they brought water from

A GLIMPSE UP NUUANU AVENUE.

the mountains to their taro-patches, some of them still utilized by the whites, we arrived at The Pali.

A "pali," in the Hawaiian language, signifies a precipice,
and this one of the Nuuanu valley is the most conspicuously
known of any on the islands. The last battle fought by
Kamehameha I. for the sovereignty of the whole group of
the Sandwich Islands, was determined here, and here it was
that he completed, by a long series of conquests, the unifica-
tion of the present kingdom under his head.

The place known as "The Pali" is a narrow gorge that
breaks, at a high altitude, through the cliffs bordering the
sea. As one approaches it from Honolulu, suddenly he
emerges, through a narrow defile of the valley he has been
pursuing, upon a frightful declivity of rocks, which drops almost perpendicularly away hundreds of feet to the plains below; while to the right and left, mighty towers of Nature's
own battlements rise far above, like giant ramparts of war
guarding the passage. It was over this place that Kamehameha drove his enemies in swarms to destruction, and at
the base of the precipice, some of their bones can still be seen,
bleaching in the sun and storm where they fell.

If, standing on this lofty height, one can for the moment
forget his immediate surroundings, and look up and out, instead of down where the picture is full of terrors, he will be
rewarded with a view of such rare loveliness, such a com-
mingling of color and of prospect, of sea, and mountain, and
plain, of plantation and moving industry, that it will not soon
be effaced from memory.

A tortuous road begins here, and hanging to the craggy
cliffs like a painter's staging, drops from level to level, until
it reaches the rolling low-lands about a mile distant below.
Over this only the venturesome dare to ride, even on horseback; to carriage travel it is impassable. Not being of the
number who prefer to take chances, we alighted from our

horses and led them down. After reaching the bottom, our route back to the city was circuitous, sweeping round a large section of the island on its south-east side.

For several miles, we traveled through thickly accumulated evidences that at one time this part of the island must have

BREAD-FRUIT.

been densely settled; abandoned taro-patches, and clusters here and there of bread-fruit trees, old and dying, designating unmistakably the location of deserted villages, or where numbers of people had formerly resided together. Now all are gone, except, perhaps, an occasional grass house, which may once in awhile be seen, dropping to pieces among the shrubs and bushes, close to the running streams that come down from the mountains.

These streams are quite frequent along the windward side of all of the islands, and there is a witchery about them which belongs forever to every running brook. The waters they contain are cold and crystal, and as you pass, they call to you with sylvan voices of laughter from a hundred hidden places, the song-notes of sprites, that charm and enslave the votary of nature, and lure him, in spite of himself, to their pleasant places. By the side of one of these, that gurgled deliciously among the porous lava-rocks forming its bed, we dismounted from our horses, and sat down to our lunch under the grateful shade of a bunch of green guava bushes; after which we proceeded on our journey, bringing up, about noon, at the Waimanalo sugar-plantation.

After passing Waimanalo, we came shortly to the borders of the sea, and for some time rode close along its shore, our path, part of the way, being over long stretches of dazzling, white sand, which glistened like polished silver, cuttingly in our faces, straining our eyes until they pained us almost to blindness.

A short distance out from the beach, just beyond the point where the sea broke most into foam over the coral reefs, were three or four huge rocks, protruding like miniature islands above the water, half a mile or such a matter apart. They however, were nothing more than great, basaltic boulders, which had broken away from the rest of the island during some mighty upheaval, and been left there stranded in the sea. On one of them were said to be some small animals and a few scrubby bushes; the others were verdureless and without signs of life.

Along in the afternoon, we came to another pali; this one just what its name indicates, a savage, frowning, precipitous

wall of fused and chilled lava. Up its ragged side a mere
goat-trail found its way, in some places almost perpendicularly, the footing everywhere to the summit being frightfully
rough, rocky and distorted. At the base of this pali lay the
ugliest, frenzied ocean that I had then seen anywhere on the
Hawaiian coast, breaking through the vaulted, sponge-like
rocks underneath, with loud, belching roars, fierce and de-
fiant. From our approach, it appeared to me utterly impossible to scale the pass, even afoot ; how we were to do so with
our horses, was a problem, the solution of which I left to the
experience of my friend.

At his suggestion, we dismounted on the level at the base
of the steep, and arranging our bridle reins in lengths, to
give to our horses as much liberty as possible, began the ascent, scrambling over and through the split and broken
boulders that intercepted our path as best we could.

We had frequently to stop, and gather fresh breath, and
rest ; but finally, after winding in and out among the black
mass of confusion, till our elevation, as we looked back over
the sea, showed us to be quite " well up in the world," we
emerged at the top, on a flat plateau, between high hills, all
of which was densely carpeted with disintegrating " aa."
Here, for a few moments, we sat down, to pant and wipe our
perspiring individualities, and to congratulate ourselves, that
probably we should never again have an opportunity to repeat that ticklish feat ; and then we " moved on."

From the top of the pali, our path, for a number of miles,
coursed through very rough places, the ground thickly strewn
with masses of friable rock of all sizes. Our horses, therefore, were left free to pick their own ways ; for the instinct
of a horse, in such difficulties, is generally safer than the
judgment of his rider, no matter how expert that rider may
be. So many horses know so much more, in many cases,
than so many men.

We saw several flocks of wild goats feeding on the hill-
sides as we progressed; there are thousands of them in the
mountains. Their preferences lead them to those inhospitable and barren places, just as the preferences of some men
lead them to Arizona and New Mexico, rather than to the
broad, fertile valleys of the great north-west, which offer,
with open-handed hospitality, all of the comforts of generous
plenty. Mountain plover also were abundant.

After a ride of a couple of hours through these broken
fields, we came out again, finally, on the ocean, and
thence into Honolulu were, most of the time, traversing its
shores.

Eight or nine miles out from the city, my friend stopped
and requested me to alight; and when I had done so, and had
fastened my horse, he led me up the side of the cliff, bordering the road, to an elevated shelf that stood out from its face,
three or four hundred feet above the sea level. It was rather
a difficult climb, but by dint of clinging to the projecting
points of the rocks, we finally reached our destination and
seated ourselves on the narrow ledge.

What he had brought me there to see, was a shallow cave,
eighteen or twenty feet deep and seven or eight feet in
diameter, rudely excavated in the side of the bluff, its aperture
partly closed with rough boulders of stone. It was an ancient
Hawaiian sepulchre.

Inside was a confusion of debris anything but inviting;
skulls, a bushel of them, and human bones; also broken and
rotted remnants of native canoes, shreds of mouldy tapa-cloth,
and matting, all in a jumbled-up mess scattered about. This
was the manner of burial that prevailed among the natives
prior to the advent of the whites. The cliffs were thickly
dotted with similar places, unopened, which we could see,
from the road below, spotting the brown face of the hills.

Close by the edge of the ocean, a little farther on, a num-

ber of bubbling, fresh-water springs oozed up out of the
ground, so close down to the shore that the high tides covered
them. Again I alighted, in order to test the quality of the
fresh, artesian fluid so temptingly offered, and after taking
an old-fashioned drink, in the rare, old-fashioned, school-day
manner of boyhood, prostrate on a frontispiece rather too
convex nowadays to be handy for that kind of pastime, I
wandered out on the exposed rocks, uncovered by the low
tide.

On my approach, there was a great scampering of something, which reminded me of enormous black spiders, leaping
from rock to rock by hundreds in their efforts to get away.
I afterwards discovered them to be soft-shell crabs, but before I could reach them, they had every one disappeared into
the crannies of the rocks. I managed, however, to dislodge
one or two, for being the first I had ever seen on their native
heaths, I was anxious to inspect them. There was, likewise,
an endless variety of salt water crustacea, with which I was
wholly unfamiliar, and shell-fish, of various kinds and sizes,
fastened to the rocks.

I was particularly attracted by a peculiar, little jumping-
fish, which I discovered lying in the hollow places of the
rocks, in considerable numbers. They were not more than
three or four inches long, and each was equipped with a pair of
flipper-like fins, placed well forward on the under side of the
body. By the exercise of these, and the force of the tail, which
was always held ready prepared for a spring, they could dart
long distances through the water, or over intervening spaces
of land, with extraordinary dexterity and swiftness. Their
eyes were set far up on their foreheads, and protruded like
those of a frog, and they watched every movement that I
made with the greatest evident concern. If I attempted to
put down my hands into the water, as if to catch them, there
was a splash and a flash, and they were feet away before I

knew they had started. I found it utterly impossible to secure any of them without a net, so was denied the close personal inspection I very much desired.

We arrived home about six o'clock, tired and sore from our long ride, but nevertheless highly gratified with it. A native "lomi-lomi" was suggested, to drive away any possible stiffness of the joints that threatened for the morrow; but I was satisfied with an ordinary American bath of salt water, and a good rubbing afterwards, and the next morning felt like a new silver dollar just passed through the mint, very fresh and bright but considerably crowded together.

A "lomi-lomi" is simply a native massage, and consists in manipulating the joints and muscles of the body in a peculiar manner, that is said to be very effective in dispelling pains or soreness. Many tourists, unaccustomed to riding, take it on arriving at Hilo, after the long and tiresome trip down from the volcano, and are greatly benefited.

As a rule, such persons are ready to adopt anything that will bring back their bodies to their normal shapes; for by the time they reach their destination, especially if they have come all the way through on horseback, their listless legs dangle along the course of travel, like slaughtered game brought in from a hunt on broncos, their collar-buttons settle down and occupy the seats of their saddles, and they pray to the gods out of the depths of their agony, " give us Hilo or give us death."

CHAPTER XIII.

JANUARY 8th, 1892, was a lovely day, as had been nearly
all the others that preceded it during my stay in Honolulu.
It was, moreover, the day of my departure for the volcano
of Kilauea; and as I sat on the deck of the little stern-
wheel steamer, W. G. Hall, one of the Inter-Island Steamship Company's boats, at the foot of Fort street, "Old Sol"
beamed down in a most benignant and congenial manner.

It was nearing the hour for the boat to start, and a mixed
crowd had gathered on the dock to see her off; some to wit-
ness the departure of friends, many out of idle curiosity;
and during the interim, I occupied the moments sizing up
my compagnons-de-voyage. There was quite a large list of
passengers aboard, representing all classes and conditions;
among them several men of eminence in the kingdom, law-
yers and politicians. Besides these, there was also the
average share of native Kanakas, men, "wahines" and
babies; and quite a number of tourists and others bound for
the volcano, or for points on the other islands. Garlands of
"maile" figured conspicuously about the necks of the native
passengers, and leis of pleated ferns and flowers, and of the
yellow ornamental "hala," all of which had been placed
there by friends with many a tear and sad "aloha."

There were five white passengers on the boat, who, inasmuch as they are going to figure prominently in what I am
about to relate, if the "truth and the whole truth" is to be
told, ought to be introduced and described.

First on the list was "Old-Forty-Niner," a man about sixty years of age, from California, and the "papa" of the expedition. There was nothing going on which he didn't take a hand in, and as will be seen later on, he came to be quite a figure-head among our number.

There was also aboard a young Irishman named Mc-Cleverty, and a very genial, quick-witted and social young fellow he was, too. It was one of the pleasantries of his

OLD-FORTY-NINER.

nature always to be loaded with a rare, good story, and he could reproduce from his stock on hand in great form. On occasion, too, he could sing a song with the best, either comic or pathetic, and he never tired of wrestling with a joke.

As "Mack's" right hand man and traveling companion, we had with us a Mr. Littlepond, but the name being rather clumsy for close fellowship, by mutual consent we abbreviated it to "Pondy," and by this title he went to the close of our pilgrimage together. He was a genteel, black-

eyed young man, about thirty-five years of age, and sported
a magnificent mustache, which so adorned him as to be an
object of profound admiration and envy on the part of all
the balance of us.

Next on the list came Mr. Sykes, a European. Though
the youngest of our party, he had yet completely circum-
navigated the globe on his wits and talents, and still possessed an ample supply for further adventures. His varied
experiences and uprightness of character had won for him
the confidences of men, and secured him a lucrative place in
an important business enterprise of Honolulu, which at the
time of our travels together, he was still representing, and
which led to the title of "The Secretary," that by common
consent was given him. He sang bass like a German bar-
tender, and as a story-teller was behind few of our number.

But, by all odds, the most eccentric one of the quintette
was a man about the age of Old-Forty-Niner, a commercial
tourist in clocks from the state of Minnesota, who, as he
himself stated it, had all his life long "been busy encouraging strikes and keeping up step with Time."

He bore all the outside appearances of an exceedingly
nervous man; his hair, quite dark, stood in a multitude of
angles about his head, as if from repeated thrusts of worry
through it; his face was thin, and one of his eyes, in color
between a blue and a gray, stared continually out at you,
with a wild, hunted expression, that was comical beyond description. This last peculiar oddity of his face was afterwards explained. The organ proved to be an artificial one,
and the artist, in attempting to copy after nature, had
simply made a failure.

He wore a pair of gold-rimmed spectacles across his nose,
and when anything occurred that particularly interested or
excited him, he had a habit of closing his good eye with a
snap, and staring at you with the other till you fairly shiv-

ered in your boots. His mouth, too, was everlastingly twitching and smacking, as though an artesian fount of lemon-juice was somewhere hidden between his lips.

In spite, however, of all these physical derangements, which taken physiognomically, would seem to imply a cynical rather than an optimistic temperament, his face wore continually an indelible smile, one of the prime secrets, no doubt, of his steady successes in business; for it certainly

THE SQUID.

was magnetic, and I might say, was almost bewitching. All in all, he was really a very agreeable man, fond of chat and chaff, and though quite a stickler for his opinions, if at any time he saw a tendency in the crowd to drift in another direction, he was sure to join in and follow the procession.

He loved a good story better than any other man I ever saw, and while one was being spun, his good eye usually remained closed, the other evidently being deputized to manifest all needful interest for both; and he was as full of yarns himself as his clocks were of ticks.

His chief eccentricity, however, consisted in a set phrase of which he made use continuously: "for instance, you understand;" and this he interjected into his conversation at all times and seasons, without any regard whatever to sense or application; and he would bob from one unfinished subject to another with such reckless agility that Mack nicknamed him "The Squid," which title adhered to him, determinedly, all the time we were together.

He was, above all, an out-and-out, true-blue American, and took the keenest delight in singing the praises of the great Republic on all occasions, and he kept constantly at hand a copy of "Triumphant Democracy," to which he confidently referred, for whatever statistics were required to bolster up his arguments and opinions.

Some one spoke of the production of pork in Australia. The Squid took it up at once. "For instance you understand," said he, "as to hogs, the wool raised in Australia doesn't compare with the United States, and when you talk about cattle, there isn't a breed of horses in the world equal to those of California;" and he hastened away for his book to verify his assertions.

Up to the time that the band of voyagers I have described came together on the Hall, only a few had ever met before, but in the customary way of ocean voyagers, they soon found the common center of congeniality, and forthwith all of them gathered round it.

A few boxes of merchandise had to be elevated over the side of the boat with a steam crane, also a couple of horses, and two bulls that struggled mightily in the air as they were being swung from the wharf to the deck, and then the final whistle was given, and we cleared away for Punaluu, our ocean destination, about two hundred miles distant, at the extreme farther end of the island of Hawaii.

We now had a chance to see who our fellow passengers were. The Kanakas to a man, and for that matter to a woman as well, were all deck passengers. This was equivalent to steerage on other boats, except that they were not obliged to go below, their place being in the open passageway forward of the after-cabin, and between it and the officer's quarters. And here they were spread out on the floor, fifty or more of them, on mats and blankets, for the voyage across to the other islands.

They were a tidy, polite, and happy lot of voyagers, too ; and hardly had we left the shores of Oahu, when an accordeon was produced, and a guitar, and except during the rougher parts of the passage, and in the deep hours of the night, music and singing blended with the swash of the sea in a concert of good feeling throughout the entire journey.

As time wore on, and the trip, to them, became wearisome or monotonous, they would often lie concealed under their blankets, their heads wholly covered up, and thus hidden from view, would pick dolefully on the guitar, accompanying its notes with low, vocal melodies, till they fell asleep or were completely exhausted ; then it was passed to another, to be by him repeated. And so the hours went by.

Taking a seat, shortly after starting, with Old-Forty-Niner and The Secretary, on the port side of the boat, we had an excellent view of the harbor, the shipping that lay within, and the shores of Oahu.

An immense school of porpoises met us as we went out, hundreds of acres of them, affording an excellent opportunity to watch their graceful movements, as they darted into the air all about us, describing semi-circles of brown flashes in the sunlight, and then disappearing again into the water, leaving scarcely a ripple to show where they went down.

We could also see them under the water, racing parallel with our direction, as if measuring speed with us, or powers of endurance with their steam rival, the Hall. Flying fish, in great numbers, also darted athwart our course, and skimmed along the blue surface of the water, in sparkling scintillations of silver, to our right and left.

The sea appeared to be very calm, and everybody was congratulating himself on the good fortune attending our trip, for almost always the channels between the islands are extremely rough. There is, probably, however, no other of all the works of creation, that can " assume a virtue though it has it not," equal to the ocean. If Hamlet had only taken a sea voyage before pleading with his mother to resort to that dastardly practice, he would, without hesitation, have sacrificed the whole royal clan, ghost and all, rather than have said one word to induce her to it. The ocean, like her, is a hypocritical, brazen, old fraud ; and when I say this I know what I am talking about.

He will lie so calm, and saintly, and so confidingly smooth sometimes, as you approach him from the harbor, that you are induced, almost, into a sincere feeling of respect for his majesty and glory ; but just you wait till he gets hold of you, and then see to what contemptible devices the powerful will sometimes resort, to wreak their devilish tribute from the weak and lowly. That was just the way we were used in crossing Oahu channel. A happy, joyous throng of congenial spirits, was, in less than twenty minutes, turned into a dismal band of wailers, and so remained for a number of hours till we got under the lee of Molokai.

One of the most agreeable and intelligent of the many Hawaiians whom I had the pleasure of meeting on the Islands, was the Hon. L. A. Thurston of Honolulu. His father was one of the early missionaries to the Sandwich Islands, and there Mr. Thurston was born about forty years ago. After being thoroughly educated, he took to the practice of law; but soon drifted into politics, receiving as a reward for his character and abilities, the highest positions of honor and trust in the kingdom. In personal appearance, he is a willowy, black-eyed man of medium height, and in conversation is clean cut, quick-spoken and intellectual. No one in the Hawaiian kingdom is better informed than he in matters of current history, and none a more complete compendium of its present affairs. We fell into chat on the steamer, and finally drifted upon the subject of the native people, their past and present condition and rapid decline.

The question had repeatedly haunted me, as I looked at those miserable, leprous outcasts, huddled together on the deck of the Hall: "What has Christian civilization done for this race, to benefit and advance it in the scale of human happiness?" for, after all, our happiness, here and now, is primarily the one thing we are all seeking; and, as we argue it, civilization affords the highest opportunities that humanity can attain to possess that end. Self-sacrifice for others is all right and commendable, and under certain limitations, is greatly to be approved; but there are boundaries set even to that. One is under no obligation to dance on molten lava, just because that act is going to afford pleasure to the devil. What we are all after is our own individual happiness; and what is true of us as individuals holds equally good of tribes and nations. The ancient Hawaiians desired happiness as anxiously as we. Did we advance their opportunities for it, when we lifted them out of their barbarism and gave them Christianity and civilization?

A hundred years ago, they were in exclusive possession of these beautiful islands; the fertile lands embracing their territory were divided into taro-patches and gardens; out of the sea they got their fish; and of the fruits that grew spon-

taneously there was an abundance, and all were abundantly
fed.   What little protection was demanded against the
elements or the weather was supplied by the growths from
the hill-sides and mountains; clothing was not a necessity
at all ; and as for labor, they were as nearly free from every
obligation to that as it is possible to conceive.   All in all, it
is fair to presume that they were a reasonably happy and
contented people ; for, physicially, they were remarkably
vigorous, and as a race, exempt from all settled disease.
They sang, and danced, and whiled away their lives in a
perpetual round of merry idleness, subject only to the
demands of their king, or of their chiefs, in periods of war
or invasion.   What more could the animal part of man
desire ?

It has been said by a notable writer, that such a thing as
fixed morality in the world, does not exist ; but that every
nation and race of people formulates and establishes its own
rules of conduct, from local customs and through public
opinion, the most powerful and far-reaching of all social
enactments, to control human beings.

The Sandwich Islanders were not the only people whose
code of morals deviated widely from that which Christianity
has sought to establish among men ; but none, perhaps,
were ever more lax than they in the one special require-
ment of personal purity.   They had no word in their language expressive of chastity ; they had never known the meaning of personal virtue, as we are taught to understand it ;
hence they wholly disregarded it.

If a man committed theft he was punished ; if he violated
the law of his king, or failed to respect the demands put
upon him by his chief, he was required to answer for his
delinquencies, frequently to the extent of his life ; but in
their domestic affairs, the sense of right and wrong did not
enter ; there was no sacredness in the family relation.

While in the midst of this state of existence, the white man came among them; and with him came disease, the most insidious and horrible known to our kind. Their blood which before had been pure and free from every germ of corruption, became virulent and foul with syphilitic taint and infection, until to-day, as is stated by the highest medical authority of the islands, the contagion has disseminated itself among the entire race, and none are exempt.

And not only did the poisons of the blood come to damn and ruin this contented and ignorant race of human beings, but another agent of modern civilization, almost, if not quite as deadly, stalked uninvited in at the same door, to help consummate the crime that was to be inflicted upon them. That agent was the white man's trusted embassador in quieting the savage, the world over,—gin.

Then came the harpies who prey upon the confiding under the guise of friendship; the Judases, who betray even their Saviour for tinkling silver; and the original possessors of the soil, deprived of their heritage, were driven out; until, at the present time, they hold but a fraction of the real estate of the islands, and less than thirty-five thousand men, women and children are left to represent the multitude who at one time made their homes on the Sandwich Islands.

I thought of these things, over and over, as I listened to the plaintive songs of those hapless refugees, packed closely together around the grimy smoke-stack of that great, throbbing steamer, and caught the notes of music with which they sought to beguile the fast-fleeing hours that are hurrying them on to extinction; and the question would rise in spite of me: "What has civilization done for them?"

While in this reflective mood, Mr. Thurston came upon the scene, and I put to him the question that had been disturbing me. He was prompt to respond, and gave free exercise to his faith in clear and unmistakable words.

"In former days," said he, "the Hawaiians were serfs and slaves, most abject, to their chiefs. They were obliged to work for them, whenever and wherever they demanded, and nothing they possessed was sacred against them. What the chiefs wanted, they took, and asked no questions. They were obliged, also, to hold themselves perpetually in readiness to go out to battle; for the chiefs were incessantly at war, instances of continuous conflict for mastery, extended over a period of twenty years, being on record. Their numbers, in this manner, were being rapidly reduced, and, in time, they would have been completely wiped out of existence. Finally, it was the progress of civilization, the supremacy of the white man over the colored, which has marked the course of modern advancement the world over; in other words, it was 'the survival of the fittest.' "

I have endeavored to give Mr. Thurston's sentiments correctly as he uttered them, and am sure I have done so, for I was much impressed by them at the time, and immediately jotted them down among my notes and memoranda. What he said did not strike me as a sufficient answer; but I give it as I received it, and my reader is free to form his own conclusions.

CHAPTER XIV.

AS we sailed along the west, or leeward shore of Molokai,
the sea became less turbulent, and the passengers were
able to come out of their state-rooms on deck. High above
us, on our port side, towered the lofty up-lands of that noted
island, whereon is located the most celebrated leper settlement of the world, the place where Father Damien sacrificed
himself to Christian duty.

It has few inhabitants, aside from the lepers, due, mostly,
to its insufficient supply of water ; but there is a sugar plantation at the east end of the island, and also a few scattered
residents. The balance is given over to wild animals and
game ; cattle, hogs, goats, deer, wild turkeys, peacocks,
pheasants, quail and plover. Owing, however, to the inac-
cessible lay of the land, they are but little hunted.

The leper settlement of Molokai is located on the north
side of the island, and consists of a strip of land running out
into the ocean, a miniature peninsula, five miles long and
about two wide, fertile and beautiful.

Back of it are high, precipitous bluffs, that shut it off from
the remainder of the island, and which being guarded besides, bar escape. The location is all that could be desired,
the climate salubrious and healthful, and here more than
eleven hundred imprisoned victims of the most loathsome
disease known to man, live, and await death. The average
life of a leper is five years.

The solicitude manifested for these unfortunates, and the love and sympathy shown them by their countrymen, is one of the most beautiful and touching illustrations of human divinity, if I may call it such, existing anywhere on the face of the earth in this nineteenth century. Mr. Thurston is my authority for the statement, that ten per cent. of all of the revenues of the kingdom is annually devoted to the amelioration of their unhappy state. They are provided with churches, hospitals, and neat homes, and nearly or quite a hundred horses are kept for their use and pleasure in the settlement. Officers are deputized, and on guard over the entire kingdom, to keep vigilant watch for new cases, and places are provided, at convenient points, for the segregation of suspects, until a competent medical examination can be had at the leper hospital in Honolulu.

One of those concessions to crime, however, which occasionally crop out, even in more enlightened communities than this, and which sometimes are permitted to go on, uninterrupted, for long periods of time, though of most vicious and baneful complexion, may be found in the Molokai leper settlement, sanctioned by a misguided sympathy which is damnable. It consists in the intermixing of the sexes, and the occasional birth of children, who are obliged to remain with their parents. If this isn't an immolation of the innocents as pitiless as the slaughter of Herod, then am I, indeed, destitute of human feeling. Far better would it be to sink the whole colony of Molokai in the three-mile depths of the Pacific Ocean, over whose mighty chasm it hangs, than that such a practice, with its horrible results, should be permitted to continue a day or an hour longer.

There is, at the present time, a man convicted of murder, incarcerated in the settlement. The choice was given him, either to hang, or be subjected to leprous vaccination for medical study and commitment to Molokai. Of

His skin grew dry and bloodless, and white scales,
Circled with livid purple, covered him ;
And then his nails grew black, and fell away
From the dull flesh about them, and the hues
Deepened beneath the hard unmoistened scales,
And from their edges grew the rank white hair ;
And Helon was a leper.

—N. P. Willis.

the two evils he preferred the latter, and the doctors have been stabbing and inoculating him ever since, but at last accounts he was well and taking his meals regularly, happy in the expectation of some day being pardoned out, as the disease had utterly failed to make its appearance on him.

After the Hall got into smooth water again, the passengers, as usual under such circumstances, all felt magnanimously happy; everybody then wanted to get acquainted with everybody else, and began, right away, to carry his desires into execution. It was at this opportune time that the five tourists who have been described, and myself, came together. McCleverty, especially, was urbanity itself. Dodging here and there among the passengers, he extended to each a handful of cigars, with the question, "Are ye smokin'?" till everybody was supplied, or if not, might have been at Mack's expense.

We made no landings on Molokai, the first being at Lahaina on the island of Maui, at about five o'clock in the afternoon. There are no wharfs at any of the island ports, except Honolulu, and landings are therefore obliged to be made in whale-boats, or canoes from the shore. All freight has to be transferred back and forth in the same way. The Hall, therefore, dropped her anchor, and lowered her four boats into the water, into one of which those of the passengers who desired to go ashore scrambled. The wooden ladder on her starboard side, for ascending and descending from and to the whale-boats, was a convenient device, and safe even for ladies in getting in and out.

Lahaina at one time was the seat of government and home of the early kings, and was the most important point of the kingdom, being the principal whaling station of the Pacific seas; now it is greatly reduced, the population numbering only a few hundreds. There are two sugar plantations back of the village, and on these whatever of life it has left largely depends. It is charmingly situated, in fact I may say romantically; the high mountains back of it, and its abundance of verdure giving to it an air of enchantment very delightful.

Some little time was consumed getting away from Lahaina, so after returning from the shore, I occupied it on the stern of the boat, amid the varied scenes of loveliness that were there presented.

To the west lay the little island of Lanai, rising obscurely out of the sea, its summit buried in a mass of rolling black clouds, through whose straggling rifts the sun, just setting, forced a flood of gold and crimson inexpressibly beautiful. Higher up, this rich coloring gradually dissolved into other and softer shades, until, half way to the zenith, it melted completely out, leaving only that superb, azure-blue tint of the sky so often seen in the tropics.

To the north lay Molokai, from where I sat, much resembling Lanai, except that it was larger; its entire upper portion wholly concealed from sight by a thick robe of fleecy-white clouds, which, like snow-drifts, lay banked against its side and along the surface of the water between the two islands. The ocean, all about, was dark and still, and before the boat started, the moon appeared in the heavens accompanied by a few radiant stars, making altogether, with mountains, and sea, and sky, a rare combination of effect, and one seldom duplicated to the voyager, no matter where he may travel. I confess that I was completely enamoured with it; and one who cannot be hypnotized by such scenes, into that delicious state of enchantment where all is dreams and visions of pleasant things, must be, indeed, other than mortal man.

We took supper on the boat at Lahaina, and then our party gathered aft prepared for a smoke. One more landing had to be made, at Maalaea Bay, after which came the "Hawaii Channel," separating Maui from Hawaii. This is almost uniformly very rough; but we did not expect to reach it until the middle of the night, and therefore relied on all being asleep to avoid its discomforts.

As we sat smoking, well astern, in the full glow of the moon, and watched the stars and sparkling water shimmering in our wake, we fell, naturally, into that happy state of being so common to the average man, who having just been well fed and watered, seeks respite from all troublesome cares. Each was anxious to enjoy himself in the best manner possible.

Mack sang a song, an old familiar one, to which The Secretary lent his rich sonorous voice; the balance of us listened silently, or dreamily hummed the chorus in tune with their final refrains.

Did you ever notice how easily, and how, by a sort of mutual, general consent, a lot of men thrown together, either as friends or chance acquaintances, will drift into spinning yarns? It never fails, you can always depend on it; and that reason alone is sufficient to explain, why we, too, soon found ourselves employed in that manner, laughing and joking in the customary way.

There were so many good story-tellers in our party, and they were so full of anecdotes, legends and squibs, and they told them so well, that, for my part, I was quite content to remain in the background and listen. Finally, however, my silence attracted attention, and by general demand, it came my turn to say something.

I couldn't, just for the moment, call to mind anything, which I thought would be at all new with a crowd such as this, that seemed so to abound in every modern fable; so I sprang one that Billy Armstrong told me, years and years ago, about three newspaper men, who, in order to test their several powers of exaggeration, in which each through force of his profession claimed pre-eminently to excel, placed five dollars apiece in a common pool ; the one who, by mutual consent, should get farthest away from the truth in the fewest words and shortest space of time to take the pot.

I thought the story would prove to be a fresh one, away out there in the Pacific Ocean among the Fejees, and I spread it on with all the flourish and decoration I could command.

Finally, I came to the " nub." " The first contestant," said I, " began his story after this fashion :   ' Once upon a time there was a very wealthy editor—— immediately the other two threw up their hands.

" ' Take the money,' they whimpered in an imbecile tone of voice, breaking off the progress of the yarn, and almost dropping from their chairs at the supreme audacity of such a statement ; 'take the money. That is the most outrageous, infernal, d—d—d—d onslaught on truth we ever heard in all of our lives.' "

I expected a terrific outburst of applause, when I had concluded, a regular Sioux war-whoop, that would hurry the purser out of his room to see what was the matter, and make the devil-fish on the reefs break for deep water ; but it didn't come. There wasn't even the glimmer of a smile apparent on any of their faces ; on the contrary, there was a look of colicky pain and disgust, which mortified me. What had I said or done, to cause such a sudden change from mirth and hilarity to dense, overwhelming gloom? I was utterly at a loss to interpret the mystery.

At last Mack took up his chair, and walking over by the side of the vessel, sat down. Resting his elbows on the guard-rail, his chin in his hands, he looked abstractedly off over the water. The Secretary and Pondy soon after followed suit, and gazed vacantly away into the distance ; while The Squid, nervously screwing himself about, put his feet up on a bench and began to whistle. Old-Forty-Niner said nothing, but looked at me with an expression of surprise.

Presently, Mack arose, and came over again where I was sitting.

"Did you say you were from Ohio?" said he, in a doubting tone of voice, looking me over, from top to toe, quizzingly.

"Yes," I answered proudly, "that's what I am; the greatest state in the whole American Union, too; the home of Garfield, and Hayes and McKinley; we elected McKinley Gov—— "

"Boys," he broke in, in a very uncivil manner, interrupting me and calling their attention away by pointing to the land, "some people pretend to say that mountains are the most indestructible works of nature that the world contains. Now look at Maui! a solid mass, ten thousand feet high, nearly two miles, nothing but rock! one would naturally infer that Maui would outlast everything else on earth; but it won't. The earthquake comes, not oftener, perhaps, than once in a million years, but it comes; and then those mighty rocks are torn asunder, whirled and split into atoms by internal commotions, and that island, so fixed and invulnerable, sinks away into the sea, never to be known again till the day of resurrection.

"Now take the case of some old chestnut of a story, and mark its everlasting qualities in comparison. True, it is often rent with opprobrium, and like the mountain, is sometimes ripped to pieces with popular indignation; maybe for awhile it sinks entirely out of sight; but it rises again; even though covered with the moss and barnacles of ages, actually fossilized, so to speak, by the arts of time; yet it comes up just the same. Frequently, too, it re-appears in strange and unexpected places; possibly disguised in unfamiliar tongues to conceal its antiquity; yet it always returns, and always as smilingly as the new-born spring, and no power on earth has ever yet been discovered that was able to squelch or prevent it. Let's go forward, fellows, and see the Kanaka babies and get a fresh whiff of gin."

So speaking, they all arose, and with one consent went mournfully away and left me. In the course of half an hour, however, the deserters returned, and we were seated as before, smoking and chatting together.

The Squid, who had been sitting a little to one side, now commenced hitching up his chair to the middle of the ring, as if prepared for something he desired to say. He also opened and shut his good eye, several times, and gave to his lips a specially osculatory smack, as if there was something between them particularly pungent and refreshing.

"For instance you understand," he suddenly blurted out, " what do you think of that cave on Molokai ? "

" What cave do you refer to ? " responded one of the party who sat nearest him, turning round and looking at him in an inquiring manner.

"The dickens ! " answered The Squid, with the alacrity of surprise, " why, haven't you heard of the Cave of Molokai ? well, that's funny ; it's one of the curiosities of the islands ; you've heard the story of it, havn't you, that's as well known as Punchbowl ? "

None of us had ever chanced to hear a word, either of the cave or the story, so we prevailed on The Squid to relate it.

"For instance you understand," he commenced, drawing himself up a little closer into the company, and tilting back his hat at an angle with the incline of his head, " this cave I speak of lies on the south side of Molokai, and up to the time of the circumstance I am about to narrate, was entirely unknown. It appears to have been, for instance you understand, the result of some submarine action, or something of the kind, when the island was formed ; but whatever the cause, the cave is there just the same, a great, immense cavern, right in the mountain side, close down to the sea.

"It's a beautiful cave, too, so they say; all hung with stalactites, the floor as smooth as glass. The only opening into it is through and under the water, and it takes a long, strong dive and swim to reach it; but when you are once in, it's simply grand, for instance you understand, that's what they say; I never have seen it myself."

CHAPTER XV.

"DURING the reign of Kamehameha the Great, there resided in Lahaina, a young man by the name of Pokee, the son of a chief. For instance you understand, I don't know why they called him that, but I presume it was because that was his name.

" Pokee was an exceedingly convivial young fellow about town, a regular high-stepper ; and for shape he stood six feet full in his bare, brown color, and was straight as an arrow. He was an awfully sociable fellow, too, was Pokee, and a great favorite with the Lahaina ladies; in fact, they say, nearly all the girls in town were fairly wild about him.

" He was an athlete, too, for instance you understand, and in a foot-race, could out-run any other fellows on the islands, especially when the fish-horn blowed for lunch, and when it came to dancing, or singing, or playing on the taro-patch fiddle, they weren't in it at all. He was what they would call in Minneapolis, a superfine quality of double-bolted, jam-up, choice goods.

" Well, things had been running extremely smooth with Pokee for a long while, and though still a young man, he had got pretty well squared away for business on the high-road to matrimony; for the first thing he knew, he found himself engaged to thirteen different girls, all at one time. All of them were belles of the town, too, so they say, the creme-de-la-creme of Lahaina society, sweeter, every one of them, for instance you understand, than monkey-pod honey ; and more than all else, Pokee had worked his cards so consummately fine that not one of the thirteen had the remotest idea he had any other sweetheart in the world, but thought herself alone, the only, exclusive favorite.

"Well, it so happened, that one day old Kamehameha chanced to be walking down one of the main streets of Lahaina, when who should he meet but one of Pokee's thirteen sweethearts. She was a gorgeous girl, too, dressed as she was in a thin, gauzy, gown of fleeting summer sunbeams, the stripes running up and down, and she immediately attracted the old king's attention. As soon as she noticed this, she peeked around her shadow in an awfully catching manner, and bowed to him with such a sweet smile and "aloha," that it fairly took the old man off his feet; she did it so all-killing 'cute and cunning. For instance you understand, she was a deucedly bright girl, as well as a clipper to look at, and she was just shrewd enough besides, to lay her ropes ahead for Pokee, in case he should ever be a candidate for any favors from the old king, after they were married. That's the kind of a girl for you, Mack; hitch onto one like her and you may some day go to Congress or be street commissioner.

"Well, that little, innocent flirtation brought about more subsequent trouble than all the delays of a telephone girl; for just at that particular time the king was a little short of help, so in order to replenish his stock, he loosed his grip and fell, heels over head, madly in love with this one. For several days, things went on in this way; in spite of all he could do, he couldn't get Kickywicky out of his thoughts, but kept continually revolving over in his mind how everlastingly frisky she was, and how kittenish, and all that, until finally, the old fool was completely befuddled, and didn't know whether he was afoot or canoe-riding half the time. For instance you understand, if he was a king he couldn't stand everything.

"Well, at last he had to give it up. So calling his grand chamberlain, he sent him out to find the girl and bring her to the palace, intending to make her "a-lady-in-waiting-for-the-queen-to-get-ready," or something of that kind. I don't know just what the position was going to be, but it was something grand.

"When the grand chamberlain brought the girl to the king's palace, and she learned that she was to be separated from her lover, it nearly broke the poor thing's heart. For days and nights she did nothing but sit in her room, and weave around, and wring her hands, and cry, ' Pokee! Pokee! Pokee!' and nobody could comfort her.

"Kamehameha wasn't used to such didoes as that, for it had always been considered a great honor before to be chosen by the king to live in the royal palace, and to be treated in that manner by a nobody of a girl made him boiling hot. So he told the chamberlain to fire her out of the establishment, and find some other girl to take her place who had a little half-way-ordinary, common, good horse-sense.

"'The chamberlain did as he was directed, for instance you understand, but the girl he brought in place of the first proved to be another of Pokee's thirteen, and acted exactly as she had done ; fretting, and stewing, and crying all the time for Pokee, till the king finally got disgusted with her, too, and gave her the sauer-kraut waltz just as he had the other.

"Notwithstanding, however, all of his back-sets, the old king wasn't at all discouraged, for like mankind the world over, he thought it couldn't be possible that any woman could resist *his* charms, unless she was out of her head; so he kept right on, sending out for others in rapid succession, one after another, all of whom, when they were brought in, turned out to be Pokee's girls, and refused to look at him, or speak to him, just as the first two had done.

POKEE BEFORE THE KING.

"Old Kamehameha wasn't exactly an archangel, boys, and being somewhat mad to begin with, by the time he reached number six of the girls, for instance you understand, he was so infernally overheated, they had to put devil-fish on his legs to draw the blood away from his head, so it wouldn't explode.

"This man Pokee, whoever he was, it appeared to him, had got a corner on all the pretty girls in the kingdom, and intended to monopolize the market; and he proposed to break that combine, or ride all the gods of the Kanakas to dinner, with his spurs on, that very day.

"Accordingly, he sent for his grand chamberlain again, and informed him that he wanted him to find out quicker'n a shyster could skin a greenhorn who that sweet-scented, japonica-blossom Pokee was, that all the girls of Lahaina were so dead stuck on; and he hinted, by telling him so right out, in so many words, that if he didn't get the information he wanted in just two hours, the best thing he could do would be to cast his shadow on the royal presence, and prepare to die, for, by thunder! he proposed to grind him.

"The grand chamberlain, for instance you understand, was rather quick to take a hint in an emergency, especially when Kamehameha was full of glycerine, and in less than half the time given him, he had Pokee corralled and before the king. The poor fellow was frightened nearly out of his tights all the way up to the palace, for he hadn't the faintest conception what was the matter; but when he was ushered into the presence of the king, and saw the dreadfully savage look on his face, he nearly fainted away. He knew, however, that he hadn't done anything wrong, so he braced up, stared the old fellow square in the face, scratched his off leg, and smiled. For instance you understand, it wasn't as you and I smile together, Mack—what? did I hear you say something? no? well, all the same, Pokee smiled whether we do or not.

"When Kamehameha saw Pokee smile, it angered him more than ever, for he thought he was poking fun at him; but when he saw him scratch his off leg, he sent up a howl that sounded for all the world like a Sprecklesville sugar-planter talking about McKinley, and shook down half the cocoanuts in the palace grounds. That's what they say.

"'Take the leper from me,' he roared, 'to Molokai with him, away! away!'

"Of course that was only a mean, under-handed ruse to get rid of Pokee, for he wasn't a leper at all; but the scheme worked, and that was all that was necessary.

"Well, poor Pokee was hustled out of the royal presence, and locked up till he could be transported, and nothing his friends could do, no pleadings nor explanations, had any effect to soften the old king's heart. The news, as a matter of course, soon spread, like fire in the Chinese quarter, all over the city, and in less than no time, Pokee's thirteen sweethearts got hold of it. Then there *was* wailing. A Kanaka funeral was nowhere, compared with it. But they didn't dare to go near him, for strict orders had been issued to toast anybody who attempted it. Finally the time came for him to be taken away. He was in the depths of despair, but nevertheless, still plucky, and as the boat left the dock, he raised his right hand to heaven, and swore by the '*ipu-kuha onionio of he diabolo*' he would never go to Molokai alive.

"The boat had a pleasant voyage, and was just ready to round the west end of the island, when all at once, for instance you understand, up jumped Pokee to his feet, ran across the deck, and before anybody could stop him, dove, 'helatyscoot,' off into the sea.

"Maybe there wasn't commotion on that boat then! Every sailor aboard almost got wind-galls on his larynx, yelling for help, for they knew if the king learned that Pokee had es-

THEN THERE WAS WAILING.

caped, their lives wouldn't be worth as much as cold goose-grease ointment is for rattlesnake bites, and in less than ten seconds, every fellow had a pike-pole, or grappling-hook, or something of that sort, and was hanging over the edge of the boat waiting for him to come up. For instance you understand, they thought they could grab him that way, and drag him aboard. But he didn't come up. So, after waiting around a long while, the Captain concluded he had been gobbled up by a shark, or some other sea monster, and, worried almost to death, turned about and went back to Lahaina.

"When Pokee jumped into the water, he expected of course, to be drowned, but as that was what he was after, it wasn't likely to be much of a disappointment to him, and he wasn't fretting over it to any great extent. Right here, boys, the strange part of the story comes in. For instance you understand, I can't vouch for the truthfulness of it, although it looks plausible enough; in fact, it really looks *very* plausible. For myself, I wasn't there; so I haven't any reason to doubt it.

"It appears, that right where Pokee went down, there happened to be, at that very minute, lying fast asleep, one of the all-blastedest, biggest sperm whales you ever heard tell of in all of your lives; and the instant Pokee struck the water and spied him, he struck out for him livelier than a Georgia shoat for a hole in a ten-rail fence. He knew well enough, though, that he had got to be extraordinarily careful or he would wake him, for Pokee had been a whaler a trip or two himself, and understood, thoroughly, just how almighty skittish sperm-whales are; so, as he approached him, he moved with extreme caution, and finally, when he reached him, crawled, still as a materializing seance, up over his tail, and along, till he got to his head.

"By this time, for instance you understand, Pokee was

pretty nigh tuckered out and fagged for breath; but he didn't dare think of going up after more, for fear of being nabbed. If he wasn't in a ticklish fix about that time, boys, which one of us here was? Answer me that! which one of us was? It was a dreadful fix. Well, now, what do you think he did under those terrific circumstances?" And the speaker stopped short, long enough to look us over with an air of profound inquiry, as if waiting our answer. The question, however, was too profound, so we all shook our heads, but otherwise, remained still.

"Well, I'll tell you just what he did," continued The Squid earnestly, paying no further heed to his own interruption of his story, "and it was about the cunningest thing ever done by mortal man. What Jonah did wasn't a patching to it. Well, sirs, for instance you understand, he just quietly sneaked himself down, astraddle of that whale's neck, and putting his mouth right up close to his blow-hole, watched his chances; and whenever the whale blew out air or took any in, Pokee just laid for his 'divvy,' and caught it as it whistled past, on the fly.

"I don't know just how long he kept on in that way, stealing wind that belonged to the whale and spitting it out again, but it certainly was a good long while, for the boat laid around there an hour or two, and he was at it constantly during that length of time, to say the least; then he gave old Cachalot a kick and dove for the shore.

"By some miracle or other, when he came up, for instance you understand, he found himself stranded in that big cave I was telling you about. He didn't, of course, know where he was, but the place was light as day, so, after awhile, he got himself comfortably fixed, and was as much at his ease as a summer boarder. In one corner of the cave he discovered water trickling down through the rocks, so he wasn't troubled for drink; and as for food, there were lots of fish in the sea, all he had to do was to catch them; so he was all right there, too.

"After Pokee had rested a little, and had pumped out the whale-wind that he had confiscated while under the water, he began to hunt around in a search to satisfy his curiosity. Then it was that he found occasion for surprise; for the cave was absolutely honey-combed with rooms, some with connecting doors between them, and all, to a certain extent, furnished with a rude, household equipment; the construction of many of the articles being by weaving, like the bottoms of old-fashioned chairs. There were, besides, many other things in sight, and some of them that he discovered mighty quick let him into the secret of his new abode.

"Then he began to tremble in earnest, for he knew that the place belonged to the kahunas, for instance you understand, the priests, and that it was one of their sacred rendezvous, by them called 'praying temples;' and he knew, too, to a dead certainty, that if they caught him there, they'd pray him to death quicker'n wind can be turned into music by a German brass band. He didn't fear being hurt, for he knew he could lick the whole lot of 'em, but he couldn't bear the idea of being prayed to death; that touched his feelings almost as much as going to Molokai.

"Well, for instance you understand, after awhile, night came on, although Pokee couldn't tell just exactly when, because the cave, as proved to be the case, was always light; every stalactite seeming to be precisely like the dials of my celebrated, patent, magical, eight-day, night-illuminating, phosphorescent clocks; shining like a cat's eyes in the dark, fourteen holes for jewels, minute and second hands, warranted for five years or money refunded, do you want one? speak quick or——I beg your pardon, boys, for instance you understand, I was slightly digressing.

"But to return; the cave was, in fact, a secret chamber of

the kahunas; but was only known to a few high ones of the order, by whom it was used as a place of hiding whenever the king made things too hot for them outside. On such occasions, they took a vacation and skedaddled there. At what other times they visited it I don't know, and I reckon nobody ever found out.

"About nine o'clock of the night Pokee arrived, he went to bed, and as he was a healthy sleeper was soon in the arms of Murphyus, snoring to beat the band. Along about midnight, a noise in the other room woke him up. At first, he couldn't make out just what it was, but as soon as he got his eyes fairly opened, he distinguished the cause; it was somebody walking around out there.

"Now, Pokee wasn't the kind of a man to be afraid of anybody but his king, and feeling perfectly confident that whoever it was it certainly wasn't him, he jumped up very cautiously, and guided by the noise, stealthily crept out where the object was, and grabbed it. For instance you understand, everybody, in those days, looked alike, when their backs were turned, so he couldn't tell who it was he had hold of; but presently there was a little scream, and the next thing he knew he had one of those thirteen girls from Lahaina lying in his arms.

"Well now, you never saw a more surprised or tickled young man in all of your lives than Pokee was that very minute. He danced, and capered about, and sang, oh! how beautifully he sang, boys; equal to you Mack, or Pondy; (I wish I were better able to describe that glorious, asthmatic wind-wheeze, fellows, and make it more explicit; but the comparison is quite sufficient; quite sufficient; and, I am sure, will answer every purpose) and when he had tired out both himself and the girl, he sat down and began talking to her. He asked her all manner of questions, and finally he asked her how she found her way over there. I shall never tell you her answer, boys, but for instance you understand, she got there; and as that was enough to satisfy Pokee, it ought to satisfy you.

"All the balance of that night, and all the next day, the two did nothing but talk and visit, and it seemed to Pokee, he never before was so happy since the day he was born. But he was bound to be happier in spite of himself, for the next night, about the same time, another of the girls came, just as the first one had done. Strange to relate, but nevertheless true, however, the two got along all right together, and harmoniously; no trouble, nor quarrels, nor jealousies; the Kanaka girls are so good natured they wouldn't for the world be guilty of such civilized freaks.

"The next night, another of the girls came; then there were three. And so it kept on going, a new girl every night, till the whole thirteen were there, all together. You can't imagine what bliss Pokee was in. For ten, solid days, he, nor the girls, neither ate, or slept a wink; they just danced and sang, and played games, and enjoyed themselves.

"For instance you understand, Pokee was a very sociable fellow; but, of course, the girls couldn't stand everything, and after awhile, they naturally became tired and sleepy; so one of them, number five I think it was, suggested that they take a rest. Pokee wouldn't listen to it, at first, but begged and plead, and said everything on earth he could, to keep them from leaving him there, all by himself, alone. Finally, however, they prevailed on him to say, 'au rivver!' and then all of them went off into another room, by themselves, to bed, leaving him suffused in tears, the most lonesome, young man, without a doubt, that ever existed on the Sandwich Islands.

"The next morning, for instance you understand, the girls got up, and after putting on their clean holakus, came out as fresh and modest as thirteen German ring-doves, laugh-

ing, and giggling, and cooing, ready for their raw-fish break-
fasts, and then for another frolic; but Pokee was nowhere to
be seen.

"They were awfully annoyed at this, for they expected, of
course, that he would be up and dressed, waiting for them.
But they didn't for a minute think he had deserted them;
oh, no! and they were mighty right about it, too; for while
Pokee was a very Ward McAllister sort of a young man, for
instance you understand, he wasn't at all the kind of a
chimpanzee to leave thirteen pretty, young humming birds
in their nests, and wander away after addled cuckoo eggs.

"Well, after sitting around and waiting for him for some
time, the girls began to get uneasy; so they commenced to
make a little noise, thinking maybe that would rouse him;
but he didn't wake. Then they began singing together, in
chorus, but like all the balance of their little schemes, that,
too, failed to fetch him.

"Then one of the girls, number eleven I think it was,
said, for instance you understand, 'I'll go and rap on his
door.' But the others thought that would be too immodest,
and not at all proper; so she abandoned the suggestion. Finally, however, they reconsidered the suggestion, and, after
talking it all over, decided to go in a bunch and arouse him;
then if the act really was immodest, the disgrace would
have to be divided up among thirteen of them, and none
would get enough to do her any harm. After this weighty
decision, they started for Pokee's bedroom door, for instance
you understand, thirteen of them.

"When they arrived there, they decided to hold a sort of
female Sorosis, outside, and listen first before rapping; but
there was no sound within. Then number nine was deputized by the club to call him to order, sort of low-like; but
no answer came back. Finally, they gathered courage, and
together pushed the door open a little; and then they gig-

gled, and snickered, and ran out into the other room, and came back again, and put their hands over their mouths, and did all sorts of things, just as girls do, nowadays; but Pokee never moved.

"Then one of the girls commenced to get riley; and pulling her hair down over her eyes, so she couldn't be seen, bolted, brave as a lion, right into the room where Pokee lay. Boys, if anybody else on earth, but me, should tell you what I am going to say, you wouldn't believe it; would you, now? So help me, for instance you understand, if right on the bed there, didn't lay Pokee, sweet and placid as an innocent, little child, but deader than a landlord's conscience; yes, boys, he was dead; dead. On his breast lay a torn scrap of thin, white paper on which this note was inscribed:

"'Dear girls: It's no use talking. I can't stand this cruel separation any longer. Your heartless neglect is killing me. But though dying here, all alone, still

> "I love you, sweet thirteen,
> 'Pon honor I do,
> All come to my wake,
> And I'll try and come too.'

"Did he come to at the wake?" quickly interrupted Mack in a loud tone of voice, rising to his feet in an excited, eager manner, and stumbling forward over where The Squid sat, "did he come to, I say? tell me, you old hyena you, tell me!"

The Squid looked at his interrogator, scornfully, for several seconds, opening and closing his good eye meanwhile with the snap and celerity of a baby trip-hammer. Finally, he burst forth in a wild, sputtering explosion:

"No!" he yelled back in reply, "come to? no; of course he didn't! The man died of lonesomeness! Did you ever know any one to come to that died of lonesomeness?"

"But," he continued, modulating his tone of voice, "for

instance you understand, Pokee was sociable to the last
and ——

"'For instance you understand,'" frantically bellowed
Mack, jumping up and down and shaking his fist at The
Squid, "shut up, you infernal, sin-smuggling, rickety, old
smoke-jack you, shut up, I say! if you had a thimbleful of
brains in your dry, old gourd of a cranium, you never would
have wound up a story like that, anyway; for a nickel I'd
heave you overboard." And he stalked savagely away.

The Squid continued silent for some time, his eyes sparkling between their lids, as they opened and closed, like the
flash-lamp of a lighthouse in quick motion, his lips smacking with unusual gusto; and then he arose and went to his
state-room. The story he had told cast a feeling of disappointment over us all, and the whole company soon after retired for the night.

CHAPTER XVI.

I WAS aroused early the next morning by The Secretary.
The boat was just preparing to drop anchor at Kailua,
a landing on the island of Hawaii; but before I could get
ready, the whale-boats had started for the shore. I was
therefore deprived the opportunity of inspecting the place,
except from the deck of the steamer. The morning was
clear, however, and I could see the village quite plainly from
where we lay. Kailua is the summer place of residence of
the Queen, and the buildings she owns, and occupies during
her vacation, stood out prominently on the main street,
fronting the water; and insignificant, cheap-looking affairs
they were, too.

Back of the town is Hualalai, the third highest mountain
of the island, 8,275 feet above the sea. The cultivation of
coffee is beginning to flourish in this neighborhood, since
the decline of the sugar interest, the soil hereabout and the
climate being favorable to it in a high degree. So superior
is the quality of the berry raised here, that it is said to
bring five cents a pound more than that grown anywhere
else on the islands. Pine-apples and oranges are also raised,
and cattle grazing is given much attention.

Two public highways run parallel with the ocean, all
along this coast; one close down to the shore, the other a

mile or two back on the mountain side; each clearly defined from the steamer by the white houses and occasional church spires that are dotted along them.

At 7:30, we reached Keauhou, one of the most romantic spots that I saw on any of the islands. Lava flows, of great volume, which, at some remote period, rolled down from the mountains back of the village, to the sea, have helped to render this place extremely picturesque and attractive in natural beauty, homely and semi-barbarous as are its buildings and people.

You pass into the village through, what appears to be, an an artificial bay, formed by two arms of dark, tangled lava-rock, extending quite a distance out from the shore, and which rise in distorted masses of angry confusion above the water. These arms were formed when the flows referred to came down red-hot from their ancient, volcanic eruptions and poured headlong into the sea, and demonstrate, force-fully, by their grotesque formations, the action of the two elements when thus combined. The village was charmingly clean and neat, and as we passed among the people on the dock, we were greeted with many welcoming "alohas," that made us feel quite at home.

Without any previous intimation or direction, we all wandered to one particular spot of the village; and here spent nearly the entire time of our visit ashore. What attracted and chained us there, was a simple, rustic temple, nothing more; a rude grotto; its walls, twenty or thirty feet high, black, and gray, and jagged, and fretted all over with vines, and ferns, and blossoms; a grass hut in the foreground; a pool of clear water at its base; its canopied roof naught but the clear, blue sky. Yet the picture was sufficient to hold us fast almost all of our while till our boat left. It was only a condensed, little trifle of Nature's fancy; but Nature loves trifles fully as much as she does majestic characters; and

this, clearly, was one of her tid-bits on which she seemed
to have expended a world of studious taste.

All of the villages of the islands are, in the main, uniformly alike.   They are located close to the water; some of them
have small docks for handling goods to and from the whale-

NATIVE FISHERMAN'S HOME.

boats; and back from the shore, a few cheap, wooden houses
are nestled among the tropical trees, vines, shrubs and flowers.   There is generally a store or two in every village, usually kept by Chinamen, and these constitute the main features of the towns, excepting, always, of course, the native

people; who, while they offer little variety in their habits and manners, dressing, talking, and acting much the same wherever you meet them, are yet always pre-eminently interesting.

Our next stop was at Kealakekua Bay, at the village of Kaawaloa, noted as being the place where Captain Cook was murdered by the natives, in 1779. A monument marks the spot, a plain obelisk of concrete surmounting a solid pedestal of the same material. Around it is an iron fence, the posts composing it being upright cannons set in the ground and fastened together by chains. It bears the following inscription:

In memory of
The great circumnavigator,
Captain James Cook, R. N.,
who
discovered these islands
On the 18th of January, A. D. 1778,
And fell near this spot
On the 14th of February, A. D. 1779.
This monument was erected
by some of
his fellow countrymen.

While waiting here for the whale-boats to unload, we watched the native children catching fish from among the rocks, and devouring them alive, a pastime which they seemed greatly to relish.

Our next landing was at Hookena, a characteristic Hawaiian village. Steamer day, at all of the ports of landing, invariably empties the surrounding country, bringing in the people from the kulianas, or farms, by hundreds; and this little village of only two stores exemplified the general rule. I counted from the dock, ninety-eight horses and donkeys, barebacked and saddled, fastened near by, that had been ridden in by the natives to see the steamer arrive.

The Hawaiian Islands are all of volcanic origin, the result

of volcanic forces. They are, substantially, naught but solid aggregations of fused, basaltic rock, projected up from the bowels of the earth, during the outbursts of former days, and chilled into mountains of stone here in the midst of a great ocean. In some places, however, the accretions of centuries have so covered them with earthly deposits, and vegetable growths, that one is not unduly reminded of their origin as he passes along.

Most of the flows of the later periods, since the great original convulsions, date into the ages far back; and are generally covered with timber and undergrowth. Others, not so old, show only clumps of bosky chapparel, kukui, lahui, etc. At Hookena, however, and at many other points along this coast, it was different. As far as the eye could reach, up and down and along the mountain sides, broad stretches of exposed lava could be seen, in some cases recently expelled, glistening and shining in the sun, like acres of black paint or varnish, and covering miles in every direction. The records of Mauna-Loa show an outbreak, somewhere, either at the peak, or along his smoking sides, about every five years; and such has been the experience for long periods of time.

Wherever one travels, in Hawaii, the matter of volcanoes is always a subject of discussion; the eruption of 1868 being the one most frequently referred to by the natives. This outbreak was preceded by great numbers of earthquake shocks. Some estimate the number as high as two thousand, many of intense severity following each other in rapid succession. After these wrenching throes, came the burst of fire through the mountain, and the rush of hissing lava down its blistering walls, sixteen miles to the sea, in a stream two to three miles wide. This, however, lasted only three or four days, and did no real damage, as the territory over which it ran had been frequently flooded before, and there was little value upon it.

It is the prevailing impression, among persons unacquainted with the subject, that the emission of lava, during eruptions, is always from the peak of the mountain. This is erroneous; on the contrary, it is seldom so; the discharges, ordinarily, being from the side. The burning lake of Kilauea is only about 4,000 feet up the side of Mauna-Loa, while the extreme summit of that mountain is nearly 14,000 feet above sea level. It, however, has a crater at the peak, and sometimes breaks out there.

Eruptions sometimes continue for months at a time, their flows coursing the mountain-sides completely down to the sea, engendering, of course, where they pour into it, terrific confusion in the water, and creating, by means of the bitter conflict of the two elements, fierce, raggy, and slag-like formations of huge proportions along the coast. At such times, the glamour of the fire, at night, attracts large numbers of fish to the shore, which, venturing too near, are slaughtered by millions by the heat of the water; the surface, close to the land, being often densely strewn with their dead bodies.

Tidal waves are also frequent accompaniments of these internal tumults. One, in 1868, did much destruction to life and property on the island of Hawaii; the entire town of Punaluu being swept away, and many of the people drowned. Some eruptions are merely blow-outs of mud and other subterranean deposits, without fire. One, simultaneous with the tidal wave at Punaluu, engulfed a large number of natives, who chanced to have a settlement, five or six miles back from that place, in the immediate neighborhood of the disaster.

Flows of lava move slowly, and except where constantly renewed, soon harden into rock. One may stand very close to them without any fear whatever of danger.

After leaving Hookena, the twin summits of Mauna-Loa,

(Long Mountain) 13,675 feet high, and Mauna-Kea, (White Mountain) 13,805 feet, could be seen from our place on the steamer, presenting, at the extreme height of the gradually rising terraces between us and them, a magnificent spectacle.

Vegetation extends nearly, if not quite, to their highest altitudes, but the zones embraced between 2,000 and 6,000 feet above the sea are most diverse and luxuriant in plant life. There is little of the soil of any of the islands that is productive, or of much value for agricultural purposes, except what is found in the valleys and along the coast. For grazing, the higher uplands are utilized, but the grass that grows there is sour and unnutritious, and stock does not thrive on it.

We arrived at Hoopula in the afternoon. The sea was running high and we experienced some difficulty getting into the whale-boats, but, by exercising a little care, we made it all right, and with four stout Kanakas at the oars, were soon rowed safely ashore. We had only a few moments allowed us to look through the village, and we occupied them examining the interior of a native grass hut, which sat on a slight elevation of ground a few rods distant from the landing. In it were two old women, one with a baby in her arms, whose body was covered with large, rank sores. "Leprosy!" some one whispered; and immediately every fellow threw up his hands, so to speak, and almost declined to breathe while in the child's presence.

The house was a one-story, common, gable structure, about 14x24 feet inside, and contained one room. There were no openings in either end, and it was wholly without windows; two doors, front and rear, constituting all the apertures of the building. Between the doors, there was a broad passage-way, probably eight feet wide, which was employed as parlor, sitting-room and kitchen combined; the spaces on either side being occupied, to the ends of the

building, with beds. These spaces were filled up solidly,
eighteen or twenty inches from the floor, with numbers of
home-made mattresses, woven and manufactured, after pat-
terns purely Hawaiian, from the leaf of the wild-flag, which
grows abundantly along the mountains; thick blankets of
matting, of native workmanship, being spread on top. The
place, throughout, looked not only cool and clean, but exceedingly comfortable and inviting. Everything else about
the house was also tidy and in a state of good order. The
women offered us some hats, ingeniously braided by themselves, which they had on sale, but we did not buy.

The waves had not quieted while we were on shore, and
going back lashed us savagely, some of our party, in the
bow of the boat, getting a good dousing. The sun, however, and the stiff breeze that was blowing, soon sifted the
water out of their garments, so they suffered no particular
discomfort from the drenching.

We reached Honuapo aboat 4 P. M., and here disembarked
some horses by lowering them over the side of the boat into
the water, whence they swam alongside the whaleboats to
the land, where they were lifted with a derrick to the dock.
Then we proceeded to Punaluu, our steamer's destination.

The ocean front about Punaluu has a wonderful formation,
the result, in times past, of herculean lava-flows, which here
rolled down from the mountains, in living torrents of flame,
and poured fiercely into the sea; the coalition, thus effected,
instantaneously hardening the burning mass into thick walls
of black and shaggy rock, full of blow-holes, rents and
gorges, through which the wind and tide now surge and
roar in a savage, bellowing manner.

As I looked at it, I could think of nothing but the mould-
ering jaws of some huge, legendary monster, that had here
fallen head-foremost into the sea, and, unable to extricate
itself, had wasted and crumbled away, leaving naught be-

hind but grinning rows of massive grinders imbedded in
the land; so nearly did the rocks resemble teeth of enormous size, dark above the water line, light below. I visited
the place the following morning, and the impression remained the same. The sea was growling angrily in the
open spaces, where it worked its way in and out through
the fissures, and throngs of creeping, soft-shell crabs clung,
everywhere, tenaciously to its crinkled walls, giving an un-
canny aspect to what, even without them, would have been
anything but a pleasant picture.

The location of Punaluu is attractive only for its marine
and landscape views; aside from these, it has no charms to
offer. There are two sugar plantations near by, and a little
railroad, over which runs a dummy engine to "Pahala
Mills," five miles distant, on the road to the volcano, drawing freight back and forth between the mills and the coast.

After supper, the landlord invited us out to view the town
by moonlight. We took it in from a slight eminence east of
the hotel. Twenty-eight miles inland, the blazing shadow
of Kilauea hung luridly over the mountain top, reminding
one of some great conflagration seen at night from a distance.

Often, by day, a heavy, detached mass of thick, fleecy
clouds hangs suspended above the burning lake, as if fastened to the sky; and at night, it seems to absorb and hold
the red glare of the pit, till it looks like an enormous ball of
fire floating in the heavens.

In viewing these different effects, at separate times, while
at the volcano, a passage of scripture persistently haunted
my memory. I couldn't, for the life of me, identify it, at
first, it was so old and rusty; yet I knew it was there, and
by vigorous search, at the Volcano House, finally unearthed
it from a copy of the Good Book, which I fortunately found,
among many unfingered volumes of lesser value, in the book-
case collection of the hotel.

Nowhere, could a Bible quotation and its illustration be brought more vividly together. The text is in Exodus XIII:21-22:

"And the Lord went before them by day in a pillar of a cloud to lead them the way; and by night, in a pillar of fire to give them light to go by day and night."

"He took not away this pillar of the cloud by day, nor the pillar of fire by night from the people."

The only discrepancy I was able to discover in the illustration was in the matter of the people who were to be led the way and given the light. They were lacking. Everything else was there in good form.

After our return to the hotel, we sat for some time out in front of the veranda, on the grass, smoking and chatting in the moonlight; and while thus engaged, discussed in a social way various matters of general interest. Most of us being tourists, we very naturally dropped into chat about home affairs, or our voyages out from San Francisco, and several funny incidents were narrated by different members of our party. One was the story of a sea-sick, gambling traveler, who believing himself absolutely certain to die, offered big odds to the other passengers, on the final chances of his ultimate demise; the ruling passion still predominating. Circumstances that had occurred since arrival on the islands were legion; the main question being, who should tell his experiences first.

Mack had come out, as the representative of a great American daily newspaper, to write up the resources and industries of the Hawaiian kingdom; Pondy, to see what openings presented for a young man whose fortune had yet to be made. The Squid was partly on pleasure bent, but more particularly was he interested probing into the chances that offered for a trade in clocks. The Secretary, as before stated, was making the trip exclusively on business. These facts were disclosed in the desultory conversation we were having together. At last, Mack glanced over at Old-Forty-Niner.

"What brought you out to this God-forsaken country, old man," said he, in his joking, comical way, "all by yourself, and two thousand miles from salvation?"

Old-Forty-Niner gazed up in response, with a sidelong, indifferent glance, as if rather indisposed to talk; and then he dropped back again into his old attitude. Soon after, however, a deeper show of interest overspread his face, and a merry twinkle stole into his clear, gray eyes; but still, for a moment or two, he said nothing.

We had about concluded that he was going to ignore Mack's inquiry, altogether, when suddenly he began moving his chair along, as if desirous to get a little more into the hearing of the company. Then he took off his hat, laid it on his lap, and with both hands, graciously rubbed the bald surface of his shining upper story, as if the full moon that was beaming down upon it soothed and comforted him.

"Who said salvation?" he half whispered, something in his throat seeming to obstruct articulation, which he immediately removed with two or three little hacks, "do I look like a man in search of kodak pictures? I guess not! What I want is present reality. A two ounce vial, to-day, suits me a blamed sight better than a jug full, however big the jug, if I can't have it till after I'm dead. I'm a treasure hunter; that's what I am; and that's what I'm here for; a treasurer hunter, boys!" and he wiped his resplendent old thinker with a glaring, red bandana, and smiled as serenely as though there wasn't a thing in the world that could ruffle or divert him.

"It appears to me," said Mack, ingeniously drawing the old man out, "that this is a mighty poor country to come to after treasures, especially at this particular time; why didn't

you come out here when sugar was booming, instead of now,
when everything is flatter than poi?"

"It ain't sugar I'm after, my boy," quickly vociferated Old-
Forty-Niner, "that is to say, I ain't after any particular
quantity of sugar; a little of it is all right, in its place, and
very useful when properly applied with lemon, and cinnamon,
and things of that kind; but look here!" he continued, drawing a well-worn, neatly-bound, little book from his sack-coat
pocket and holding it up for Mack to gaze at, "did you ever
see volume two of this publication? I've been looking for it
for twenty years."

We all closed up, around the speaker, to see what the name
of the strange book was. It was bound in black leather, the
corners and edges were rusty with constant handling, and it
contained about a hundred pages. On the front, outside cover,
the title was imprinted in faded, gold letters:

American Drinks
and How
To mix Them.
Vol. I.

CHAPTER XVII.

DISAPPOINTMENTS AND ANXIETIES—TRIP TO THE VOL-
CANO, OVERLAND—POOR MINAH—THE " LAHUI "
—AND SEVERAL REFERENCES TO THE
VEGETATION OF THE
MOUNTAINS.

"THAT book was given to me, " resumed the old man,
"twenty years ago, and I've got more real comfort
out of it, since that time, than from my conscience, my abilities, and my religion all put together. It contains over three
hundred sweet, soul-slumbering, choice receipts, every one of
which I have thoroughly tested, time and again ; and not
one of them has ever been found wanting."

"Did I understand you to say, for instance you understand, that you detested 'em?" broke in The Squid, shutting his glass eye and keeping it shut.

Old-Forty-Niner was absorbed and didn't notice the question, but continued his remarks.

"Yes, time and again ; and never found one yet that
wasn't all that it was recommended to be. Now I'm hunting after volume two. Boys, if I can only find that book
before I die, I shall pass away in peace ; but if not, I shall
go down the most disappointed, miserable skeptic, as to the
goodness and wisdom of Providence, on this earth. I went
clean out to Manitoba once, after that book, thinking I had
it on the string, sure ; but when I got there, it was another
thing altogether: ' American soups, and how to make 'em.' "
Bah ! I had all my trouble and expense for nothing.

" Then I heard of a copy in Texas ; Galveston, Texas ; and
I wired about it there ; telegrams cost me four dollars ; but
it was volume one, and I was disappointed again.

" I was reading about the Sandwich Islands, lately, in one
of the San Francisco papers. It told how the missionaries
came out here, years ago, and mesmerized the natives with
their Eau-de-cologny religion, and paralyzed 'em with their
Hoop-la-de-Old-Holland Gin, and got their lands away, and
all that ; and as it appeared from what I read, that this work
was mostly done twenty years or more ago, it flashed into
my mind that maybe those missionaries had monopolized
the whole edition of volume two of my book. It certainly
was a reasonable supposition, to say the least, wasn't it ?
So thinking a little sea air would do me good anyhow, I concluded to take a run out here, look over the field, and see if
I couldn't find a copy. But I haven't, though, not a single one
anywhere.

" I met a fellow out on the fo'castle deck, coming up on the
Hall. Somehow, he looked to me like a missionary, so I
asked him about the book ; not with much hope of finding it,
to be sure, for I've inquired of pretty nearly everybody I've
met on the islands during the two months I've been here, all
without any success ; but I thought no harm to ask him anyhow. He got ripping mad at me right away, and swore he'd
decorticate me if I ever asked him that question again. I
don't know what that means, but that's what he said. He
said I had stopped him twice already on the streets in Honolulu, and had asked him the self-same question both times,
and he wouldn't stand it any longer. He said he wasn't no
missionary, but an honest saloon-keeper up at Hookena, and
if I wanted anything out of him to come right down into the
hold of the vessel, I could have it quicker'n lightning.

" Of course, he was an dod-ratted, old fool ; but I humored
him, and begged his pardon, told him I didn't mean any harm,

and came away. But I tell you what it is, boys, if any of you can find that book, it'll mighty nigh make your fortune, certain; American drinks and how to mix 'em, volume two; remember! volume two." We all agreed to keep an eye out for the precious relic, and immediately thereafter separated for the night.

On retiring to my apartment, I discovered a large moth flitting from corner to corner along the ceiling, and up and down the walls, and called the landlord's attention to it. It proved to be a welcome and familiar insect, known by the popular title of the "mosquito-hawk," its name having been acquired from a playful habit it indulges of feeding on those annoying little pests. The inhabitants, for that reason, regard it very kindly, considering it a good omen whenever one comes into their homes, and treating it with the utmost consideration.

There is a delicious satisfaction in seeing an enemy come up with; especially when it doesn't devolve on you to do the coming up part, and some other fellow takes all the chances. And that was just the spirit that possessed me, while I watched my friend, the mosquito-hawk, going for my enemy, the mosquito. I think I could have sat up all night and watched him do it.

The following morning, at 7:30, we took the train for Pahala Mills. As the road was built and is run for the purpose of bringing down sugar to the wharf, and for no other use, I shall spare it a description. The engineer was very accommodating, and stopped a number of times, during the five-mile ride, to enable us to get off and examine specimens of lava, and other curiosities, and in the course of an hour we reached Pahala. Through this courtesy, and the charming scenes of land and water frequently presented along the route, the trip was rendered extremely enjoyable.

It was Sunday (January 10th) when we were in Pahala,

and the mills being idle we did not stop, but proceeded on
with the conveyance provided for us to the volcano. Our
·route, thus far from Honolulu, had been along the west side
of the islands ; now we were crossing, overland, sixty miles to
the east shore, taking in the volcano on our way; thence to
return, by another course, to our starting point, which would
give us, substantially, a complete circuit of Hawaii. The
whole round trip is between five and six hundred miles in
length, and the excursion cost of it, including travel. hotel
bills, guides, etc., is seventy dollars.

The conveyance to which I was assigned at Pahala was a
two-seated Concord wagon, with red-running gear, covered
and curtained. There were four animals attached to it; the
wheel team consisting of one horse, and one mule called
Minah, and the lead span, a pair of horses. The driver was a
listless, uninteresting kind of a fellow, and didn't appear to
know beans. Minah was the only one of the outfit that
seemed to have sense enough even to kick; but she knew
what was best for Minah all the time.

We got away from Pahala, at a snail's pace, at 8:30, with
twenty-three miles before us ; and as the entire territory over
which we travelled to the volcano is owned by the Hawaiian
Agriculture Company, and is most of it fenced in, we were
opening and shutting their gates every few miles to the end of
our journey. The property is simply an immense ranch, and
much of the fencing is of barbed wire, the posts being set
upright on the ground and supported by piles of stone massed
around their bases. Post-augers are rather at a discount
where all underfoot is solid, volcanic pahoehoe. Herds of
cattle, in large numbers, ranged along the way as we progressed, many of them in excellent condition ; but there
was no other agricultural development of the ranch that we
saw.

There are two kinds of lava-rock, one or the other of which

is always in sight wherever one travels over the islands ; and in going to the volcano from Punaluu, the tourist becomes very familiar with them. They are known by the native names of " aa," and " pahoehoe ;" the former broken, crumbling and chalky ; the latter, firm, solid stone, in some instances so fused by the fiery ordeal it has passed as to be almost vitrified.

Stunted shrubs and wild grass were abundant on both sides of the road, but as we neared the Volcano House, both became more profuse and of larger growth. Mountain plover, single and in flocks, were met in great numbers.

The road, generally, is good, but in some places, pahoehoe was rolled up in our way in such enormous masses as seriously to obstruct travel ; and our teams not being over-vigorous, on account of having just been taken off pasture, took substantially their own gait, and kept it. Minah, particularly, didn't propose to be crowded or worried a particle.

She was the near " wheeler," and regularly, about once in every fifteen seconds, it appeared to me, the driver's long whip-lash was sent whirling into the air, and, by an adroit twist of the stalk, descended with a sharp, cutting sting, somewhere on her sole-leather cuticle. It didn't, however, seem to have any more effect to accelerate speed, than if he had been whipping the bushes, or the lava-rocks along the way. The only acknowledgment she gave the event at all was with her ears. Those she carried, uniformly, always in the same position, like two, enormous, tin trumpets, inclined at a handy angle back ; and there she kept them, from Pahala to the crater, without apparently varying their direction the thirty-second part of an inch. When the lash went into the air, she appeared to stiffen them, just a trifle, and that was all the testimony she gave that she cared anything whatever about it.

The continued, heartless punishment of the meek and ill-treated brute, and the manifest show of partiality, on the part of the driver, to her disadvantage, after awhile, aroused the ire of Old-Forty-Niner, and he poured out his expressions of sympathy for her unstintingly.

"Poor Minah!" he would whisper, as the thing of torture went cavorting into the air on its mission of savagery, "poor Minah! damn it, driver, let that mule alone!" to which display of anger he ordinarily got only a mute stare, or a sickly, sullen smile; and that was all.

"I'll lick that fellow, or he'll lick me, at the Half-Way House," he growled under his breath, "if he don't quit abusing that poor, dumb, critter; by thunder, I'll do it if he kills me!" and then he retired into himself, to watch the enemy further in sullen mood.

We stopped at the "Half-Way House," about noon, for dinner, and all the passengers lumbered out, tired and stiff from the ride, and glad enough of an opportunity to exercise their legs. Old Forty-Niner alighted with blood in his eye for the wrongs inflicted on Minah; and immediately he was out of the wagon, started round the team, to carry out his threat, and make the driver either promise kinder treatment thereafter, or settle scores with him on the spot. As he went by the mule, he laid his hand softly on her flank, with the same gentle, sympathetic exclamation that had got to be almost chronic with him, but which, nevertheless, was expressive of a depth of humane feeling highly creditable to his better nature.

"Poor Minah!"

Hardly had the words passed his lips, or the touch of his hand been felt by the animal, when "poor Minah" crouched a little in the harness, and then lifting herself, shot out one of her hind legs like a thunderbolt, against his body. Fortunately for him, he was near her when she struck, and in consequence did not receive the full force of the blow;

only a savage thrust. It was ample, however, to fire him
like a football into a lot of low, thorny bushes about ten feet
away.

If a fresh eruption had broken out on Mauna-Loa, or an
earthquake had come to shake up the island, it probably
would not have excited half the consternation or surprise,

THE VOLCANO HOUSE.

that this ungrateful act then and there produced in the old
man's breast. He rose from his couch in the bush, a raving
maniac; and while rubbing his side with one hand, rushed
frantically about, like a cocker-spaniel on scent, looking for
something with which he might slay the hateful beast that
had wronged him.

"Give me a gad!" he screeched, "a club; a gun; anything! I'll teach the infernal, long-eared, miserable, lazy,
kicking brute a thing or two; goll-blast her sneaking, contemptible, low-down, ornery disposition! where's a club?"
but before he could find a suitable weapon, Minah had been
safely stalled and was quietly eating her barley.

From that time on, however, the old man and the driver
were on the best of terms; and the more the latter flogged ·
the poor animal, the more plethoric grew his stock of cigars
at Old-Forty-Niner's expense. "I always did hate a cussed
mule, anyhow!" he said to me; "I wouldn't trust one of
them as far as I could throw a four-year-old steer by the
tail; they're so devilish quick and tricky!"

We arrived at the Volcano House about five o'clock in the
afternoon. It is a handsome, two-story, frame structure,
fronting the south, and is nicely and comfortably furnished.
One room, on the ground floor, is used for lounging, and
contains a large wood fire-place for chilly days, a billiard
table free to the guests, books, lounges and easy chairs.

As we rode up to it, we passed over a long stretch of ground,
through the bramble-covered fissures of which quantities of
steam were exuding in hundreds of places; the smell of sulphur was also very pronounced in the air. Afterwards, before leaving, the immensity of the terrific, underground
forces at work there was made manifest to me; but not until
several days spent in close proximity to the crater, was I
able to realize what indeed is a fact, that the comprehension
of man, even in imagination, is wholly inadequate to grasp
or fathom a fraction of its mystery.

Not only are there acres, and hundreds of acres of territory,
under which this great bed of fire forever rolls, like a subterranean sea, close to the surface, liable at any moment to
break through and overflow the land, but hundreds of square
miles, with a depth which nobody knows, are embraced in

its compass.   One of the guides at the Volcano House, when I asked his opinion of its depth, thought it was more than twenty-five thousand miles; but I seriously doubt the accuracy of that estimate.   To the thoughtful mind, however, any attempt to comprehend its hidden immensity results only in bewilderment and defeat.

Notwithstanding all that I had read and heard of Halemaumau, which, in sum, was by no means small, I found on personal contact that I had a very imperfect conception of it, indeed.   It was not at all as I had thought it to be.   How the two elements of fact and fancy differed, I cannot now tell; but this I do know: that when I came to view it, the real so completely supplanted every former imagination in my mind, that all else sank out of sight and was wholly forgotten. Thenceforth I could only remember the magnificent stupendousness and glory of the great wonder itself, as in truth it actually exists.   I could not, from that time on, reproduce in memory, even faintly, any one of the impressions with which I had formerly clothed it; a thing, with me, truly quite remarkable.

The hotel stands on the brow of an abrupt ledge, five hundred feet high, overlooking the crater.   All around it are green trees, shrubs, grass and vines; while in front are heliotrope bushes of immense size, their blossoms as fragrant as the rarest extracts of that name bearing the choicest labels of Lubin.   Down to the right was a jungle of wild roses, climbing up over the rough, rocky, hill-side in great clusters, rich in perfume; and there were also nasturtiums that more than rivaled any I had ever seen elsewhere, in their perfectness of growth and abundance of bloom.

Wherever one goes in the neighborhood, or however far, except it be down on the crater of Kilauea, the most superb ferns imaginable carpet the ground, or rear their weeping, fragile branches in the air, sometimes twenty or thirty feet

high, like palm trees, only of a milder growth.   The beauty
and rich variety of coloring which decorates tree, and shrub,
and vine, also diverts and engages the attention.

There is a tree called the " ohia " that grows in wonderful
spontaneousness all over the mountains ; it is also found as a
shrub ; and from the size of an oak, down to the trembling
stem which peeps timidly out of the ground, perhaps only a
few inches high among its more pretentious neighbors, all
bear crowns of color so beautiful that I was not surprised it
had been adopted as the national flower of the people.

Each blossom is about the size of a rose, and, from a distance, much resembles it.   Closer inspection, however, shows
it not to be composed of leaves at all, but of little groups of
pea-green cups, filled with delicate, thin, scarlet needles ; each
needle tipped with gold.

The effect of great numbers of these flowers on a large tree
is incomparable, attached as they are, like plumes of brilliant
flame, to the branches.   When the season is at hand, the
forests where they abound appear to be aglow with fire.   The
blossom has a name peculiar to itself, " lahui, " and is much
used for leis by the natives.   It has no perfume.

There is a shrub known as the " ohelo," which bears a
delicious, edible berry, red and yellow, resembling our cran-
berry in shape and size, but less tart, and which is utilized
for food, in pies, jams and jellies ; it is also eaten with cream
and sugar.   The plant itself is of low growth, and when in
full berry, is as beautiful as a bouquet of flowers.

Many of the bushes which one sees in the woods are variegated in color; dark and light green, pink, scarlet, and crimson, all being frequently found on the same branch, and generally in the order given, from trunk to outermost tip of the
laterals.   One can easily imagine how ravishing must be the
sight of great numbers of such together.

There is a bush, something like our huckleberry, which

bears a fruit similar in size but not in color, called the " turkey berry." Different shades of the fruit are often found on the same bush ; white, purple, and mixed ; and frequently, individual berries will have all of these colors blended together.

A rank, trailing vine, bearing lustrous, black fruit, which for lack of a better name we called "lava custard," grows profusely. The ground, in some places, was thickly matted over with them, the berries glistening in the sun, among the green leaves, like strings of black beads in clusters.

CHAPTER XVIII.

THE CRATER OF KILAUEA—THE GREAT LAKE OF FIRE—
ALSO A VARIETY OF THOUGHTS AND IMPRESSIONS
THAT RUB, SOMEWHAT, UP AGAINST
THE HEREAFTER.

TO the east of the Volcano House, the landscape is flat; but on the other side towers Mauna-Loa, and back of him Mauna-Kea, more lofty still, and more grand and impressive, his billowy crest outlined artistically against the sky. At the time of my visit, Mauna-Kea wore a crown of snow; a circumstance almost as interesting to the natives as a lava flow, and decidedly much more pleasing.

There is a peculiar quality to the atmosphere that surrounds these mountains, which, it may be, is largely due to the difference in rainfall on the east and west sides of the island; it being almost continuous on one, while quite infrequent on the other.

The whole distance across is only about seventy-five miles; and the ever-changing combinations of temperature, occasioned by the winds as they sweep back and forth round those mountain summits, and by the force of the sun's heat under varying conditions, aid in producing multitudes of scenic effects, which, like views through a kaleidoscope, are forever shifting.

I have seen the mountains, early in the morning, stand out bleak, bare, and unattractive. Two hours later, their mottled sides, half way up, were draped in long, horizontal columns of rolling clouds; their tops and bases uncovered and clear of all obstructions to the view. At noon, a faint blue, only a trifle deeper than the dome itself, suffused them with a filmy shadow; as if the deeper coloring of the glorious sky had been sifted out, to give to the azure tint of the firmament a hue more soft, and mellow, and sublimely perfect. Before night, a score of other changes, equally grand, all took their turns; a magnificent procession of moving marvels traveling with the sun. Kilauea is not the only wonder one sees on Mauna-Loa, nor the only source of pleasure to be derived from a visit there. The atmosphere is pure, balmy and bracing, and the temperature being equable, Honolulu people make of the Volcano House quite a resort for recuperation and rest.

Directly in front of the hotel, which stands on the brow of the cliff, fifty feet or such a matter back from its edge, is a bridal path leading down to the crater. This is about a mile in length, somewhat winding, and can be traversed either on foot or horseback. In going down, the sturdy tourist ordinarily prefers to walk, for the road is a good one for pedestrian travel, and most of the way, lies among rich growths of vegetation, affording many observations that render the trip on foot exhilarating and delightful.

The appearance of the crater, as you descend to it, is at first smooth, like a vast plain of some black, inky substance; bitumen or tar; and will attract little comment. But as you approach closer, its rough, broken and tormented surface slowly unravels to the eye, and by the time you have reached its border, prepared for the three-mile journey across it to the burning lake, you will begin to realize something of the forces which have rendered such a perplexing entanglement of nature's elements possible.

If you ride down to the crater, you will leave your horse at its edge, and for the balance of the way proceed on foot. A good pair of easy shoes, in addition to the regular ones which the tourist wears, ought always to be taken; for the walk is a long one, the path tortuous, and pahoehoe has a faculty of cutting away sole leather with the speed of an emery wheel.

If you chance to come from the frozen regions of the north, where the voices of winter have impressed themselves indelibly on your recollection, you will notice at once, as you walk over it, the strong similarity of sound between encrusted lava, and sharp, crisp, crackling, frosty snow; and you may also be reminded, perhaps vividly, of those keen, early mornings of boyhood, when, muffled to the jowl, like an Esquimau, and loaded down with imprecations against winter, you used to sally forth at daylight, to let out the colts to water and fodder the shivering cows. And, if you are at all an imaginative and observing man, it will pay you to keep your eyes about you; for, if you do, you will certainly see more objects, animate and inanimate, illustrated by the hand of Nature on that black, rough floor, than you ever before thought possible in all the days of your life. What I saw you might, and you might not see; but there will be thousands of objects that will force themselves on your attention, whether you will it or not.

I saw fallen horsemen, armored and helmeted, lying prone upon their sides, dead beside their dead steeds; beasts struggling together; birds-eye views of cities and towns in black plaster; huge and hideous serpents crawling in and out among the fissures of the rocks; monsters of every form that nature or the fancies of man have ever created; gnomes, hobgoblins, and devils; saints, prophets, dancing dervishes, and priests; angels with wings and angels without them; birds, fishes, and reptiles; in fact, one may conjure up whatever he chooses as a thing possible to exist, and he can find it here outlined quite to his satisfaction.

In some places, the gaseous forces from below have forced up obstructions across the path of travel, little hillocks around which one must go; in others, the surface has fallen

KILAUEA, PRIOR TO OVERFLOW.

in, exposing caverns and dangerous holes. Earthquakes, too, and other causes, have checker-boarded the whole plain with cracks and seams, some of them deep and ominous, that gap at you threateningly as you pass. Such is the crater of Kilauea; but you have not yet reached "the burning lake of fire and brimstone."

This rankling place of horrors lies about three miles from the edge of the crater, where you first approach it, in a south-westerly direction from the Volcano House; and after you have walked over the distance, wondering, a good part of the way, how much farther you must travel to get there, and asking your mind, numberless times, whether Hawaiian miles are really three times as long as those of any other land on earth or only twice, you come to "a hole in the ground."

A step or two more brings you up close to its awful margin, and then you look down over smoking, frightful walls, three hundred feet or more, into a great, boiling, bubbling, sizzling hell of fire, whose face, wrinkled and distorted, seems to peer back at you from below, as if inquisitively surveying your age and condition of health, to know when to depend on your coming.

To fittingly describe this place is an utter impossibility; and yet it is not, or was not when I was there, turbulent to an extreme degree; it partook more of the powerful, the majestic, the mighty, the sublime.

Its surface is the perfection of magnificent beauty; such artistic lines, such shades of varying color; shifting, changing, fading out, intensifying. And so it holds, charms, fascinates; just as does a serpent its fluttering victim, by the sheer force and occult demonism of its wicked, hateful, fiery, dazzling eye. You know and fully realize the peril that environs you while you sit and watch it, and you wish in your heart to draw away from and avoid it; yet you stay, and stay, and continue to stay, till the magic spell is broken.

The tendency of the current, if it may be called a current, is centripetal, though at times it varies, flowing to one side; while along the borders of the pit, up-tossed waves of slumbering lava, apparently as immovable as those over which you have just crossed coming from the hotel, lie in wrinkled folds and masses, heaped against the shore.

If you watch those waves closely, however, you will presently observe what appears to be a fiery, red serpent coming up out of the lake and creeping stealthily through and under them, like a chain of brilliant flame, its form lengthening as it goes, until it has circumscribed a large share of the entire basin. Then it will begin to spread and flatten, as though the body had burst asunder and was dissolving back again, along its whole trail, into the fierce flood of turbulent fury whence it came.

Continue to observe, and you will shortly discern the broad, thick mass of lava, thus surrounded, and which you before thought fixed and immovable, slowly drifting off from the shore to the center of the lake; reminding you forcefully of detached cakes of broken ice, such as are often seen in winter when the thaws come, or during spring freshets when the streams burst their encrusted chains.

If you do not lose sight of those cakes, the force of this comparison will be strengthened when they reach the center, for there they go to pieces exactly after the manner of large pieces of ice, and turning upon their edges, disappear into the ravenous vortex below, which forever is swallowing up all that approaches it, giving nothing back in return.

Evidently, two kinds of lava form on the face of the lake. One is stony, hard, and brittle, such as I have described; the other, flexible and tough, similar to India-rubber. The flexible kind formed exclusively on one side of the basin and spread over it like an immense, sombre blanket; and, as it floated down in slow procession to the central abyss, would occasionally rise and fall with a flapping motion, by force of the generated gases underneath, like a sheet shaken in the wind.

Occasionally, the fire would force its way through this covering and launch huge, spluttering fountains of red-hot liquid lava high into the air, with a noise that resembled distant bombs exploding; and again, multitudes of smaller founts would burst into blossom all over the lake, like water-rockets, presenting a spectacle of wild, rampant beauty across its entire surface. The main eruptions, however, were confined to two places, where, from time to time, with quite precise regularity, enormous belches from below cast up great volumes of lava, and hurled them confusedly about, in thick, bubbling masses, over rods of space.

Two hundred and fifty feet down from the bed of the crater, where visitors ordinarily view the spectacle, is a broad platform running completely round the lake. This is known as the "black ledge" and is rarely visited, because of the dangers attending the descent, over the rocky debris and gorges which throng the sides of the embankment one must travel. Besides, the dense, sulphurous fumes of the place are liable, at any moment, to settle and suffocate the intruder.

In the center of this circling platform, which acts as a wide parapet to enclose it, is the "burning lake," at the time of my visit, about a hundred feet down from the ledge. This distance, however, is not arbitrary; sometimes it is much more; while at others, it rises to such an extent as not only to overtop the black ledge itself, but to fill the entire chasm up to the very level of the crater, distributing its fiery contents over acres of plain.

Notwithstanding, however, the perils of the trip, five visitors, myself included, after soberly discussing the matter,

decided to take the risk and make the descent, down to the
black ledge, for the sake of the better view there to be obtained ; and a short time subsequent we were on our way
thither. We were led by a skilled guide across three immense, intervening fissures, opened by earthquakes, or during
throes of the volcano, to the edge of a large, splintered crag,
which hung suspended in a threatening manner over the pit.
This, however, was the only spot where it was possible to go
down, and we there prepared ourselves for the descent.

Divesting ourselves of all clothing, except our shirts and
trousers, we commenced the wild, zig-zag journey.

First, we clambered down through one of the enormous
clefts of which I have spoken, and crept around under a
shelving palisade of fierce, black rocks, which, at some time
anterior, had burst from its moorings, and now seemed to
hang only by a tremble, liable at any moment to come down
upon and crush us to the bottom, like straws.

The savage aspect of our surroundings here, was too much
for the nerves of the majority of our party, and they all beat
a hasty retreat. Being myself next to the guide, who continually assisted and encouraged me forward, I had no opportunity to see what the others were doing, nor time to in-
dulge in any thoughts of danger ; otherwise, undoubtedly, I
should have turned tail with them and gone back.

It was, indeed, a hazardous, aye, even more than hazardous, it was a perilous thing to do. One single keystone dis-
placed might have precipitated hundreds of tons of rock, of
all sizes, upon us ; for avalanches of loose debris lay menac-
ingly above, which the moving of a single stone might have
started ; besides this, a mis-step or a fall, and the life of a
man could have been torn out, as easily as that of a robin by
the discharge of a gun at short range.

But, like many another of those circumstances which are
passed and gone, we ask ourselves, afterwards, why we took

the risk, and would not, under any stress or inducement, repeat the thing.

But if the risk was great, so likewise was the reward. To stand on the very edge of that great sea of fire; to hear its rumblings, its gurglings, its sighs and its groans, as it surged up from below and sank away no one knows whither; to watch its gleaming outbursts of artesian flame gushing in

CLEFT IN THE CRATER.

torrents from its writhing body, like life-blood from the ruptured veins of some inhuman Pluto; to stand close by the side of such a phenomenon of marvelous wonder and fierceness, and catch its ever-recurring changes of voice, and color, and motion; and to feel that indescribable something in the breast, which cannot be analyzed, but which new and striking displays of nature always reanimate into bounding life; this, indeed, was an experience well worth all, and more than all, that it cost of difficulty and peril to visit it.

As I stood on its smoking, precipitous borders and gazed down into its tumultuous basin, a thousand conflicting fancies, like wayward hallucinations, took possession of my thoughts and held them captive. These, subsequently, assumed the more sober phases of reflective revery; until, at length, I was wholly absorbed, unconscious of all things else around me, held only by the spell of my own imaginings. The spectacle was one of such sublimity, so potential and overwhelming in its mysteriousness, so fascinating and beautiful, I wondered how it was possible for any one to look on a cold and barren, canvas reproduction of it, and with that remain satisfied and content.

Musing, I asked myself: 'is there in the whole world a man so dead, or lame in spirit, that he can look for the first time on a living picture such as this, framed by the Almighty in those walls of stone, and by His hand sketched and colored as never man, even in fancy, can hope to color or design, and not be drawn away from his own rough nature, to higher thoughts and nobler realms of feeling?'

And then I thought, how vain and futile are even the best of pictures for a scene like this. A beautiful painting may serve as an outline of it, both in form and color, but nothing more; for who can paint that brilliant oriflamme of gorgeous, rainbow hues, and do it justice? who limn the life, the majesty, and the radiant glory of its tempestuous motion, or draw, with truth, those walls that frame it in?

A painting, a grand composition of music, or a poet's theme, all serve their parts in lifting man up from this groveling earth to loftier heights of soulful human being; and all are worthy. Yet they are but make-shifts, after all; artifices, devices, go-betweens; to satisfy the cravings of man

for the true and real.   Just as city trees, dotted here and
there, must serve the purposes of woodland and forest; or a
bit of rock-work or tiny waterfall, the romatic beauties of the
glen.   Why not then cultivate the natural first and most, by
closer contact in her open places? for Nature is the mother
of Art, and, even at the best, her children are never more
than nurslings.

Wordsworth's house-maid, while showing visitors through
the poet's home during his absence, was asked to let them
see his study, and replied: " I can show you his library, but
master studies in the fields."

Sir Joshua Reynolds, than whom no artist ever studied
nature closer, contributed his testimony along these lines
when he wrote: " The more the artist studies nature,
the nearer he approaches to the true and perfect idea of art;
and when you have clearly and distinctly learned in what
good coloring consists, you cannot do better than have
recourse to Nature herself, who is always at hand, and in
comparison of whose true splendor the best colored pictures
are but faint and feeble."

And Rogers said of music:

> The soul of music slumbers in the shell
> 'Till waked and kindled by the master's spell ;
> And feeling hearts, touch them but rightly, pour
> A thousand melodies unheard before.

The simple study of a sky-lark's song may be the stepping
stone to melodious joys greater, by far, than a score of Mozart's
ever could confer; because Nature is illimitable in her resources, and lavish of them ; and Mozart was but one of her
millions of interpreters.

Wordsworth, with an appreciative spirit and a facile pen,
sang, in his day, as scarcely any other man ere sang before ;
yet he told but the story of the trees, and of the mountains,
and of running brooks; he was utterly incapable of repro-

ducing their voices; those only can be heard in the heart, where they themselves speak. We have only to listen and absorb their lessons.

All of the art galleries of Europe combined, would be found insufficient to inspire a soul, equal to the thrill producing by one of the simplest of Nature's pastels painted on the eternal hills, if but the study of her works were half so persevering and industrious as is that of the "old masters;" for one is the sun, the other, flickering gas jets; one, reality, the other, shadow; one, God's work, the other, the work of man.

I have in mind now, a once rugged, strong and mature man, so acutely sensitive to the charms of nature, that unfamiliar scenes of grandeur and of beauty would oft-times overwhelm his emotions, and in spite of his best endeavors, move him to tears. At such supreme moments, he stood, with heart uncovered, in the presence of a personal deity whose glory, and immensity, and goodness, he, as a little child, could fall down and worship. He realized then, if ever mortal man did, that lofty uplifting into godliness interpreted by Wordsworth when he sang:

> Not in entire forgetfulness,
> And not in utter nakedness,
> But trailing clouds of glory do we come
> From God who is our home.

After some time spent on the black ledge, we returned to the bed of the crater. The climb back was much more perilous in appearance than the descent, the rocks, jumbled topsy-turvy together, seeming to hang more threateningly overhead than when we went down; but by dint of perseverence, and care in dragging ourselves up over the rough and dangerous spots, and across the yawning gaps that were necessary to be passed, we finally reached safe footing at the top. Then we returned again to the Volcano House.

CHAPTER XIX.

SEVERAL VISITS AMONG THE EXTINCT VOLCANOES — A BRIDAL PARTY—A VOLCANIC SHAVE—KILAUEA AFTER DARK.

THERE are three, large, extinct craters in the neighborhood of Kilauea, all of which I visited; also a " flow," of very recent date, where remains of lava, hurled red-hot into the air, can still be seen lodged among the branches of the dead trees. We visited this latter place and two of the extinct volcanoes in one day.

The trip was made on foot, and was a long and tedious one, fully fifteen miles, through tangled underbrush and ferns; and for part of the way, the utmost precaution was required, to avoid the many openings in the earth, screened by over-growing plants, into which we were liable by any imprudence to be hurled. Our course, at the beginning, traversed the face of the crater-cliffs, half way up their sides, and was extremely difficult to follow; particularly on account of the rocky debris which intercepted the way, and the multitude of creeping shrubs and vines that grew among it. In some places, too, precipitous hills had to be climbed, where only the wild, mountain goat is safe to travel; and giant lava-beds, and broad ranges of crumbling "aa" had to be crossed, the journey, altogether, lasting from early morning till late into the night. But the views and pleasures of the trip well repaid the exertion.

Kilauea-ike, (little Kilauea) located about a mile from the Volcano House, was the first one visited.

We were accompanied on the trip by a honeymoon couple from Punaluu; he, a sturdy young Scotchman, a "luna," (foreman) on one of the sugar plantations there ; she, a bonny, plump lass, whose dimpled cheeks and merriment of laughter would be worth a husband to any girl alive.

The dew of the mountains still lay thick on the grass under our feet, as we walked down across the heath that led to the little crater. All along our path, bunches of ohelo berries, yellow and scarlet, shone and glistened, like prim-

KILAUEA AT REST.

roses, among the moistened leaves. The dainty little bride was enraptured with them; so "we plucked them and brought them to her."

"Maiden-hair" ferns, too, and leaves of many bushes that equalled the rose in beauty, drooped so affectionately near as to brush our clothes and faces as we passed them by. The happy bride from Punaluu was enraptured with them; so "we plucked them and brought them to her."

The " lahui," scarlet red, the most ravishing in combination of fragile delicacy, rich color, and abundant profusion, of all the blossoming life of the islands, glowed on a thousand tree tops. The sweet, little bride of the Scotch luna was enraptured with them; so " we plucked them and brought them to her."

In consequence of all this lavish courtesy, the smiling little woman was very soon naught but a smiling martyr to the competitive graces of our jealous gang; but she continued to receive, so we continued giving; until, at length, both she and her "old man" were simple embodiments of floral sweetness; and if we hadn't reached Kilauea-ike just at the time we did, what they would have done to avoid further onslaught from our bold attentions is a puzzle.

Kilauea-ike is very deep, its bottom partly overgrown with trees of quite large size, and its sides fringed with vegetation. Six extinct boils (I can think of nothing else so appropriate, with which to compare them, and hence must beg pardon for the indelicate simile) stand, in a horizontal row, part way up its bluffy incline, showing where internal forces, of late, have " burst their cerements " and poured into the cold bed of the crater floods of burning lava. Small flecks of steam are all that now exude from those places.

While here, the Scotch-luna-bridegroom gave us a bit of entertainment not down on the bills, by loosening from the edge of the cliff, a huge rock, weighing some tons, and sending it down to the bottom. It was an exciting spectacle to see a boulder so enormous leaping like a demon through the air, fifty or a hundred feet at a spring, tearing away trees in its path as if they were but blades of grass, and plowing up the earth in clouds of dust, with terrific confusion, till it finally rested in the center of the basin below, a mere speck in the far distance.

After returning to the hotel, our party of gentlemen, armed with alpenstocks, canteens, and lanterns in case of absence after dark, started for Keanakakoi, another extinct volcano, several miles distant, where, on a projecting ledge of rocks, near its most conspicious border, we lunched in the shade of some large lahui trees. A flock of wild goats, on the opposite side of the chasm, kept close watch of our proceedings, and scampered away when we resumed our journey.

The bottom of this crater is very smooth, and from where we sat, glowed in the sun like polished, black marble. The deposit constituting its floor is said to be specially hard and flinty, and in former days, was much utilized by the natives for battle axes and other implements that required to be particularly tough and strong. It is about a thousand feet deep.

A day or two later, in company with the manager of the Volcano House and a native guide, I visited Kamakapuli, eleven miles from the hotel, and about half way, southward, to the sea. We went on horseback, most of the way over a rough trail of pahoehoe. Kamakapuli is the largest extinct crater on the island, and is said to be two thousand feet in depth. A stone, large as a man could hurl, cast over the edge of the cliff, was lost to sight long before it reached the bottom. One half of the crater is much deeper than the other, abrupt palisades describing the line of demarkation between the two parts. Steam could be seen issuing from half a dozen spots in the bottom of the deeper section.

There is a wonderful solitude about these deserted craters; no bird-cries or voices of any kind are there; no water-falls, or rustle of branch or leaf; only dead stillness. They seem, indeed, to be fit homes of the departed spirits with which the natives have inhabited them. There is a weirdness about them, too, and a fascinating, frightful impulsion, that seems always to incline you to the edge of their cavernous jaws, urging you ever to forget yourself in the wizard enchantment which they weave about the senses.

January 14th was a day of rain and storm; the wind, known as a "kona," because from the south, blew a regular blizzard which kept the inmates of the Volcano House in a state of siege from morning until night. Some passed the hours reading, others, writing to friends at home, while others still, played cards for Anhauser at a dollar a bottle, or billiards for the fun of the thing. Old-Forty-Niner reclined on one of the lounges, and snored like Vesuvius. Finally he aroused himself.

"I wonder if I could get a shave here?" said he, rubbing his grizzled cheeks affectionately with the palms of his two hands. "I haven't had one for a week, and danged if I can wait a week longer; how is it, landlord, do you suppose I could get one?"

"I don't know," said Mein Herr Lee, reflectively, anxious to please yet realizing the difficulty of doing so, "we have no regular barber, but Otto, the barn man, sometimes does such work; do you think you could stand it to have him shave you?"

"O, I can stand anything!" said the old man, "I'm no spring chicken; bring on your Otto, I'll chance him for once, anyhow."

"All right," responded the landlord, "I'll get him for you." And he hustled away to scare up the little, bow-legged hostler, who was to be brought into service as tonsorial artist of the occasion.

Presently, Otto arrived in his shirt sleeves, arrayed in a pair of rubber boots, held in place by a hemp cord tied round his waist, in his hands a plain, white shaving-cup, in which he was vigorously endeavoring to work up a lather.

"Take this chair, sir, please;" said he, as he set out a low-backed, ancient structure, close by the window.

The old man took the seat, loosened his shirt collar, and fixed himself in position. A copious supply of lather was then spread over his face, and the quondam barber began rubbing the lantana fields of his placid countenance with all the graciousness of an old timer; then he put on another coat of calcimine.

"Is this performance by the hour, or job?" spluttered Old-Forty-Niner through the stray tid-bits of lather that had somehow wandered into his mouth, "I don't want to be curried here all day! why in thunder don't you go ahead with the shave?"

"All right!" responded Otto, a trifle flurried, "I'll be with you, sir, in just a minute; wait till I sharpen the tool a bit."

The razor was now brought out and given an extra whirl or two across the strap, but whether he was sharpening the edge or back of the blade, I verily believe the barber hadn't the faintest notion. Then he got behind the old man's chair and proceeded to business.

Reaching over in front, he caught his customer by the nose, fastening two of the fingers of the left hand into his nostrils, like grappling hooks, effectually closing them; then, with a determined yank, he forced back his head till both eyes stuck out like a cow strangled on raw turnips. When this was complete, he slipped the cold blade of the razor down along the dewlaps as far as he could go, and then, reversing its course, gave it a ferocious rake up that sounded as though a fresh kona had just struck the house. Before his adversary could garner the proceeds of his first foul swoop, or prepare for a second swath, the old man rent the air with a war whoop, and slid out from under him, flat on the floor.

"Blistering volcanoes!" he snorted, scrambling to his feet and staring at the now thoroughly frightened barber like a mad bull; "what under heavens are you trying to do with me, anyhow; skin me? if you are, why in Helen Blazes don't you take me out to the slaughter house and do it up in shape, and not try to pull it off; hey?" and he capered round the room, rubbing his face with agony.

"Was it very painful?" at length timidly asked the barber, getting his traps together ready to leave the room, as Old-Forty-Niner passed him coming down the home stretch.

"Painful!" roared the enraged victim, squaring himself about and glaring at his tormentor, "painful, did you say? damn you, look here! I've seen more hardships in my time than any other four men in Californy; I'm a '49-er; I've been in three railroad accidents; I've had my leg broke; and once a grizzly chawed me for fun, and I had to have seven pieces of bone taken out of my shoulder before I got over it; but never, in all my life, did I have anything hurt me like that infernal razor; take it away or I'll strangle you." And he vamoosed out of the room, upstairs to his own apartments.

The next day, our party went over to Kilauea for a final visit. In order to get the effect of the volcano both by day and night, we started at four o'clock in the afternoon, and on our arrival, discovered that the lava had risen quite perceptibly in its basin, and besides was much less active and turbulent.

The flow had also changed. Instead of centering, as it then did, in the middle of the pit, and being there sucked down into the vortex, it now seemed to drift to the north edge and disappear into an opening under the black ledge.

Besides this, the brittle lava which had formerly occupied one side of the lake, had now disappeared, and the whole surface was covered with the other formation, which seemed to wrinkle into shape like a fan, as it was drawn through the opening I have mentioned, handle first, by some underground power.

The colors, too, were more gorgeous than they had been before; three only, however, seeming to predominate, gold, old-gold, and royal purple; the whole bespangled with living jets of spouting fire. The guide said he had never seen anything like it before, and prophesied a fresh eruption soon; but as he was the same individual, who on a former occasion estimated its depth to be more than twenty-five thousand miles, none of us ran away to escape the outbreak.

While we were seated together at the west end of the lake, waiting for the sun to set, in order that we might once more see the face of Madame Pele shining through the blackness of night, we were attracted to Old-Forty-Niner, who sat on the end of one of the benches, alone, apparently oblivious of all that was going on around him, intently gazing down into the red, boiling pit.

Nothing that was being said appeared to have any effect to move or divert him, and his customary jokes and sallies of good humor were for once hushed in the calm of a deep self-absorption. Several of the fellows spoke to him, but he paid no attention to their remarks, nor seemed to hear them.

So striking was his conduct and manner, that whispered comments soon began to pass from one to another, accompanied by nods and becks in his direction; but still he remained in the same attitude, apparently neither hearing nor seeing anything whatever of it. Finally, Mack got up, and passing round the balance of us, went over where the old man sat. Putting his hand on his shoulder, he spoke to him:

"What in the old Harry is the matter with you anyhow?" said he, "wake up here! you'll have lock-jaw if you keep mum this way any longer; wake up and say something."

And he shook him lightly, in the rollicking good-natured manner always proverbial with him.

Old-Forty-Niner started, as if just awakened from a sound nap on one of the Volcano House lounges, and looked around in a dazed and puzzled manner, as one will when disturbed from a profound sleep.

"By jimminy, boys!" said he, rubbing his eyes, "I believe upon my soul I've been out of my head; I do, by cracky! it must have been a sort of a trance. That dream I had last night has knocked the underpinning clean out from under me, and I can't think of anything else, and haven't all day long; whenever I am still a minute, I go right off thinking about it, and can't get it out of my head."

"What dream was that?" responded Mack, "you didn't tell me of any dream; did he tell any of you?" he inquired, looking from one to the other of us as he spoke, in a perplexed and questioning manner.

"No," said we all in chorus, becoming interested and crowding over where they were, "we haven't heard of it; what was it?"

"Upon my word!" continued the old man, "I actually believe I'm going crazy; I thought I told everybody about it; I did, I hope I may never die if I didn't."

The thing now commenced to get exciting, and we were all worked up to a high degree of interest, in our anxiety to learn more of the mysterious dream that had so metamorphosed the mind of our old friend; so we prodded him to relate it and he was very ready to do so.

Facing about on the bench where he was sitting, he took out his handkerchief, and after wiping away the perspiration from his brow, began to talk; slowly at first, like a rank trotter that must score a little before he can settle down to business and hold his gait.

"I want to ask one thing in particular," said he, "before

I begin ; and that is, that you won't interrupt me, with any questions till I get through.   I want to bring it all back just as I dreamed it, and if you keep bothering me it might confuse my chain of thought.   Promise me that and I'll get under way."

We were quick to grant his demand and he commenced as follows :

CHAPTER XX.

THE STRANGE DREAM OF OLD-FORTY-NINER.

"I WASN'T feeling very well last night; that infernal barber upset my nerves so. I never was so mad in all of my life, and when I got over it, I was all broke up; I seemed to sort of collapse. I don't know what it was that got hold of me, but I was stupid and sleepy-like, and every bone in my body felt as if it had a wooden leg; so I crept up to bed pretty early, and was soon sound asleep.

"I don't think I'd been abed half an hour, when it appeared to me, some one was shaking me. I opened my eyes to see who it was, but the light was out, and the room was dark as pitch, so I couldn't discern anything around me.

"Presently the bed shook again. 'What's that?' said I to myself; and then it flashed into my mind, that maybe some of you fellows had come up to play me a trick, so I concluded not to say anything, but just lay still and keep a dark eye on you.

"Pretty soon it shook again, this time a good deal harder than before, and the windows rattled like an ice wagon. I had been so drowsy, at first, that I didn't more than half have my wits about me, but that last shake acted for all the world like an invitation to take something; it was a regular eye-opener.

"'By gosh!'" said I, 'that's an earthquake, sure;' and up I jumped and ran to the window to look out. I pushed open the blinds, and then could see a little something what was going on outside ; but everything seemed to be quiet and regular, so after a minute or two, standing there, I concluded it was all over and prepared to go back to bed.

"Just as I was about to close the blinds again, so I could sleep in the morning, jeeminy-crimeny! but there came a shake that beat anything I ever heard tell of. Back I pitched, heels over head, on the floor, down came the window ker-slam, and for about five minutes, the bedroom furniture capered around the room like prize horses at a county fair. Then it got darker than ever, and if forty thousand tom-cats had been playing hide-and-go-seek down in the crater, they couldn't have created a bigger yowling than seemed to be going on out of doors.

"Well, now, you can very well imagine, that about that time, anywhere else on earth except that room was good enough for me, even if I didn't have anything on but my pajamas ; so I commenced hustling around, mighty lively, to find the door, intending to make a break down stairs ; for I thought every minute the house was going to tumble down, and I wanted to get out before that time came.

"The racket had jumbled all the furniture together, topsy-turvy, and the best I could do was to crawl along on the floor, among chairs, and cuspidors, and over the bedding, how long, I don't know, but it seemed to me all of an hour ; and finally when I reached the door, and took hold of the knob to open it, I hope I may never die if it wasn't stuck tighter than Jay Gould's pocketbook, and I couldn't budge it to save my life.

"Then I began to get scared, and the dew-drops stood out on me like water on a sugar vat. I pulled, and tugged, and yanked, and swore, but it was no go ; the door had got wedged in, somehow, by the surging and twisting of the earthquake, and was just like an iron door, riveted solid to the wall.

" Well, what to do then, I didn't know; I was getting frantic; but, after a while, it occurred to me that maybe I could jump out of the window and save myself that way. So over there I scrambled, quick as I could, and peered out to see how far it was down to the ground; but whether it was a foot or a mile I couldn't tell, it was so infernally dark.

" During the time I was standing there, the noises outside, that before had somewhat abated, commenced again to grow louder, and immediately after, a terrific clap came, that seemed to tear everything all to pieces. The house rocked, and weaved about, and shook in every joint, like a New-foundland dog just out of the water, and while I was hang-ing to the window with all my might to keep from being upset again, right down in the crater before me, a great, red crack opened in the earth, big enough to take in all the sinners in San Francisco; and you know, boys, that would have to be an awful big one; an aw—ful big one; and then, snap! it went together again, and everything was just as dark as it was in the first place. Well, when I saw that, I said to myself, ' old man, you get out of this; and caper lively, too, do you hear?' and I started for that door again, double quick.

" About half way across the room, I ran jam up against the wash-stand, that somehow had got tumbled in the way, and down I went over it, on all fours, striking my head, as I fell, against one of those big, iron-stone-china, wash pitchers, that they have in hotels, which hold about three pints of water and weigh as much as a baby; and for a minute, I thought the earthquake had got me, sure. It didn't last long, though; and presently I came to, all right, and got on my feet again. Then I felt of my head. There was a lump on it as big as an egg-plant; I could feel it, too, just as plain as I don't feel it now, it was so smooth and natural; but I'd

made up my mind to go out of that door, and I was agoing,
egg-plant and all, even if I had to dive out head-foremost
like an unshipped bicycle rider.

" Well, after awhile, I reached the door again and got hold
of the knob; and then I took it in my two hands, and bracing my feet against the casings, began to pull, till I thought
I'd surely uncouple somewhere, in spite of all creation. I'd
give forty dollars for a kodak picture of me at that time;
I reckon I looked about as near like one of them big, red-
headed wood-peckers you sometimes see in the orchards,
yanking out grubs from the old, dead trees, as any human
being ever did since the world began. But I pulled, you bet
I pulled for all I was worth; but it didn't seem to do any
good; till finally, heaving a long breath till I almost bursted,
I gave the most infernal double-twist to that lock that you
ever heard tell of; when off came the knob.

" I got over being scared then, and commenced to get
mad; and I verily believe, before I got through with it, I
could have gone out of that building if every blasted door
in it had been made of solid brass; I was riled up to such a
gory pitch of everlasting, bald-headed excitement. What I
wanted then, was something to smash somebody with; and
happening to think of that water pitcher I made for it in-
stanter.

" While I was on my hands and knees, crawling round the
room feeling for it, another big shock came, a regular mer-
ry-go-round, that knocked all the glass out of the windows,
tore off every bit of plaster from the walls, and slammed me
up against the partition with the mattress on top of me. I
thought my time was up then, sure, and was just getting
ready to pray, when happening to put out my hand, I hope
I may never die, if there wasn't that water pitcher lying
right beside me on the floor. That gave me new hope; so
grabbing it, I crawled out from under the mattress and

started once more for the door. It didn't take me long to find it this time ; I'd sort of got used to it, I reckon.

"As soon as I reached it, I began to feel carefully around in order to locate the exact center, for I wanted to make no mistake when I fired. Then I stepped back two or three paces, and taking the pitcher in my two hands, commenced swinging it round and around over my head, like a Scotch athlete heaving the hammer. When she got to going like lightning I let her fly. Well, if ever you heard a noise, that was one ; forty claps of April thunder all at once wouldn't have been a patching to it ; and then everything began to rock backwards and forwards, and sway about, and finally commenced to sink right down into the earth.

"I knew then I ought to make my peace right off, so I began praying without any further ado ; but all I could think of, or had time to get out, was "Boom-te-rah-la, boom-te-ray,' when down went the whole thing in a heap. I felt something or other strike me on the head, as I went down, and that ended me. Everything got black after that, and I lost all my interest in what was going on.

"How long I remained that way I don't know ; but after awhile I came to again, and found myself lying at the bottom of a deep cleft in the ground, which appeared to be a split opened by the earthquake, a thousand feet or more down.

"There was a smell of sulphur all around, and hot steam was hissing out through the cracks between the rocks and debris. I scrambled to my feet and looked around. General devastation was spread on every hand ; broken timbers, window sash, plaster and furniture ; showing that the house and all its contents had gone down together. Lying a little way off, was the door of my room, smashed to flinders, but on top of it was the water pitcher, sound as a rock ; there wasn't even a crack in it, or a single chink broken out.

"I knew then that there had been a fearful catastrophe, and I immediately began stirring about, to find out whether anybody was hurt, or dead, in the ruins. I couldn't see how in creation anyone could possibly have escaped in such a disaster, and remembering that all of you fellows were in the building when it occurred, I was afraid some of you had got caught. How I had escaped without a single scratch was a mystery to me.

"While I was hunting around among the debris, almost suffocated with the steam and sulphur-fumes of the place, suddenly, a little gleam of something red, under some broken joists, opposite where I stood, caused me to hurry over there with all the dispatch possible. There was so much lumber scattered about, criss-cross and every other way, that I had considerable difficulty in reaching it at all, but finally I got there.

"Boys, if I should live to be as old as Methuselah, and my grandchildren, and great-grandchildren, and their children's children, should come back, after they were dead, to ask me what I saw there, I should have to tell them just what I'm going to tell you. It was a sight that made me bleat like a billy-goat caught in a gate, and I couldn't help it to save my life.

"Right there before me, lay a man that looked exactly like myself; just my size, age, height and complexion, and I hope I may never die if he didn't have on my old bald head, and wasn't wearing my red-and-white pajamas; and he was as dead as a politican's promise, and as stiff and cold as a Honolulu porter-house steak.

"Gosh-all-hemlocks! but I was scared. The hair on top of my head didn't exactly stand up, for a very good and sufficient reason; but I tell you what, the little fringe around the border flew out so straight and stiff it actually tickled my ears, and made me cackle like a guinea-hen in spite of my fright.

"Who in the dickens could that corpse be? that was what puzzled me. I knew I hadn't any twin brother, and even if I had, how in thunder could he have got hold of those pajamas, in time to die in 'em, during that racket?

"But I didn't wait for any explanation; I didn't even go down to examine the remains to make sure they weren't mine; I just commenced climbing out of there; and if ever you saw a fellow leap lively, from rock to rock up the side of a hot gully, that fellow was me. All I needed was the horns to be a regular mountain sheep.

"After I arrived at the top, though, I was all right and felt safe; so I turned round, and went back to the edge of the chasm and looked down into it. But the steam was so thick I couldn't see anything, so I hunted out a comfortable place and sat down on the grass, intending to rest a few minutes, and then make up my mind what to do.

"While I was sitting there, racking my brain over the strange experiences I had just passed through, I thought I heard voices near by, and rising to my feet, who should I see, but all of you fellows walking along, together in my direction, a short distance away. You can't imagine how glad I was to see you, and to know that you had all escaped with your lives; and every one of you appeared just as much pleased to see me. We shook hands all round, and then got to talking about the earthquake.

"'Did you die easy, old man?' said Mack, sort of sympathetically, coming over and sitting down by me on the grass.

"At first, I looked at him a little quizzingly, wondering what new gag he had on tap now; surprised, too, that he couldn't, for once in his life, be sober, especially under such serious circumstances; but his face had a look of sincerity and earnestness about it that was unusual, so I thought I must have misunderstood his question.

"'Beg pardon?' said I, trying to get the English accent on just right, for I never like to be outdone in manners when I'm dealing with people, candidly; 'what did you say Mack?

"'Did you die easy?' he repeated, as if he didn't care a continental whether I told him or not, or whether I was dead or not.

"'Die?' answered I, 'what are you giving us? do I look like a dead man? I haven't a scratch on me, and I never felt better in all of my life.'

"'That may all be,' replied Mack, indifferently, 'but you're dead just the same; there's no getting around that; we're all dead, every mother's son of us.

"Imagine, fellows, how that last remark took hold of me. It came just as a truth always does, that you don't want to believe but have to. First, I smiled at it, incredulously, and turned my back on it; but it came round on the other side and looked me square in the face. That rather nonplussed me, still I wouldn't believe it; I thought it must be a dream. Then I flirted a little with it; like an old maid with a proposal of marriage, just a little; but that didn't do any good. So, when I found I couldn't get away from it I did just as she would have done, gave up completely, and threw myself bodily into the arms of my captor.

"Sure enough, I was dead; every one of us was dead; and this new flesh, so life-like, with which we were now trying to cover up our spiritual shortcomings, wasn't the apparel of mortal men at all, but robes of immortality.

"Having so recently adopted these new garments, and for the first time put them on, it wasn't at all to be wondered at that they didn't exactly fit or suit, or that we didn't feel entirely easy in them. But after we found we had got to wear them, whether we wanted to or not, we made the best we could of the situation, and finally got to talking the matter over quite seriously.

"Pondy was more worked up over the situation than any of the balance of us; it was so discouraging, he said, for a young man, of ambitious aspirations, to be stranded in a strange country, without friends or relatives, dead. He didn't mind the country being dead, he liked Honolulu fairly well, but to be dead yourself, however fair the prospects, was tough; and having no handkerchief handy, he wiped his eyes on his mustache, and for some time, sobbed so acutely that his weeps might have been heard around a corner.

"As we sat there together, discussing our new relations, suddenly, a slight blast of hot air came wafted across our faces, and we all turned, involuntarily, to see what had occasioned it. The sight that met our eyes was appalling.

"A gentleman of noted reputation, dressed in red, two cupolas on his cap, hoofs cloven, and a barbed-wire tail with an arc-electric light on the end of it, stood close beside us leading a string of mules, all saddled and bridled, as if just ready for the trip to Hilo. The instant we turned around, he recognized us, bowed pleasantly, said 'good morning,' and remarked that he had come after us.

"For a minute or two, I thought I should certainly drop in my tracks; and then I was taken with a sort of buck-fever, and hopped up and down as stiff-legged as a Kansas hayseed practicing the heel-and-toe polka, and the perspiration ran off from me in a stream and sizzled on the ground where the new-comer stood. Presently, however, I saw Mack go up and whisper something in his majesty's ear, that made him smile; and when I saw him reach round, as if for that bottle in his coat-tail pocket, I pricked up courage. But he failed to find it there, as he expected, so after that, there was no more parley, on the part of his majesty, with any of us, and no more smiles; but we were told to pick our mules, and grease 'em, and to be mighty lively about it, too.

"We didn't any of us just understand what was meant by

'greasing the mules;' so his majesty condescended to tell us, that on the pommel of each saddle would be found a little tin box filled with Standard Oil, and this we were required to smear over our animals, every inch of them, in order that our ride might be made easy and smooth to the end of the journey we were about to take. So we went around to pick out our mules and get ready for the excursion.

"I was a little behind time when I got there, and the balance of you had already picked your mules and were busy greasing them; so I stood and watched you for a minute or two to see how it was done; then I went over where my animal was.

"Boys, I hope I may never die, if the mule that was left for me wasn't Minah, that cussed, ungrateful she-thing, that kicked me into the bushes coming up from Punaluu. I recognized her in a minute; but you had all got ahead of me, and she was the only one left, so I had no choice but to take her. When I came up to her, she looked at me, sort of catty-cornered, out of her eyes, and brayed two or three times, like a Brooklyn brewer; as if to show that she, too, recognized me. Hence, as a matter of prudence, I thought best not to tackle her without making an effort to avoid it.

"Accordingly, I went round to his majesty, and requested, inasmuch as this was the first favor I had ever asked of him, if he wouldn't please fire me right through to Hades by some other cut, and save me the trip on Minah. The only answer I got was a savage slap from his tail, which again very forcibly reminded me of the Half-Way House; so I concluded the only thing I could do was to make the best of it, and I pulled off my coat and went to work.

"Well, you ought to have seen me when I got through with that mule. I thought I had learned to dance every kind of a double-shuffle, sashy-de-sashy, thunder-and-lightning racket that was known, while I was on earth; but

Minah taught me some new steps I never heard of before. It was the liveliest mix-up of Virginia Reel, Devil's Hornpipe, and the Hula, that I ever struck in all of my life. My eyes were full of mud and mule-grease, and I had more than a bushel of pahoehoe stuck all over me, till I looked like a hedge-hog just through waltzing with a cyclone, and—

"'Did you succeed in greasing her?' broke in The Squid at this juncture of the story, his whole frame quivering with agitation caused by the narrative, and both of his eyes staring wide open, as he rose to his feet with the question; 'for instance you understand, did you grease her? Truth now and no lying.'

"'Grease her?' retorted the old man in a tone of voice that bespoke his utter disgust at the simplicity of the question; 'grease her? yell at me, boys, and wake me! grease that mule? well, now, you bet I greased her, dammer!'

There being no further interruptions, Old-Forty-Niner proceeded.

"Well, after we had finished our jobs of greasing, we all got onto our mules and formed in line, single file, like ducks going to water, his majesty ahead; Mack came next, where he belonged, and I brought up the rear.

"The first thing that infernal Minah did, after I mounted her, was to reach round and take a piece out of the calf of my leg, and then she brayed and kicked up. Great Scott! but I was mad. I'd have given every acre of the land in Tulare county, just then, if I could only have had a bowie knife, about a foot long, strapped to my heel; but I didn't have anything at all, so all I could do was to simply kick and yell."

CHAPTER XXI.

"WHEN everything was ready, his majesty gave the order, 'forward!' and we started. Immediately, we began to rise into the air, like a kite, Minah and I constituting the tail. Up we went, higher and higher, until we reached an altitude of about five hundred feet from the ground; and then we sailed right along the edge of the crater.

"His majesty must have had something all-killing important on hand, for he lit right out at a terrific gait; but I was glad of it, for it hustled Minah to keep up and prevented her feeding any more off from my leg.

"First, we followed in a circle clear around the edge of the crater, the whole nine miles, and I think we made it in about nine minutes. Then we closed in a trifle, and went round again; this time quite a little faster. And so we kept going, round and round, each time a little closer to the center, and each time a little faster, till I am willing to swear, positively, that the rate of speed we were traveling was, at least, a thousand miles a second; yes, boys, at least; and then we lit right down there on the black ledge, close to the edge of the fire.

"I was pretty well warmed up, I tell you, when we stopped; dizzy, too, and thirsty; so I asked his majesty if I couldn't have a drink of something to wet up on. He smiled, and said, 'certainly!' and asked me, very politely, what I preferred. I told him if it made no difference I'd take beer.

He said he was awfully sorry, but the beer was out—he didn't say where, but it had stepped out somewhere—but if hot lava would do, I could have a mug of that, in fact all I wanted. He said he kept that always on tap for his friends. I thought I'd try a mug of it, anyhow, I was so all-fired thirsty; so I told him to send up a schooner, but to be sure and have it on ice. Just my luck, the ice was all out, too, and so I've got to wait till some other time to learn how that drink tastes.

"As soon as we got off the mules, every one of them took a header down into the lake, and disappeared. Minah brayed again as she went down, and tried her level best to kick fire over me; but I was onto her tricks, and dodged it.

"When the mules were gone, we felt quite relieved, and took seats, as directed by his majesty, all in a row, near that big lava-rock you see down there on the left. We didn't know what was coming next, but we thought it would be perfectly honorable to wait, so we waited.

"Presently, here came a lot of shrivelled-up, skinny-looking 'deputy devils,' who looked for all the world as if they had been over-done in cooking, thirteen of them,—'same old thirteen'"—and the speaker looked sideways over at The Squid, who faced him, bolt upright, both eyes closed, his mouth revolving like a brass electric ventilating fan. But he said nothing, so Old-Forty-Niner kept on with his story.

"Those thirteen deputies scrambled up lively out of the lake, onto the edge of the fire pit, and after shaking off the hot lava that adhered to them, came round and stood back of us and grinned. One was a Chinaman, one a Jap, and one a Kanaka; the balance were all from Chicago.

"Pretty soon, there was a fearful commotion in the lake, and then hundreds of imps and common devils began to pour out. As soon as they reached solid footing, and, like the deputies, had shaken themselves, they ran up the side of the cliffs and squatted on the rocks, till they were thicker there than grasshoppers on a western ranch, all sitting and chattering together.

"After all of the rank and file had got in place, out came a big, proud, burly looking fellow and strutted along till he reached that great rock you see sticking out over. there, half way up the bluff. He swaggered along so important-like and pompous, that I thought he must be one of his majesty's partners in the business; so I turned to the deputy devil who was standing behind me and asked who he was.

"'Why!' said he, 'don't you know him? why, that's Ignatius Donnelly, of Minneapolis; he leads the choir!'

"He had hardly finished speaking, when up raised Donnelly on the rock where he was sitting, and taking the end of his tail in his right hand, like a baton, began to beat time. As he beat, he repeated these words; I remember them just as plain as day:

> "Boil, stew, and toast, and in your own fat fry;
> You'll ne'er again his majesty deny."

"I thought, at once, that he had reference to Lord Bacon, and as I had never denied that Bacon wrote Shakespeare, I jumped up to explain; but before I could get a word in edgeways, Donnelly struck fire on a rock with the end of his tail, and immediately all the common devils that were perched around on the cliffs began to sing, and drowned out my voice.

"The tune was the same that is played in Honolulu when they dance the hula, and was a sort of chorus to Donnelly's prelude, which he kept repeating, over and over, as long as they sang. There were several verses, but I can only remember two or three of them; one ran this way:

> "'Ny, 'ny, never more deny,
> You ought to thought of this afore
> You took the freak to die.

"And another,

> "'Ny, 'ny, never more deny,
> Ain't you mighty sorry now
> You weren't a better boy?

"They kept on singing in this way, for several minutes; first Donnelly would tantalize us, and then the chorus. All we had to do was to sit still and perspire.

"When they finally quit, I turned to the deputy who was standing behind me, and asked him why the poetry was so execrable, and why it was that they didn't have better music? I never shall forget his answer, it struck me so forcibly.

"'Because,' said he, 'there ain't no thoroughbreds here; no Shakespeares, nor Miltons, nor Mozarts, nor Mendelssohns; not one; see? all them fellers went the other way; nothing but dunghills jine our gang.' Before I could ask him any more questions he had slipped away.

"Just then one of the Chicago deputies stepped out.

"'Take off your hats!' said he, in a voice as tough as John L. Sullivan; hain't youz got no manners? be youz all from Pittsburgh?' Every fellow took off his hat.

"'Now, gentlemen,' said his majesty, politely, stepping out in front of us, 'I am going to examine your heads phrenologically, in order to determine what branch of my service you are best fitted for. Please remain very quiet.'

"When he got through speaking, I thought I'd just take a squint down along the line and see how you all stood it. Everyone of you was as brave as a lion, except Mack; he was in a pitiable state, wringing his hands and crying, his face for all the world looking like a basket of unwashed clothes.

"I felt awfully touched to see the poor fellow in such a plight, so I said to him, sort of quiet-like, in a half whisper: 'Mack, what in the wor—, what in h—,' and then I happened to think that I didn't know just where to put him till the thing was over; so I changed my phraseology and said, 'what are you crying about, anyhow? none of the other fellows are making such babies of themselves; brace up; even the devil himself abhors a coward; come out and face the music and be a man.'

"When I referred to his majesty in the complimentary manner I did, Satan bowed to me, very profoundly, but I didn't pay any attention to him; I was all wrapped up in Mack.

"Mack looked over at me, and then burst out sobbing in the most doleful wails.

"'It's all right with you fellows,' said he, 'boo-hoo-hoo! you've all been married and don't fear a thing like this; you've been through it before, and it's nothing new to you; but, boo-hoo-hoo-hoo! I'm a single man and I can't stand it; I haven't been educated up to it.'

"'Don't pull any slivers out of your fingers, young man, till you get some in,' said his majesty, going over where Mack sat and putting his two hands on his head.

"He felt around a little while, and then he spoke.

"'That's a fine head,' said he, 'a mighty fine business head for this kingdom;' then, after hesitating a moment, he continued, 'conviviality is immense; and taste is as delicate and discriminating as a humming bird's; try him, for awhile, with a clerkship in Distillery No. 44,000.' Then he went over to Pondy.

"'J. B. Weaver and the People's Party!' he exclaimed, jumping up and down, joyously, 'just the man! just the man! a mugwump, and the truth isn't in him! put him on the Hades Sun.'

"The Chinese deputy now stepped forward and took Mack and Pondy by the hand; switching his queue around them, to hold them faster, he was just making ready to dive into the burning lake, when Mack arrested him long enough to

THE EXAMINATION.

throw a last parting salute to me. His expression of countenance had all at once completely changed; instead of tears he was now all smiles, and his face was again beaming, as of yore, with joyous good humor and fellowship.''

"'Ta-ta, old man!' said he, extending his open hand, palm down, and waving it; 'ta-ta! I'm satisfied; good, easy, congenial job; see you later;' and down the trio went, and were buried out of sight.

"The Squid was next examined, but where he was sent I couldn't find out, for the minute his majesty commenced to feel of his head, the chorus began to sing, and I couldn't hear anything, except what they were saying. I could hear that though, perfectly plain; and I thought I never saw a man look so proud in all of my life as The Squid did while they were singing. They only sang one verse, but they kept repeating it, over and over, as long as his majesty was at work on him. That was what puffed him up so. I shall never forget the words.

> "'Ny, 'ny, never more deny
> Glory to the author
> Of the Cave of Molokai."

"The Squid got something good, I know that; a big, fat job, somewhere; for his reputation had preceded him, and besides, he was entitled to it.

"Next came The Secretary's turn. When his majesty got through with him, he motioned to one of the imps up on the side of the cliff, who had a taro-patch fiddle in his hand, to come down; and when he arrived, he took the instrument away from him and gave it to The Secretary; then he turned him and The Squid over to the Jap, who disappeared with them, as had the Chinaman with Mack and Pondy. Then it came my turn. As quick as his majesty put his two hands on my head, he began to bellow.

"'Who's been hammering this old man's head?' he shrieked,

'I'd like to know! infernal outrage! best talent always tampered with!' and so on, and so on; and he danced around the ledge, three or four times, wild with rage, every once in a while running down to the lake and bathing his head in the fire, till he looked like a victim of Texas justice burning at the stake.

"The deputies immediately gathered around and looked me carefully over, as though I were some new and strange phenomenon in nature, such as they never before had seen, and one after another felt of my bumps.

"Then, one of them, a former phrenologist from Detroit, ventured the opinion that my head was a natural one enough, but that it came under what was known as 'freaks,' and that his majesty was in error in thinking any one had attempted to violate, in any way, the original handiwork.

'That can't be possible!' ejaculated his majesty, in a low tone of voice, beginning to tremble, 'why, the bump of Truth sticks out quite a little on Eli Perkins' head, and here on this one, it drops in; don't you see it does?' and he rotated his fingers so rapidly over the spot that the place began to smoke.

"'Besides,' he continued, 'there isn't nearly as big a bump of Reverence as on Bob Ingersoll's; not the tenth part as big; and as for Respect for Authority, why, there's a washout where that ought to be; can't you see it? can't you see it?' and he rushed, again, in wild confusion, down to the edge of the lake, where he tore out a red-hot rock from the bank, which he brought up and sat down on; and then he wept, till, really, I felt sorry for him.

"Pretty soon, he got up, and in a hoarse tone of voice, whispered, very low, to one of the deputies, but it was sufficiently loud so that I caught what was said.

"'That man can't stay here, Jonah; never! never! why, he'd supersede me in less than three days, and in a week's time would have Hawaii annexed to the kingdom; seize, and away with him!'

"'Where shall we take him, your majesty?' said the deputy, deferentially, but in an awful state of excitement; 'where shall we take him?'

"'Anywhere! anywhere!' responded his majesty, in great trepidation, 'so you only get him away from here.' 'But get him on ice, somewhere, quick; freeze him till he can't wiggle, and keep him frozen; for if he ever thaws out, he'll slip you, sure; now, be quick; get him on ice! on ice! on ice!'

"At this point, the Kanaka deputy stepped out; he had heard what his majesty said and was in a frightful state of commotion.

"'No ka pono o ka lahui!' he bawled; 'even if he should annex Hawaii, wouldn't it be better than to be annexed to the United States? Ashford says it would, and Ashford knows. Don't drive the man away; wed him to the goddess Pele and give him a chance; he can keep her quiet if you can't;' and he commenced singing Hawaii-Ponoi, and dancing before his majesty, who stood paralyzed with surprise, as did all the others about him; so presumptuous and unusual was his conduct and so unexpected from one of his race.

"While all were in this state of uproar, suddenly, a fierce turmoil appeared, right over there in the center of the lake, and the whole bed burst into an enormous fountain of flame more than forty feet high. It naturally attracted everybody's attention, and I looked over with the balance of the elect.

"Boys, I hope I may never die, if right in the middle of that fountain, sitting right on top of it, wasn't Mack; and he was looking straight at me, with a smile on broader than a man-shark chasing a Kanaka mermaid. I looked at him two or three times before I could believe my own eyes, he appeared so natural; but all at once, I got a good focus on him, and just when I did, he began to drop down again into the lake.

"As he went down out of sight, he threw up his hands. One of them had something in it. What do you think it was? I hope I may never die, if it wasn't that book I've been looking for for the last twenty years; American Drinks and how to mix 'em, volume two.

"Well now, I didn't wait for any further phrenological ceremony, nor any invitation from Mack; but I just lifted myself, ten times quicker than any of the imps around me, could do it, and before they could stop me, took a header, and away I went right over into the middle of the pond where Mack went down.

"As soon as I struck the fire, I could smell what little hair I had sizzling and singeing, and my toe-nails sort of crinkled up. My ears, too, kept getting full of lava, and bothered me; but I didn't mind any of those things; I was after that book, and I was going to have it no matter what happened.

"I think we must have gone a good, full mile, down, and I was gaining on Mack like a hound on a jack-rabbit, when, all at once, he dodged, just as a rabbit will under similar circumstances, and shot down a side street like a 'Frisco morning paper after a subscription list.

"It took me just a second, by my watch, to catch myself and turn after him;—that wasn't very slow, was it?—and as I did so, I saw he was breaking for a pair of big, open, double doors about forty rods away, right ahead, and I proposed to catch him before he got there or burst a ham-string. There was a sign over the door:

> Distillery No. 44,000.
> No Admittance,
> Except on Business."

But I was on business, so I didn't pay any attention to the sign.

"I had just caught up with him, when he shot through the

THE TWO CHAMPIONS.

door ; and as he went in, he sort of kicked out behind ; I grabbed at his leg and got it ; down he went and I over him ; lickety-swizzle ; snatching the book out of his hand as I went by. Mack gave up then, right away ; and I jumped up, and seating myself on a keg near by, marked ' Missionary Gin,' began to read.

"I hope I may never die, boys, if what I tell you ain't true. That book I had been looking for for the last twenty years was a delusion and a sham, and contained nothing but a few cold receipts for temperance drinks, the first on the list being lemonade, and the last one some kind of a fizz.

" Honestly, I never was so disappointed in all of my life before, and for the first time in sixty-two years, I realized what real, genuine punishment is for one's sins. I just threw up my hands and gave up everything ; for I didn't care what became of me after that. The shock woke me up.

"When I came to, I was in bed, all right, but so weak that, actually, I couldn't kick off the cover to get up for more than an hour. Do you wonder I was in a meditative mood ?"

When the old man had finished his story, we all sat silent fully five minutes. Then Mack arose, and without saying a word, walked over and took him by the hand. Leading him back, where The Squid sat, he joined them together ; then turning to the balance of us, " allow me, gentlemen," said he, with a profound bow, " to introduce to you the two champions." No one inquired in what line they excelled.

Mack and Pondy left for Hilo a day or two before I was ready to go. The day they started was one of violent fury on the mountains, a kona blowing from the south with great fierceness. Their going broke up the party that had thus far been together most of the time since leaving Honolulu. The Secretary and Old-Forty-Niner also left on the same date, returning by the same route we came, via Punaluu. The Squid having time to spare, decided to remain a few days longer.

CHAPTER XXII.

THE morning I left the Volcano House was, indeed, a
lovely one, even for this lovely clime of Hawaii. The
atmosphere was delicious and fragrant, the sky beautiful,
and the pulsing earth seemed to bound responsive to their
numerous enticements. I really regretted leaving; not because I had not seen enough of Kilauea and its surroundings, for I had spent several days there, and besides, had
taken in all of the other places of interest about it, but Mr.
Lee, the manager of the hotel, and his good wife, had been so
very kind and hospitable to me, that it seemed like leaving
home to go away.

Mr. Lee was a German, his wife a native woman, possessed of all the warmth of nature so characteristic of her
race. Often, if I chanced to be alone, or at any time, appeared to be neglected, she would seek out the place where I
was sitting, and, placing herself at a convenient distance,
would begin weaving on her guitar some of those dreamy,
native airs which so wondrously lull the spirits and drive
away all gloomy, sad forebodings.

Often too, she would sing, in that low, melodious tone of
voice which always so reminded me of the birds, and which
strange and sweet illusion I could never disentangle from her
songs. Nor was I the exception in their acts of kindness
and courtesy; all who become their guests shared it alike.

Mr. Lee had provided me with a good saddle-horse, a

guide, and an abundant lunch; and at 7:30, I was on the way to my destination, thirty miles distant. Before I had finished the trip, I came to the same conclusion as my guide, that the miles of Hawaii are the longest of the known world.

For several miles after starting, I was in a perfect state of earthly enjoyment. Under me was an easy-going, amble-gaited horse: over me, a cloudless sky; all around, tropical vegetation, whose fragrant perfumes, fanned across my face by gentle breezes, were musical with the song-notes of birds.

For a mile, wild roses crept up over the fences, and clambered into the branches of the wild ohias along the way, and climbing ferns, of many species, hung tangled among them in profuse abundance. Wild magnolias, also, their thick, outspread leaves varnished by the mountain dew and glistening, dotted the forest; and " silver sword," a rank, tall grass, one surface of whose leaves is shining white, lined the road where I travelled, and lifted their clusters of yellow berries up to me on either hand.

If I only could have had my caroling voice along, I should certainly have burst forth into strains of melody ne'er heard in any land on earth before ; so delightful were my inward emotions. But unfortunately, the tonsil-notes I had with me were not marketable where all else was glorious, so I was forbidden to express myself or my feelings that way.

Most the way, for about seven miles, the trail was over rolling beds of hard pahoehoe, in many places rough, but yet fairly good and not difficult to travel. After this was passed, however, we came to a much more serious road, and for the next ten or twelve miles our progress had of necessity to be slow.

In some places, the rocks were like billows of the sea, black, tortuous and variform, and the pony I rode had to exercise all of his skill and ingenuity to get along with any degree of ease or comfort. Again, the trail would drop, sometimes almost abruptly for several feet down, but by letting the horse have his head, he would pick his way safely over the rough spots, and always as cautiously as a military pioneer in the face of danger.

Other places there were, where the road would so twist and turn as to necessitate travel along the sloping sides of great boulders, where the footing was narrow and where it seemed hardly possible that a horse could go; but the little quadruped never hesitated nor wavered, and no amount of urging could spur him forward, an iota, in his gait. His nose, all the time, was held close to the ground, and thus he proceeded, never once stumbling or slipping during the entire trip. As a general thing, lava rock is so rough, that in travelling over it, the footing of either man or beast is secure against slipping, no matter what the degree of incline may be. If it were not so, this road would be next to impassable, except at the peril of either limb or neck.

The government is, at the present time, engaged in the construction of a fine road between Hilo and the Volcano House, and it will be pushed steadily on until completed; then tourists can go through in carriages and with comfort.

Over the roughest part of the trail, there was little of interest to be described, a few, scattered, grass houses of ancient date, dropping into decay, being about the only things worthy of mention; except, it might be, the fern growths, which were wonderfully abundant, rank and superb, and occasional clumps of guava and other fruits which were sprinkled along the way. Near by, however, were forests of ohia, among which, in frequent places, pea-green patches of the kukui tree shone in a decorative manner.

The "Ie" vine interested me greatly, on account of its peculiar aspect along the borders of the woods, where it hung suspended to the trees in great quantities, its long, slender, spreading leaves looking like gaunt fingers reaching out for

ON THE ROAD TO THE VOLCANO.

alms. Further on, we found it wonderfully prolific, over-running all the other vegetation of the forest.

In many places, the bodies of the trees were literally buried out of sight by this vine; scores of them clustering, in thick masses, around a single trunk. Every few feet up, they threw off graceful, drooping shoots, ringed after the fashion of bamboo rods, which hung like countless serpents, trailing to the ground. Each was five or six feet long, at the suspended end of which radiated great, paw-shaped bunches of green leaves, their palms outward.

In the center of each group of leaves, were three or four brown or scarlet stamens, shaped like the fruit of the banana, or, perhaps, more nearly like the crowning tuft of the cat-tail flag. The Ie is so abundant, and fastens itself so tenaciously to the trunks and branches of the trees, and is so rank in its growth, that, in some places, it fairly laces the forest together, rendering passage through it next to impossible.

Rarely, if ever before, had I been where the voices of birds were so many as along this route; yet they were very shy, and I saw but few of them. I could hear them warbling, close at hand, in great numbers, but the foliage was so dense that I could not discern them. Those of which I did chance to catch a glimpse, were uniformly of bright plumage, and some of them, high in the air, had a habit of singing as they flew, their notes resembling, very much, those of our meadow-favorite of summer in the north, the rapturous bob-o-link.

I overtook Mack and Pondy at Hilo, and inquired of the latter if he, too, had the same delightful experiences with the birds, when they came through from the volcano. He said for a number of miles he thought he had, and it appeared to him, he never in all of his life had heard such a " concord of sweet sounds," although he had been raised in the country where birds were abundant and of great variety. All at once, however, and to his utter amazement, he discovered that what had so captivated and enthralled his senses was not birds at all; but rippling strains of heaven-born harmony, resulting from a combination between the fierce wind that was blowing and that magnificent mustache of his, which the former whipped into rhythm like the dulcet notes of a lute. I asked what effect the wind had on the tail of his mule; whether or not it worked that into the sonorous blare of a trombone? but he declined to answer the inquiry, alleging that it reflected insinuatingly on his veracity as to the other statement.

We passed, on our way, several large patches of wild bamboo, which grew in the edge of the thick woods, also wild bananas, and guavas, and, about noon, brought up at the Half-Way House, kept by a Portuguese, where were two enormous, wild-orange trees, loaded down with sweet, delicious fruit. We stopped an hour here for refreshments and rest.

For the remainder of the way into Hilo, the road was fine, equal to a macadamized highway, and lay through the most luxuriant verdure I have ever seen.

We launched first, into a verdant spread of heavy, tropical timber, principally ohia, numerously populated with bird-nest ferns, which were scattered among the trees, like nests of hawks or crows. These not only attach themselves to the branches, but are also seen in great numbers in the crotches of the trees, and, like fungus, plastered against their trunks; and out of them, delicate sprays of light-green ferns rear their heads in clusters, the effect, mixed with the shadows of a torrid sun, being very refreshing to the eye.

Emerging from this belt of timber, we came next to a long stretch of unfruitful land, covered only by ferns, which grew so tall as to overtop the height both of a horse and his rider; and then we passed again into other timber, ohia, kukui, mountain apple, bread-fruit, and many others, all draped with thick festoons of the ie vine.

Great quantities of a scraggy, little tree called the "pan-hala," which bears no leaves except at the tips of its laterals, lined our way. They were evidently very feeble, for they were propped all about by numberless, over-ground roots, attached to their trunks, extending, in some cases, several feet up from the ground, like so many braces; as if specially intended by Nature to protect the tree from being shaken to pieces. What properties of good the pauhala possesses I am not informed, but it ought to have valuable abilities of some kind, to compensate for its beggarly disabilities; for it is a cripple, alike in form, beauty, and verdure.

When we next emerged into the open, Hilo Bay and the little city were seen lying, like a beautiful picture, about three miles distant before us, and although our horses were exhausted from the long journey, they pricked up their ears and galloped forward, as if conscious they were near the end and were anxious to be done with it.

From this time on, until we reached the limits of the town, large sugar plantations lined the roadway on either hand, the cane in all stages of growth, from the green sapling just out of the ground to the mature plant ready for the cutter's knife and the mill.

Finally, at four o'clock, the little, white cottages of Hilo, and some of its more conspicuous buildings, began dreamily drifting by, as we galloped at random along its streets, framed in with lava-stone fences to which honeysuckles and nasturtiums clung, the shadows of the royal palms, and the odor of fragrant shrubbery and flowers, greeting us "welcome!" till we drew rein, at last, at the door of the Hilo Hotel.

Here a genial hospitality awaited me, from its Portuguese proprietor, and also from Mack and Pondy who soon after put in an appearance; and I may safely say, I was in capital condition for the dinner to which I was shortly after invited, and to the principal cover of which, young green-turtle steaks, fresh from the sea, fried in batter, I am sure I did ample justice.

These succulent, marine reptiles are quite common on the shores of all of the Hawaiian Islands, and constitute a liberal share of the food supply of the people. They are frequently caught, of large size, weighing many hundreds of pounds, and covered with the barnacles of many years; but those weighing about fifty pounds are considered most

A HOME IN HILO.

choice and delectable for food purposes, being uniformly delicate in flavor, tender and juicy.

Hilo is a small town, claiming about fifteen hundred population; it does not, however, appear to be so large. The chief industry is sugar.

At twelve o'clock, noon, two days after my arrival, I said farewell to Mack and Pondy, and boarded the little Philadelphia-built steamer, "Kenau," of 940 tons, bound for Honolulu. The sea was running high, and I got somewhat drenched in the whale-boat, going out to her in the road-stead; but, for a wonder, it was not raining, and the warm air soon dried out my garments and put me all right again.

There was quite a list of passengers aboard, the number in the steerage being unusually large. These were stowed amidships below, and as a matter of curiosity, I went down to interview them; but the rich odors of the place, strongly Chinese and Japanese extracts, so speedily threatened sea-sickness, that I retreated hastily.

At 1 P. M. we raised anchor and cleared for our destination, and as soon as we started, I was made painfully aware of what had been told me by others, relative to the rocking qualities of the Kenau, and which have rendered her noted, far and wide, among tourists. Lying still, she rests easily and floats right side up; but the moment her engine commences to throb, she commences to roll, and so keeps it up, like a Chinese toy image, from side to side, to the end of the voyage.

This peculiarity of the boat had an immediate effect to mesmerize me into harmony with her; and as soon as she started, and began putting in her best licks to heave along, I started, likewise, and did my best to heave too; between us both we made very fair progress. After quite a period of this "pernicious activity," however, I finally, again got my legs trained and educated under me, and was sufficiently emptied so that I had no further fears of any leaks or starts, and at that stage of the proceedings, left my berth and appeared on deck. Then, for the first time, I met Captain Clark, Master of the Kenau, and in his genial sociability and good fellowship, soon forgot the qualms, that up to that time, had persistently threatened to again upset me. For twenty-six years he had been cruising around the Hawaiian isles, and his fund of anecdotes and legends, relative to the native people, was endless and entertaining.

During the day and all the following night, our course was along the windward side of Hawaii, and we were constantly deluged with rain storms of great severity. The water appeared to come down in torrents, whipping the ocean to a thin, white foam, which lay like a network of filmy lace, sparkling on its billowy surface. All along the shore, numerous, high waterfalls could be seen, pouring down over the steep, cliffy embankments bordering the sea, their white, shimmering ribbons of silver, as seen from a distance, contrasting beautifully with the magnificent green of the hills.

The rainfall of this coast is remarkable. At Hilo, in 1891, it was 162.39 inches, or about thirteen and one-half feet. This is equivalent to nearly one-half ton of water per day to every acre of land. One trifling shower of twenty hours precipitated a fall of eighteen inches. The town is full of sluice-ways filled with running water, and night and day, interminably, one can hear the roar of its flight, as it rushes madly along through the streets of the city.

An old German, long a resident of San Francisco, who was on the boat, and who occupied a state-room next to mine, afforded me a good deal of amusement, after I had got far enough along in my wrestle with the Kenau to be entertained. He was a well travelled man, and had been in most of the countries of Europe, and in Africa and America. Now he was looking up coffee lands in Hawaii. He had been awfully sea-sick, and staggering up to my door from the rail of the boat, began giving vent to his feelings of disgust, freely.

"Dam dees conetry!" he exclaimed, "dam de Sand-vitches, islands! dam de whole peesniss, I hate 'em!" And with a sharp, whistling sound of "tscheet," he ejected through an aperture of his closed teeth, a spiteful little jet of spray and noise, over the deck of the vessel into the sea.

"I hafe beene in France; I hafe beene in Schpain; I hafe beene in Ofrica; I hafe beene in Portland, Maine; but nafer in all mine life hafe I seen such a dam place like dees; tscheet.

"Dam dees boat; she rock, rock, schust like an ole voman wid only one leg, and dare vas nafer no sea on needer; only schust a leetle schwellness; I hate deese dam boat; tscheet.

"Vat ish dare here, like America, anyhow? notings. In Californ ve hafe aferytings; ve hafe cold; ve hafe seelvare; ve hafe queck-seelvare; ve hafe fruit; afrey kind fruit; oranges, feegs, grapes; dey no hafe grapes here; tscheet.

"In Californ ve hafe amoosments; teayters, ooperas, afery kind moosic; and vine, and veeskey, and peer; vat hafe dey got in Halaluyah? (meaning Honolulu) notings; tscheet."

"They have fine fish here," I ventured to remark.

"Vat vas feesh?" he answered, "notings; ve hafe got more fine feesh in Californ, ten times more as Halaluyah; dam Halaluyah! dam dere feesh! I hate 'em."

"Don't you like shrimps?" I suggested as a sort of pacifier.

"Schreempus?" he responded, "naw; I no like any eensect out of de sea but ossters; leetle, young Californ ossters. Crabs, clams, devil-feesh, afery dam eensect from de sea, except ossters, is pisen; tscheet."

"What brought you out to the islands," I asked, "business?"

"Naw," said he quickly, "testiny; I pelieve in testiny; de whole, human family is controlled by testiny. De world used to vorship itols; after avile dey vorshiped vomen; now dey vorship dat." And he took from his pocket a bright, silver half-dollar and held it up between his finger and thumb before me.

"Dat's what I'm here for; dam Halaluyah! tscheet."

"But," said I, "how about all of these churches here on

the islands, don't they signify something more than a mere chase after the almighty dollar?"

"Naw," he replied, "de Sandvitches peoples bees all dam fools; dey bees too much ignoramous; dey got not civilicised. Aferytings here on deese islands vas religion; religion dees; religion dat; aferyting religion. Nine churches in Hilo; tree Kanaka, two Protestant, four Catolic, and only one saloon; vat you tink of dat, eh? Nine churches, and not more as nine hundred people. And only one saloon, and more as nine hundred people in de town, too.

"License in Hilo ees a tousand dollar; and peside, forty dollars hafe got to paid afery year to de Protestant church; and forty dollars to de Catolic church afery year, too; it vas a dam shame. I vas a voluntary soldier in de American var, and I no like it; tscheet." And he went off grumbling to his bed, sea-sick, home-sick and mad.

When I awakened Tuesday morning, we were lying in Kawaihae Bay, on the northwest shore of the island of Hawaii; and by the time daylight was fairly spun, we were putting in at Mahukona, where we dropped anchor. Shortly after, the sky cleared and the promise of a pleasant day lay spread along the eastern horizon in the smiles of the early morning, warm and delightful.

We were obliged to remain at Mahukona until the arrival of the incoming train, due at nine o'clock, from the sugar plantation twenty miles away on the east side of the island, and promptly at that hour, it came wheezing around the north point above the village. It consisted of a dummy locomotive, with two box and one open car attached, and the small amount of freight which it brought, together with several passengers, was soon transferred to the steamer; after which we again proceeded on our way.

Across the channel of Hawaii, about thirty miles to the northwest, lay the island of Maui; and for that point of des-

tination our rudder was set. We were now again on the
same course as was followed by the Hall on our trip up, and
had substantially encircled Hawaii.

As we crossed Alenuihaha Channel, Captain Clark pointed
out Hana, a little settlement on the easternmost jut of Maui,
where the natives say, the wind was born. We could also
see Lanai, where it matured its youth, and Molokai, where
it is said to have died. Any one, however, who visits these
shores, even at this remote date of the demise, when in all
reason the corpse should be very much dead, will come to
the conclusion it is about the liveliest wind-cadaver that has
whisked its sable pinions round his observation in many a
day. The thing that does the howling may be only the
ghost of the deceased, or like Hawaii Ponoi, merely a wind-
stiff metamorphosed into a stiff wind, backwards; but whatever it is, it howls, and howls, and howls.

It was in this channel that Kamahameha the Great used
to discipline his soldiery. Selecting periods of the fiercest
storms, he would take them out, by thousands, in their
fragile canoes, lashed together, and there unleashing them,
would set them adrift, to either float, sink, or swim to the
shore, according as they were skilled or otherwise in the art
of canoe navigation.

Such were the methods of drill which the barbaric, old
chief practised, and by means of which, combined with his
own impetuous force and example on shore, he was enabled
to conquer and subdue his enemies and bring together the
scattered islands of the group under one head.

Our last stop was at Lahaina, whence we cleared at ten
o'clock, arriving at Honolulu the following morning at five,
thus having been absent about twelve days on our trip to the
volcano.

CHAPTER XXIII.

JANUARY 29th, 1892, was the first anniversary of the accession of Queen Liliuokalani to the Hawaiian throne. It was also the festal time of Chinese jollity, being their New Year season. Together, the two events made things lively in Honolulu.

The ordinary sleepiness of the little city suddenly awakened into an atmosphere of din, and rattle, and smoke, from one end to the other; and the intensity of fun which the almond-eyed populace enjoyed, during the next few days, was something marvelous.

Chinese lanterns were displayed, in massive size and gorgeousness of color, all through the Chinese quarter, and every single pig-tailed denizen in town, doing kitchen work, hung up the dish-rag and gave notice to " missee," that until the following Monday, morning, heaven and earth and all the revolving planets might revolve and keep on revolving, but as for him, he was going to rest. And then he went out and put in four days and four nights of Chinese revel; shooting off Chinese fire-crackers, eating Chinese pig and Chinese rice, and drinking Chinese cock-tails, till every miserable bone in his yellow, crinkled-up skin fairly squeaked when he came back, and he was uglier than a caged orang-outang.

I had received, a few days prior, through the Marshal of

the kingdom, a plain white card, neatly inscribed. It was
about five by six inches in size, bordered with a silver band,
and was printed in gold letters, above which rose a gold and
scarlet crown resting on a tasseled pillow. It read as follows, *modo-et-forma* :

" The Chamberlain of the Household
is commanded by
Her Majesty
to invite Mr. Ash Slivers, Sr., to a
Luau at Iolani Palace on Friday
afternoon, the 29th of January, at 3 o'clock."

The morning of the 29th was a rainy one ; it had been
raining all night ; and in consequence, the streets were in a

LILIUOKALANI.

humid, muddy condition which was very disagreeable.
Being solicitous, however, to see all that was going on, I
arose early, put on my mackintosh, and with umbrella in
hand, sallied forth to the palace grounds.

The queen had provided an elaborate programme for the
day, beginning, at an early hour, with the receipt of " hookapus ; " and this was carried out despite the weather.

The hookapus, or gifts, customarily brought by the native
people for their sovereign, on festive occasions, consist of

pigs, chickens, fruits, cloths, nick-nacks, or whatever else of other articles they may chance to have most of, or prefer to render as offerings. They were noticably quite few on this occasion, but the fact was attributed to the inclemency of the weather, which, possibly, may have been the real cause; although I heard it frequently remarked, during the day, that the respect formerly manifested for the king, while the royal family of the Kamehamehas were on the throne, was conspicuously absent since the reign of the present queen, and during the time of Kalakaua, was indifferently felt.

Beginning at an early hour, her majesty, standing on the south porch of the palace, received the different societies that had manifested a desire to be presented; and later on, the military legions of the kingdom, fifty to a hundred strong, were paraded and put through the manual of arms and drill in her presence. In their evolutions and man-euvers, they were headed by the Royal Brass Band, little Berger in the lead, out of step, but doing the very best that his wind and jolly, short legs would permit, to keep up with the procession, and avoid being run down and trampled into the earth by the fierce, crowding cohorts behind him.

The display made by the female riding societies was in-deed beautiful. They were composed, exclusively, of native women, all of whom rode astride, robed in uniform habits of striking colors made from some cheap, flimsy stuff, their suits hanging close to the ground. Owing, however, to the wretched condition of the streets, and the galloping gait of their horses, the skirts of the riders soon became dismally bedrabbled with mud, half way up to their waists, and be-fore the parade was over, most of the members scattered and retired to their homes.

One troop was exquisitely costumed in close fitting paus of sky-blue color, with girdles of bright yellow about their

A NATIVE EQUESTRIENNE.

waists, from which gracefully depended long and loose tassels at the sides. The skirts were embroidered in large figures, also of yellow, and on the shoulders and about the sleeves, ornaments of the same color were fastened. Straw hats, with broad bands of yellow, and blue leis, and neatly fitting gloves, completed the outfit.

The gracefulness of these native women, on horseback, is something indescribably charming. They are as much at home there as on the ground, and the easy poise with which they bestrode their steeds, as they galloped by in columns of two, equalled the most finished equestrianship of the best gentlemen riders I have ever seen, anywhere. Another company was likewise outfitted, but their costumes were of scarlet instead of blue, and less elaborately decorated. They were, however, decidedly pleasing and attractive.

At eleven o'clock the Queen received members of the diplomatic corps; and later, the officers of the United States war-ship Pensacola, and others designated in the royal order. At three the general reception was held.

The American visitors were requested to assemble at two o'clock, in the reception room to the left of the main hall of the palace; and here, at about that hour, thirty or forty sons and daughters of " the land of the free and the home of the brave," were brought together. To the right of the hall was the throne room, where the Queen and her retinue were to look over the blooded stock as they trotted by.

Half an hour, perhaps, was consumed, after our arrival, before the old thoroughbreds, colts, and fillies, could be indexed and got into line, by " His Excellency, the American Minister; " but he kept industriously at it, holding the field register up against the door while he wrote, and jotted down the names as they were given to him, until, finally, all were enrolled. Then the procession proceeded to procesh into the royal presence for inspection.

An old stager from New Orleans, a trifle spavined and somewhat wind broken, whinnied a little as he went in, and attempted to put on airs; but most of us, having proper regard for the occasion, straggled along sedately, one eye peeled for the Queen, the other rolling about over the ladies-in-waiting, the floor, the ceiling, the decorations, and, last but not least, our august usher, the American Minister, who register in hand, preceded us, and took his position before the throne.

As we swept into the royal presence, we formed a marching column which, geometrically speaking, might very appropriately be termed a right-angled triangular circle; although it was, perhaps, a trifle obtuse at one end, and possibly, rather too curly-cued at the other. Some, also, of the individual members careened a little on the starboard side, as they went in, as if to show off their white vests; while others sidled along on a sort of hop-skip-and-jump tangent, as if to disguise the wrinkles and threadbare spots in their garments; for we all had on our walking, every-day clothes. Mr. Stevens, our Minister, was appropriately robed in his swallow-tail regalia, minus medals and decorations.

Contrary to the anticipations of our dignified usher, our procession trailed after him somewhat faster than he had calculated upon, he having planned to get into position in front of the throne, ready for announcements, before the head of the column arrived. But the live stock he was about to exhibit was American, and it proposed to get there, Eli, on time. To make the point, therefore, which he was aiming to do, the American Minister had to trot a little; and the balance of us, not understanding what he was up to, thought it the proper caper for us to trot, too; so we all trotted, coming down the last quarter-stretch in great shape, neck and neck with the starter.

The Queen was modestly arrayed in plain black, but

whether the fabric was of silk or calico, for the life of me, I cannot tell. I do know, however, that she didn't have on a holaku; I watched that part of it pretty close. She stood out in front of the dais, which occupied one entire end of the throne-room, her retinue of attendants back of and around her, and slightly inclining forward, sized us up as we came cavorting down under the wire.

THE THRONE ROOM.

Mr. Stevens, as soon as he reached the place of vantage which he had been so industriously legging it to attain, raised the register and began hurridly to read off the list of entries. This he had to do in a very spirited manner, for the high-steppers were going by lively, some of them " bucking " a little as they passed, in a violent endeavor to give espectful homage to the throne, that would smack familiarity with similar events in Europe, or show off their quality and breeding, and his articulation, at length, become so rapid as to be almost unintelligible. The last name on the list was that of Mrs. Rotschild, a young bride from Kalamazoo, and the usher announced it with a final flourish which was truly imposing. But Mrs. R. was near the head of the stampede and had passed on long before ; so a young, German chemist, from Milwaukee, gave response in her stead, with due and proper obeisance, he being at the rear of the line. Then we all scooted.

As we filed out, we passed into the main hall of the building, where we registered our names in a little, blank blotter, such as is frequently used in commercial houses for insignificant transactions; and the reception was over.

Then we examined the interior of the palace. It is a roomy, well-lighted, solid structure, but very bare of decorations, pictures and ornaments. The ceilings are high and the wood-work, much of it, is beautiful, being of the koa wood ; but there is scarcely a residence among our wealthy people of the States, which would not, by far, over-shadow it for artistic excellence and good taste.

The next event of interest was the royal luau, and thither we repaired. The weather had cleared, the day was beautiful, and the great feast, as it lay spread on twenty, immense tables in the palace grounds—besides the circular one assigned to her majesty and retinue at one end, and two extra-long ones for the children at one side—presented an attractive and palatable appearance. The whole was canopied over by a light, wooden structure, from the sides of which roofed extensions ran out for a number of feet ; and around these, multitudes of people were walking, or talking, or lying on the grass. The Royal Band, meanwhile, discoursed sweet music, as it had done since morning, from the pavilion at one end of the luau buildings.

The place where the luau was spread was open on all sides, and we went in, before the feast had begun, and examined the lay-out. It was very tastefully and nicely arranged. The tables sat up from the floor, civilization style, and chairs and plates were provided, at each place, for the guests. By the side of each plate was a calabash of poi and a bottle either of pop or ginger ale. The other usual accompaniments of every native luau were also present in abundance; pig, chicken, fish, raw and cooked, jams, puddings and all those other innumerable delicacies with which the Kanaka appetite is inseparably linked. Flowers, too, in great profusion, decorated all the tables.

Off at one side, under the trees, a crowd attracted our attention, and we went over to interview it. Sitting on the ground were two ancient crones, wrinkled and infirm, wreathed in leis. Behind them stood an old man, tall, gaunt, gray and toothless. All three were mumbling together, some kind of a sing-song, verbal chant, which mightily interested the lookers-on, and which, on inquiry, was found to be a recounting of brave deeds and valorous exploits by heroes of the nation in times that were past. It didn't interest the party I was with, so we moved on.

Finally, a roll of common matting, that showed wear, was brought out and placed at the foot of the steps leading up into the palace, in close juxtaposition to a strip of carpet that partially covered them. Then there was a long wait for the Queen.

The multitude after awhile began to get uneasy; the poi was getting sour and the devil-fish was spoiling; why didn't she come?

After a trifle longer delay, two Kanaka cavaliers cut the strings to the coil of matting, where it lay at the foot of the palace steps, and unrolled it across the drive-way and intervening grass-plat to the luau buildings. And then the children's mouths commenced to water, for they knew that the Queen must certainly be coming ; and they looked longingly back and forth from the palace to the feast, but still she came not.

There were a number of dogs-in-waiting around the palace grounds, for fish, and chicken bones, and bits of roast pig, the fragrance of which could almost be tasted in the air ; and one of those vandals dared to cross the royal matting, dared even to desecrate it with his dog-goned feet.

Quick as the flash 'twixt a pop-bottle cork and the pop thereof, thus quickly did a sturdy soldier in martial outfit, on guard against such and all other dastardly invasions of the royal matting, whip from its sheath the encased blade of a glittering bayonet, and with mighty force hurl it at the miserable and unseemly howler, that fled fleetly away, untouched, his tail in the air. And yet the Queen came not.

Lo, see the scramble on the palace steps ! Hail! all hail !

Harness thy respirations, Oh, Jupiter ! and hold fast all I give thee, Oh, Miss——issippi! for the Queen cometh.

Down the royal steps of the royal palace and across the royal grounds on the royal matting, came the royal promenade.

First, her majesty, very dignified, and deporting herself as the first lady of any realm could scarce have done more modestly, on the arm of some gentleman in harmony with her in color but whose name I did not learn ; she attired in plain black, he in civilian's dress. The band played.

Then followed the retinue, two and two ; old men, lame men, white men, Kanaka men ; and on every good, right arm, a smiling miss or madam. The gentlemen, without exception, were arrayed in plain, citizen's dress, and some of their garments, I am sorry to say, looked suspiciously stale ; as if they had recently done yeoman's service loading rice or sugar ; but they probably had not.

After the procession had passed, everybody on the invited

list formed round the luau tables. Before taking seats, a blessing was invoked; and immediately after, the 4th of July, or something equivalent to it, broke forth in a thousand squirts and fizzles filling the air. Think of a thousand pop-bottles all going off at once. This little prelude occupied a few moments of time, and then the meal proper was begun. The old trio of chanters now gathered again, this time near her majesty, and commenced monotonously to croon her virtues and the glory of her reign. Young girls, meanwhile, waved feather kahilis back and forth over her head. Altogether the scene was fantastic, yet not unpleasing.

Her majesty proceeded to business at once. Down into the royal calabash went the royal fingers, scooping up poi in wholesome morsels, which forthwith was transferred to the royal lining with many a royal smack. Here a piece of roast pig was sampled, there a strip of raw fish; and crabs, and jellies, and jams, and comfits, and no one knows what else besides, all floated away to the regions of the imperial duodenum in reckless confusion.

But the meal went on quietly, orderly, and in good form; and so far as I was able to observe, the Queen did nothing, either there or elsewhere during the day, that a cultivated lady might not have done anywhere, except to eat with her fingers.

But Liliuokalani is a patriotic, kind and gentle-hearted woman, if reports be true, and she loves her people. Their customs and practices are reverently dear to her, and she will never turn aside from them so long as she remains their Queen, or so long as she continues to live. It is her mission to serve them, and if she can do it in no other way than by the gift of her love, in that way she will serve to the end, and none of her subjects have any fears that she will ever wilfully wrong or betray them.

CHAPTER XXIV.

THE Mariposa was sighted off Honolulu on Wednesday forenoon, February 10th, 1892, bound from Sidney to San Francisco, and about noon reached the wharf. I had arranged for accommodations on her, and Thursday morning found me aboard, bag and baggage.

The government of Hawaii has adopted a stern regulation, that requires tourists who have been on Hawaiian soil more than thirty days, to procure passports before leaving the country. The rule might, perhaps, be submitted to with grace, were it not for the fee which is likewise exacted; "but there's the rub;" it's the fee they are after.

I had been subjected to this disgraceful, little fleece, not without some feelings of resentment on leaving, which I should have preferred not to carry away with me, and at ength stood on the deck of the good ship, gazing for the last time on the mountains and skies, the sweet valleys and charming landscapes of Oahu and Honolulu.

How beautiful it all was. The day was cloudy, yet divinely soft and entrancing. Over Tantalus and the twin peaks of the Pali, and all along the corrugated summits of the high uplands, mazy drifts of pearl-white color swam like islands of foam, indolently between land and sky.

I walked out on the bow of the boat; a rainbow, partially outlined, came down out of heaven and touched with a quiet flood of loveliness the hills in the west; while here and there, glints of checkered green shone on the mountain sides.

The Royal Band, in white caps and uniforms, was on the dock; America was played; and Home Sweet Home; and Auld Lang Syne. Women wept; men stood silently by, but

DIAMOND HEAD.

smiled not; children played with unconcern—Oh, happy days of childhood! that know neither griefs, nor partings, nor heart-aches, nor wearying, troublesome cares; only your own sweet, wilful, selfish joys.

"Sound two whistles!" commanded the captain to the first officer; and a moment later, the voice of the exultant steam rent the air with piercing shrillness, and died away in slowly fading echoes far across the sea.

The crowd surged down the gang-plank.

"Cast off!" sang out the officer on duty; and immediately the plank was loosed from the ship; the stern-line, like a thing of crawling life, crept stealthily aboard through the port hole; and the great hull, motionless and silent, floated drowsily out into the harbor, as if impelled thereto by a soft and gentle breeze.

All at once a loud splash was heard in the water, attracting sudden attention. "Somebody overboard!" I heard a lady exclaim. But it was only the usual crowd of Kanaka boys, who had plunged into the water to follow the steamer, as they do all the boats of the Oceanic Line when they leave Honolulu and square away for their farther journeyings.

Presently our bow pointed to Diamond Head, our port side next to the wharf; the bell tapped; the engine throbbed; the Pensacola, God bless her! waved the glorious "stars and stripes" in our faces; workmen hurrahed at us from the shore; "aloha! alo-ha! alo-ha-a!" and we were off for America.

Then everybody began to circulate. "What lovely weather! what a lovely sea! what a lovely trip we are going to have!" said one lady after another. Poor misguided "founts of ever blessing!" did you for a moment suppose such a thing could be possible? Did you not, "in your mind's eye," see that crafty, blistering, blustering, foul-mouthed, old, rippling villain of an ocean lying out there, waiting and watching for you, like a Honolulu hackman for a green Yankee sucker? But, after all, if you did not, you are to be congratulated; for a trifle of peace—thank heaven! —was thus accorded you, in the uncircumscribed limits of

time which lie between the was of an epoch of sea-sickness,
and the is to be.

Along about two o'clock of the afternoon of our departure,
I was standing out on the forecastle deck of the steamer,
looking forward to the east where my possessions lay, and
surveying the waterscape. Oahu had faded quite from view,
naught but the ocean was in sight, and old Neptune's muzzle altogether too frequently appeared, bobbing up and down
on the waves.

Suddenly an old feeling took possession of me. It was
not exactly one of homesickness, nor chicken-pox, nor
measels, nor mumps. On the contrary, it partook of something radically far removed from all of those things; a kind
of illness, somehow, or in some manner, intimately associated
with the great lakes of the land of my nativity. A comatose
condition, so far as all interest in affairs that relate to this
earth is concerned, stole over my senses; I gasped for
breath. Now the sensations became more pronounced; I
began to float; aha! whither am I drifting? I grabbed at
my heart—or at sections of appetite lying in that immediate
neighborhood—with a feeling I can never describe, but oh,
so far from every thought of pleasure.

As I continued to gaze down into the water, all at once, an old
familiar face which, in years past, I had met on Lake Huron,
and Erie, and Lake Michigan, was pushed up out of one of
the billows and made for the boat. A second later, its pos-
sessor stood on the deck, close by my side, clad in the same
old garments which in those days he fretfully wore, on his
ugly phiz the same satanic smile. I looked at him and
grinned. It wasn't exactly a genial grin that I gave him,
or one expressive of any particular pleasure at again meeting.
But, to be more explicit, it was nearer the smile of a hen-
pecked husband, presented by his wife with triplets, and no
bread in the house.

This may have angered him; at all events, as he passed, he gave me a most terrific counter with his left, chuck in the pit of the stomach. Ough! blurted I—for, indeed, I couldn't have helped it even if Lilinokalani herself had been present —and down I squatted on a stool. I was just preparing to dodge the next whack, thinking I heard him coming for me again, when I saw him disappear down the starboard side of the vessel, among the other passengers.

Some were talking and chatting, others reading and laughing; but he put a stop to it all, in double-quick time, when he got among them. I saw him take an old man of sixty, who weighed fully three hundred pounds, "a humper," that doubled him up quicker than a sinner's flight to Purgatory, and lost him seventeen pounds before he got over it.

After he had finished with him, he went about in a kittenish frame of mind, jabbing this one, and that one, and the other, all on the gastric juices, men, women and children alike; and then he took a header and went overboard. I never saw such a completely used up lot of people as those passengers were after he got through with them; and in less time than it takes to tell it, every one had disappeared into his state-room.

"Good idea!" thought I; "maybe he'll take a notion to come back!" So I rushed for my apartment, shut the door tight, bolted it, and lay down on the lounge to be quiet. I hadn't been there, however, two minutes, before he again appeared, smiling and smirking at me just as mean and contemptible as before. I was about to ask how he got in, but he didn't give me time; but came immediately over where I lay, and gave me an awful blow on the larynx.

"Tonsilitis," said he insultingly, dancing round the state-room, "tonsilitis!"

"Yes," I replied faintly, "I've got it; please sir, may I die?"

Then my throat began to swell, and I gagged awfully trying to catch my breath. So I got up from the lounge and lay down on the bed. He sat down for a moment, where I had been lying, and watched me; I, meanwhile, keeping both my eyes on him; but, presently, I felt so wretchedly bad, I closed them, just for a second. Seizing this opportunity, coward-like, he jumped on me again.

"There's a dose of the grippe for you," said he, giving me a thundering dig under the short ribs; "and there's contraction of the viscera!" and he reached down my throat and took me by the shoe-strings which he drew up and tied in a double-bow knot around my last meal. "There's gall displacement; ta-ta! when I come again, I'll turn you inside out and unravel your paxy-waxy," and away he went out of the room.

By this time I was completely used up, and though my supplications were feeble, yet I prayed, nevertheless, from the depths of my empty vitals, that lightning, or the great deep, or some other horrible thing might come and dissolve me, thus ending my perils and sufferings. But nothing came, so, finally, I either fainted or went to sleep.

Every once in awhile, for two days and nights, my adversary came and practiced on me in the same old manner he had done at first, strangling, wallowing, and churning me, till, at last, there wasn't anything in me to churn, and I hadn't strength enough left to strangle; then he went away, and I saw him no more, heaven grant it may be forever!

The trip to San Francisco, aside from those two days, was a very pleasant one. The sea, none of the time, was very rough, although towards the last, frequent fogs lay over the water. The passengers were mostly from the Colonies, and having been for nearly three weeks on the vessel, were naturally in a state of irritation and in good trim for fault-finding.

It is one of the sacred prerogatives of ocean travel to vent all of your surplus spleen, no matter under what circumstances it may have arisen, on the officers of the ship; and the uniformity of this custom prevailed on the Mariposa. "The captain was unsociable," so they said; "the purser didn't mix with the passengers;" and "the doctor's medicines didn't have the desired effect." These troubles, combined with the deficiencies of the table, which came in for its share of denunciation, on account of lack of size of the oranges, or of freshness in the chicken pot-pie, helped the discontented ones to while away the days until we reached the American shore.

I went out to Honolulu on the Mariposa and returned on her; and while the officers were not especially sociable, I found them, invariably, polite gentlemen. Moreover, they attended strictly to the ship's business, and their duties, so far as I was able to observe, were never neglected. On shore, it has come to be an axiom, very much applauded and regarded, that the man who can attend to his own affairs, and keep his proboscis religiously out of those of his neighbor, borders so nearly on the confines of human perfection as to be little less, in the scale of existence, than the angels. If that rule holds good on the sea—and certainly I can see no reason why it should not—then the officers of the Mariposa are eminently fitted for their places.

We came into San Francisco on the morning of February 18th. A dense fog covered the ocean for one or two hundred miles out, and our final progress was slow; but we nevertheless arrived on time. After we had passed in over the bars of the Golden Gate, and arrived safely in the harbor, we were boarded by the health and custom house officers, and about eleven o'clock, anchored at the wharf of the Oceanic Steamship Company.

CHAPTER XXV.

I ATTENDED a Lumbermen's banquet, in San Francisco, during my stay there, after my return from Honolulu. It was given by the brotherhood, in behalf of a delegation of Northwestern dealers who at that time were on a visit to the Pacific slope, and was an elaborate affair.

The elegant dining parlors of the California Hotel, on Bush Street, were the scene of the festivities; and the fraternity of San Francisco dealers did itself proud in the liberality of the entertainment.

I went, very naturally expecting, first of all, to be enlightened regarding the wonderful timber resources of that land of magnificent forestry. But I also expected, of course, to hear the usual speeches of such occasions, always more of flower than of substance, and compliments, *ad infinitum*, passed by the guests and their hosts. I even went so far as to prophesy, that before the thing was over, truth and flattery would both be so outrageously hammered and mauled, by sectional pride and zeal, that the very best friends of either would hardly know how to discern them. I went in my every-day clothes.

The elevator elevated me up one, two, three, four, five, six stories; and then I got out and was shown to the toilet rooms, where, after taking off my over-garments, I was escorted to the banquet parlors. Jews-harps and soda water! how excitedly my pulses pulsed when I entered that room. The place was full of men, elegant, swallow-tailed men; the entertainers all dressed in broadcloth, low-cut vests, embroidered shirts, and diamonds.

I said to myself: "Surely, I've got into the wrong coop, our kind of chickens don't roost on such perches as these!" and was about to retire, when I was approached and accosted by one of the reception committee, who introduced himself. I looked him all over, carefully; then I looked over the others who were present; and finally I looked over myself. Pansies and buttercups, all of them, and I the only scrub in the lot. However, I made up my mind to stay and see the thing through, so I clung to the rigging and sailed along with the rest.

Shortly the call was announced, and we filed into the dining hall. Plates were provided for about a hundred and fifty persons, and the table was charmingly spread. Flowers and smilax, in profusion, lay scattered and twined amid beautifully decorated cl.ina ware, and glistening cut-glass spangled the white cloths in the gas-light as thickly as embroidered ornaments a fancy doily.

A string band discoursed choice music from the room we had just vacated.

We took our seats.

Wine began to flow.

We sampled it; it touched the spot.

We sampled it again; it touched the spot twice.

A button-hole bouquet, and a lavender-colored silk ribbon, with the date of the feast printed on it in gold; a pine tree, hand-painted, also in gold, just above; were at the side of each plate. We fastened the bouquets and the ribbons to the lapels of our coats. Then we took another draught of wine.

Again our tickled palates got up and returned thanks.

Now, the President arose at the head of the double row of tables.

"Gentlemen," said he.

We were all silent.

"Gentlemen, I welcome you to San Francisco, and to the Pacific slope."

Then we fell upon the viands and devoured them.

Every time a waiter passed on his circuit, our glasses were replenished; every time a new course was ushered in, we exchanged vintage.

At length, quite a few of the company had lost all opinion as to whether they were in San Francisco or Omaha; and less than that number, by a very large majority, were not concerning themselves an iota to ascertain which.

Then the President once more arose.

"Gen'lemen," said he: "Welcome, t' slope, an' Fran Sancisco; Hooray! See Bro'er Jones over there. Jones, biggest liar, Fran Sancisco. Talk to 'em, Jones. Hooray!"

Jones responded in eloquent strains; damned the Southern Pacific Railroad; coquetted with the proud compliment paid him by the President; modestly denied it; said Deacon Towface was far ahead of him in that regard; would like to hear from Towface.

Towface replied; said he yielded to neighbor, Pasteum; Pasteum was the champion prevaricator of the Pacific slope, and everybody knew it.

Finally the home talent was all exhausted. Then the Northwest was called on; Mr. Potkins, of Minneapolis, first.

"Where's Min'apolis?" vociferated the President, rising to his feet and dropping back again into his chair; "where's Min'apolis?"

Potkins told him.

Potkins gloried in California; climate lovely; fruit couldn't be beat; ladies divine.

Then Walkaway, of Duluth, was called on.

"Where's D'luth?" inquired the President, looking up from his chair, but not attempting to rise.

Walkaway explained, minutely, the location of Duluth.

Then he said climate of California was just bully; fruit hunkidori; ladies took the cake.

After awhile, Slivers, of Ohio, was introduced.

" Where's O-whio? " murmured the President, opening his eyes meekly and then closing them again to sleep.

Slivers delineated the geographical status of Ohio.

Then he began to orate: "Climate of California——"

" Hooray! " shouted the President, jumping to his feet; " Hooray for Min'aplis! Hooray for D'luth! Hooray for O-whio! climate; fruit; ladies! Le's go home! Where's Fran Sancisco? "

And we all went home.

CHAPTER XXVI.

QUITS.

R EADER, in your flights and journeyings, have you ever looked out through the opposite window of the luxurious Wagner you were occupying, and imagined the picture there presented to be a painting?

Did you ever stop to think what a wondrous gallery of choicest gems a modern car of railroad travel is?

The glazed apertures of every Pullman sleeper are a matchless row of rarest works of art. Whether in city or country, or whether dashing in wild confusion over mountains, or across plains, there they always are, framed on either side in richest panellings of oak, or cherry, or of mahogany; all masterpieces of the Great Artist; living, moving panoramas of endless change and color.

And still there are those—alas! too many—, whose most exquisite delight it is to rave over the art collections of Europe; of Italy, or France, or Belgium; whose aesthetic souls, wafted by exuberance of sentiment, soar far away, like toy balloons, " out of sight," when the Louvre is spoken of, or the Ufizzi; and who at merest mention of the " Old Masters," uncoil their eyes, and sigh with depths of such profound emotion as would move a Stoic.

Yet these same connoisseurs can contentedly curl up on their cushioned railway seats, and sleep, or listlessly bury themselves in some vapid novel, while passing through scenes the grandest, most picturesque and sublime, ever spread by the Creator, before the eyes of his children, and care nothing about them.

Follow me, Sir Artist, out of the city of the Golden Horn; across the Bay of San Francisco; along the dimpled valleys of California, amid her sunshine and prolificness. Lose no glint of this radiant, western daughter, as we pass her by on the wings of our rushing whirlwind; this houri of smiles and warmth, reposing there between the Sierras and the sea; in daintiness of attraction, the fairest, gentlest, sweetest sister of all the constellation of this grand Republic.

Follow me up into the snow-clad heights of the giant Rockies, the home of fugitive summer; away! away to the east! with rattle, and clamor, and clang; past cities, through gorges, over rivers, plains, and bursting fields of plenty; and if, on that journey, you will catch for me, one only of the cheapest and least attractive of those millions of fleeting shadows, which for a moment peer in through those plated windows—make it only as large as one of their panels of glass; paint it only one-fourth as true as it is to nature—and your fame shall be greater than that of Michael Angelo, or of Raphael.

This beauty it was, this gentleness, this grandeur, this sublimity of the perfect work, that ever, during my journeyings, impressed on me the glowing words of Trench, and planted them forever deep in my memory:—

> . . . . "If God has so arrayed
> A fading world that quickly passes by,
> Such rich provisions of delight has made
> For every human eye,
>
> What shall the eyes that wait for him survey
> When his own presence gloriously appears
> In worlds that were not founded for a day,
> But for eternal years?"